It had been one heck of a kiss.

And not one that he would soon forget. Nor would he forget Delaney pushing him into the lake. The woman was plucky. Too much so.

Cooper shook his head as he glanced up towards the ranch house. He could hear faint music stealing out the windows. He wondered if she was thinking about their kiss…

The kiss had been the kind of thing he'd never done on a job before.

But he'd *wanted* to kiss her. He *had* to kiss her.

Only that kiss made things worse. Because he'd end up hurting her no matter what.

Dear Reader:

We are delighted to bring you this daring series from Silhouette.

Intrigue—where resourceful, beautiful women flirt with danger and risk everything for irresistible, often treacherous men.

Intrigue—where the stories are full of heart-stopping suspense and mystery lurks around every corner.

You won't be able to resist Intrigue's exciting mix of danger, deception…and desire.

Please write and let us know what you think of our selection of Intrigue novels. We'd like to hear from you.

Jane Nicholls
Silhouette Books
PO Box 236
Thornton Road
Croydon
Surrey
CR9 3RU

Outlawed!

B. J. DANIELS

*Silhouette and Colophon are registered trademarks of
Harlequin Books S.A., used under licence.*

*First published in Great Britain 1996
Silhouette Books, Eton House, 18-24 Paradise Road,
Richmond, Surrey TW9 1SR*

© Barbara Johnson Smith 1996

ISBN 0 373 22353 6

46-9609

*Printed and bound in Great Britain
by Mackays of Chatham PLC, Chatham*

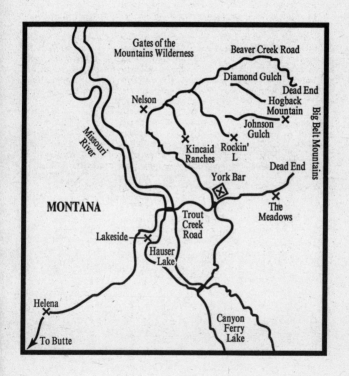

Gates of the
Mountains Wilderness

Beaver Creek Road

Diamond Gulch

Dead End

Hogback
Mountain

Nelson

Johnson
Gulch

Missouri
River

Kincaid
Ranches

Rockin'
L

Dead End

Big Belt Mountains

York Bar

MONTANA

The
Meadows

Trout
Creek
Road

Lakeside

Hauser
Lake

Helena

To Butte

Canyon
Ferry
Lake

To Harry Burton Johnson,
the man who taught me to dream.
Thanks, Dad.

Prologue

The moon rimmed the tops of the ponderosas, golden in the late darkness. As Digger O'Donnel tugged his mule, Tess, up the mountain through a narrow passage between the rocks, he fought a vague sense of foreboding. A breeze danced along the back of his neck, as hot as the devil's breath. He urged Tess to move a little faster, anxious to get back to his camp.

They'd just crested the ridge, topping the band of rocks that formed a wall above the creek bed, when Digger saw the creature. At first he thought it was the moonlight playing tricks on him. A lot of people already thought he was crazy. What would they think if he told them he saw lights deep in the lake that pooled among the rocks and something dark moving around in its depths?

Suddenly the creature surfaced, and the old prospector knew he'd never seen anything like it on earth—let alone on a horse ranch in Montana. He noticed with growing fright that the strange being seemed to be attached to a small round craft that floated on the surface of Johnson Gulch Lake.

Tess sniffed the wind and let out a frightened bray. Digger hurriedly pulled at the mule. She balked as he dragged her into a stand of trees and out of sight. He stood in the shadows, afraid. Of what he'd seen. And of what he might have just imagined. What if the creature had heard Tess and was now coming after them both?

He fought the urge to run. Instead he hunkered in the pines, listening for any hint of a sound. There was nothing but the breeze stirring the tall pines. His old, tired mind told him he should leave to go tell someone what he'd seen. And yet, who would believe him? He could think of only one person—Delaney Lawson, the owner of the Rockin' L Ranch. She had always been kind to him. And the thing *was* on her ranch.

By the light of the moon, he quickly drew a crude sketch on a brown paper sack he pulled from his saddlebag. He tried to capture both the creature and its craft before he forgot the details. After all, his memory wasn't what it used to be.

When he finished, he stared at what he'd drawn. Not even Delaney Lawson would believe this, he told himself. Ordering Tess to stay put, he sneaked around the pines and took another look. The lights in the mountain lake were gone. No strange being rippled the water, no alien craft floated on the cold, dark surface. Instead the first rays of morning began to climb the back side of the Big Belt Mountains. In the distance, the ranch was as silent as the summer night.

Digger O'Donnel felt another fear—worse than when he'd seen the creature come out of the water. He crushed the paper in his fist and shoved it into his coat pocket. Space aliens! Ha! Maybe people were right. He *was* crazy, he thought as he headed back over the ridge, the new day lightening the sky to the east.

Digger and Tess had reached the outskirts of their camp, when he sensed something behind him. That same foreboding evil seemed to fill the air around him, just as it had earlier before he'd seen the creature, just as it had the night of the mine cave-in all those years ago. . . .

"Run, Tess!" he cried, slapping the old mule on the rump. "Run!" Tess let out a startled bray and took off through the pines at a lumbering gait. "Run, old mule," Digger yelled. He heard a branch snap behind him and turned, trying to make sense of what he was seeing. "Oh, my God, no!" He felt a sharp crack against his skull and the darkness come up to get him.

Chapter One

Cooper McLeod awoke to what he thought was distant thunder. He lay prone on a warm, flat rock, his Stetson covering his face as he napped in the shade of a huge ponderosa pine. The last thing he wanted to do was wake up. He was in the middle of a dream involving the most fascinating woman he'd ever met.

Not only was this woman beautiful, but she seemed to appreciate his finer qualities. It didn't bother her that he looked a little trail-worn or that he didn't have a roof over his head at the moment. She even liked his horse.

The thunder grew closer, and he realized it wasn't from a summer storm. Reluctantly he left the woman in his dream and sat up, his hat shading his eyes against the sun blazing in Montana's big sky. Along the valley floor below him he could see a rider coming his way, hooves pounding the sun-baked clay. The sound echoed through the rock outcroppings and the tall pines as clear as a warning.

Trouble. It was his first thought. Probably because trouble had a way of finding him. It also didn't help that he was on private property—what some might consider trespassing. Cooper squinted at the rider, telling himself he must still be dreaming, because if *this* was trouble, it certainly came nicely wrapped.

The woman rode hell-bent, her hair beneath her western hat whirling in tight circles behind her as black and shiny as obsidian. He was enjoying just watching her, when she spotted him. She brought her horse up sharply, then spurred it in his direction. As she galloped toward him, he was reminded of the woman in his dream. Except even *his* imagination couldn't come up with a woman like this!

"What do you think you're doing?" she demanded, pulling up her mahogany bay mare. Her boots hit the ground before the horse had a chance to come to a full stop. Reins in hand, she stalked over to him.

Cooper stared up at her, too spellbound to speak. She was all curves, from her long denimed legs to the sweet promise generously filling out her blue-checked Western shirt. Her black hair spilled around her face like a storm cloud. But it was the fire in her dark eyes that made him smile as he got to his feet.

"Something funny?" she asked, her tone as steely as her stance.

Cooper figured he outweighed her by a good fifty pounds, was almost a foot taller and definitely stronger. None of that seemed to intimidate her in the least.

She stood, hands on her hips, meeting his gaze with one that would have made most men damned nervous. "When the Rockin' L takes on a man, we expect something from him," she said evenly.

He pulled a stalk of wild grass and chewed on the stem as he tried to imagine what it would be like having this woman take him on. "I'm afraid there's been a mistake." Cooper hated that he had to tell her so. He was enjoying just looking at her. She had the most kissable lips he'd ever seen. And he'd never been able to resist a woman with a little fire. This woman had enough to keep a man warm all winter.

"There's been a mistake, all right," she said. She let her gaze roam freely over him, from top to dusty bottom. He saw her stop for a moment at his belt, lingering on the All-

Around Best Cowboy buckle he'd won at Cheyenne Frontier Days, then she moved on down his faded jeans to his worn-thin lucky boots. She didn't seem all that impressed by what she saw. He fleetingly thought of the fantasy woman in his dream.

Suddenly her gaze darted past him. Her dark eyes widened. "What is *that?*"

He looked over his shoulder. "That's my horse."

"You call *that* a horse?"

Now that he thought about it, this woman didn't remind him at all of the one in his dream. "Careful now," he said, dropping his voice. "You wouldn't want to hurt Crazy Jack's feelings. He's real sensitive about his looks."

She narrowed her gaze at the horse snuffling grass beneath the big ponderosa. Cooper knew it was hard to see Crazy Jack's beauty at first. You had to get past his face. Crazy Jack was the best and worst of the Appaloosa breed. He had a head like a suitcase, just enough mane to look silly and not quite enough tail to look like a horse. Of course he had the Appaloosa spots. Everywhere. And in every size, shape and color. He wasn't the kind of horse you could miss—even at a distance.

"I suppose you named him Crazy Jack because of his eyes," she said, still staring at the horse. Crazy Jack was a little walleyed. At first glance, all you could see were the whites of his eyes. And as the old horsewife's tale has it, when you can see the whites of a horse's eyes it's a sure sign the beast is crazy.

"No," Cooper said. "Jack *is* crazy."

She stared at the horse for a moment longer, then turned back to Cooper. She appeared to be making up her mind, and not liking her decision.

"Get your…horse and come on. I'm sure Buck told you when you hired on that you were to start mending fence in the southwest pasture."

She shook her head as if she saw little hope for him.

Right then Cooper saw little hope for himself. This woman, whoever she was, was amazing when she had her dander up. She was all he could think about and he knew he should be thinking about how he was going to get himself out of this.

"The fence is over there." She tipped her hat toward a dark strip of pine and rocks etched against the blue horizon on the other side of the road. "I hope your work is better than your sense of direction."

That would probably have been a good time to tell her he wasn't lost or necessarily lazy, nor had he hired on to work for the Rockin' L. But something in the way she stood, the sun blazing in her eyes, her lips slightly parted as if needing to be kissed, changed his mind. This was an opportunity he couldn't pass up. Not only that, he didn't think she'd take kindly to the fact that he was on private property, especially if she found out why. He figured she wouldn't hesitate to have him thrown in jail for trespassing—or worse.

He dragged his hat from his head. "The name's Cooper McLeod. My friends call me 'Coop.'"

She nodded. "Fine, McLeod," she said, and swung up onto her horse.

He noticed her backside was just as intriguing as the rest of her and then he noticed she noticed him noticing.

"Is there a problem?" she asked, cocking her head as she settled those dark eyes on him.

He ran his hand along her horse's neck, pretending it was good horseflesh that had drawn his interest, and not her derriere. "Just admiring your ... horse." It was a fine Morgan, bold and high-spirited like its owner.

She smiled down at him, but only a fool couldn't read the warning in her eyes just before she spurred her horse.

Cooper grinned to himself as he mounted Crazy Jack and rode after her. She *did* ride a beautiful horse, with powerful shoulders, cleanly shaped legs and a cool intelligence in its eyes. Even Crazy Jack had noticed, and he was a gelding.

As Cooper followed her, he was only a little concerned about what would happen when Buck told her he'd never seen this cowboy before—let alone hired him. Cooper had talked himself out of tight places before. He had no doubt he would again.

He thought about his last assignment, his grin fading a little as he rubbed his left thigh. He'd believed he had that one aced, and look what had happened. No, he wasn't fool enough not to know he was riding into trouble. This woman was temptation in snug-fitting jeans. He'd never seen anything like her. But, he reminded himself, he'd also never let a beautiful woman distract him so much that he couldn't do his job. This woman—no matter who she was—wasn't going to be the first.

DELANEY RODE OFF, cursing Buck for hiring an arrogant rodeo cowboy. She'd spent years avoiding men like Cooper McLeod—both professionally and personally. Long, lanky rodeo cowboys who'd ridden their share of rough stock—and charmed more than their share of women with sweet talk. She knew his kind only too well. Her father had been a rodeo cowboy. Hank Lawson had broken her mother's heart and almost lost the family horse ranch with his rodeoing.

After her mother had died, Delaney took over the place and had to watch her father, loving him, but hating the wild, irresponsible side of him that couldn't quit chasing adventure, whether it was the next untamed bull to ride at a rodeo or a beautiful woman to win over.

No, she'd learned all she wanted to know about rodeo cowboys from her father. She didn't need Cooper McLeod to remind her just how dangerous they could be. And on top of that, Cooper McLeod had to be one of the worst she'd ever seen. All denim and dimples, even with his rugged sun-browned features, he had the look of something sweet and tempting. Angel-blessed innocence, her mama used to call it. Until you looked into his eyes. The devil jitterbugged in the depths of all that clear blue. No, this cowboy was nothing but walking trouble.

Cooper caught up with her and shot her a grin that should have been outlawed in every state in the Union. "You didn't say what I should call *you.*"

Delaney slowed her horse and looked over at him. If she wasn't so badly in want of a ranch hand, she'd send him packing. This cowboy was the last thing the Rockin' L needed right now the way her luck had been running. "You can call me 'Ms. Lawson.' "

"Ms. Lawson?"

From his lips, it sounded like a caress.

"Then you must be related to Delaney Lawson, the owner of the Rockin' L."

Delaney smiled. "No, I *am* Delaney Lawson." She watched surprise wipe the grin from his face, heard him curse under his breath and realized Buck must have failed to mention the boss was a woman. She smiled to herself. This cowboy didn't know it yet, but he'd just met his match.

DELANEY LAWSON? Apprehension coiled like a rattler in Cooper's belly. Delaney Lawson was a *woman?* A young, beautiful, headstrong woman. He'd never dreamed this woman could be the owner of the Rockin' L. But he *should* have known. He should have known *everything* about the Rockin' L. His mind raced as he tried to figure out how this kind of mistake could have happened.

He'd been given the wrong information. That was the only thing that made any sense. Why else would he have been misinformed that Delaney Lawson was a man? An elderly man with one foot in the grave. He hadn't wanted to take another job so soon after the last one. The only reason he'd taken this assignment was that his employers had promised him it would be quick and simple.

Suddenly worried, he rubbed the almost healed gunshot wound in his left thigh, reminding himself how badly things had gone during his last job. And now he was getting the wrong information. Why hadn't he double-checked what Jamison had given him? Because he'd never had to before. Because he trusted his employers not to make mistakes. A mistake could have serious consequences, he reminded himself. Especially with a hellcat like this one.

He studied Delaney's slim back, quickly regaining the calm that made him the best at what he did. He could handle her. Actually, this could turn out better than he'd expected. He'd always had his best luck with women. But it did change things. Especially if his employers had failed to tell him anything else.

He considered for a moment coming up with another cover story. The problem was, he kind of liked the idea of being Delaney Lawson's hired hand. It could work into his plans quite well if he was careful. When she found out the truth, of course there'd be hell to pay. But it was a price he'd paid often enough before.

Cooper was admiring the way his new boss sat the saddle, when he noticed they were about to have company. A blue Ford pickup rattled up the dirt road, leaving a trail of dust a mile long. Delaney reined in, and Cooper did the same, hoping this wasn't the man who'd "hired" him.

The pickup rumbled to a stop beside them. As the dust settled, the driver rolled down his window. Cooper noted with relief that the painted lettering on the truck door read Kincaid Ranches. From the look of the man's expensive western suit, Cooper figured he had to be Kincaid.

"Afternoon, Del," he said, tipping his gray Stetson as his dark eyes shifted to Cooper, then settled possessively on Delaney again.

"Jared," she said with a slight nod.

Jared Kincaid looked to be hugging fifty, with a little gray at the temples and a slight paunch that strained the snaps on his western shirt. Kincaid could have been ten years younger and he'd have still been too old for Delaney, Cooper thought, but the rancher didn't seem to realize that.

"Sorry to add to the troubles you've been having, Del," Jared said, almost sounding as though he meant it. "But I was flying over the ranch this morning and I spotted about twenty head of horses I think might be yours up above Diamond Gulch. Problem is, they looked kinda...strange."

Troubles she'd been having? What was this about? Cooper wondered as he watched his new boss out of the corner of his eye. Twenty head of horses? Something told him this wasn't a cattle ranch and that he'd been given more misinformation.

She looked toward the mountains for a moment, her face appearing tranquil. But he could feel anger coming off her in waves.

"'Strange'?"

Kincaid stopped to tug at his mustache. "They were all down, Del. Didn't look good."

When Delaney spoke, her voice had an edge to it as cold and hard as a good knife. "Well, thanks for letting me know, Jared."

"It's a damned shame. Seems you've hit a real streak of bad luck."

"Seems that way, doesn't it?" she said.

"I'll get my horse and ride up there with you," he said. "It might not be pretty."

"Thanks, but I can handle it," Delaney said.

The determination in her voice and in the set of her shoulders made Cooper want to smile.

"I wouldn't go up there alone if I were you, Del," Kincaid said, biting off each word. "There's likely to be some rattlers in those rocks and I recall you're not all that partial to sidewinders." Kincaid shot a glance at Cooper. "Usually." His eyes narrowed. "*This* a new hand?"

Cooper didn't like the implication or the rancher's tone. Delaney didn't seem to take offense, nor did she seem all that excited about introducing him. He admitted he didn't look like much, but still—

"Cooper McLeod, Jared Kincaid," she said by way of introduction.

Cooper tipped his hat.

Kincaid studied him a moment, then quickly dismissed him. "You know hiring someone wasn't necessary, Del," he said.

His tone was so patronizing it made Cooper grit his teeth. Delaney looked as if her jaws were permanently locked.

"I told you I'd lend you a hand." His lips curled into a smile. "You know I'm always ready to help a little lady in need."

"Thanks anyway, but as I told you, I can take care of myself."

Delaney's tone worked as effectively as a bucket of ice water on the rancher, much to Cooper's delight.

Kincaid's smile faltered and died. Something mean flickered in his eyes, then skittered away. "You're a capable woman, all right, Del, but there're still a few things a woman needs a man for. Maybe it's been so long, you've just forgotten." He shifted the pickup into gear, touched the brim of his hat and left them in the dust.

"Seems like a nice enough fellow," Cooper said.

Delaney shot him a look. "McLeod, if I were you, I'd have the good sense to keep my mouth shut."

He doubted that, but at least he had the good sense not to say so.

She shifted in her saddle, eyeing him darkly. "You think you can find that fence now," she said, pointing to some downed barbed wire a dozen yards away. "You'll find the wire stretcher and a roll of wire in the barn."

The last thing he wanted to do was mend fence. He needed to know a lot more about what was happening on the Rockin' L. "You sure you don't want me to come along with you?" he asked.

Her expression was deadly. "McLeod, we'd better get something straight right now—"

Realizing his error, he held up his hands in mock surrender. "I just thought if there was a problem, you might want someone along, even me. I didn't mean any offense." He gave her his best grin. "I'll get to work on that fence now."

For a moment, he was worried that he'd lost his touch. But her features softened slowly. The anger eased out of her ramrod-straight back. She brushed a wisp of her dark hair back and looked over at him.

"I suppose I might need some help." She sounded resigned not only to finding her horses probably all dead, but also having to put up with Cooper. "I'll pick up my doctoring bag and meet you at the bottom of Diamond Gulch." She pointed to a narrow cut of rocks in the distance. "Try not to get lost, McLeod."

He tipped his hat at her and gave her another grin. "Whatever you say, boss." She swore as she spurred her horse. He breathed a sigh of relief. If he wanted to keep being Delaney Lawson's hired hand, he'd have to be more careful.

As he rode toward the gulch, he couldn't help wondering. Wondering about this woman. About her bad luck. But mostly wondering why Jared Kincaid seemed so happy to hear about it.

One thing was for certain, Cooper reminded himself, Delaney Lawson's luck wasn't going to get any better now that Cooper McLeod was in town.

Chapter Two

Delaney felt the air change around her as they rode up the gulch toward the east corner of the ranch. It grew thick and hot, scented with the dark aroma of death. Her mare shuddered beneath her, then snorted and tossed her head. Fear danced around the horse like electricity in a lightning storm. The mare had never been spooked around dead animals. But she was spooked now. And Delaney could think of only one other time she'd acted this way—when they'd come across a grizzly with two cubs. She brought her horse up and glanced at Cooper.

He sat astride his strange-looking beast, staring up the mountain, eyes squinted against the sun. Crazy Jack stomped the ground, ears back, nostrils flaring.

Delaney pointed to a meadow of wildflowers, high and to the left of a massive shale butte. "That's where we should find the horses." She motioned to a narrow canyon that cut through a corner of the butte. "The fastest way to get to the meadow is up that dry creek bed, but we'll have to leave our horses here and walk."

Cooper swung down out of the saddle and pulled his rifle from the scabbard. She saw him check to make sure it was loaded. He dropped his reins, ground-tying his horse, then whispered something in Crazy Jack's ear. The horse let out a whinny, as if it understood. Delaney swore under her breath. It was bad enough that Buck had hired a rodeo cowboy, but a rodeo cowboy with a crazy horse was too much.

"You want me to go take a look?" Cooper asked her. "Whatever got into the horses might still be around."

Delaney sat for a moment, suddenly afraid of what they'd find on the mountain. The steep butte shone white hot. Nearer, pines shimmered, cool, dark and green in stark contrast. Heart pounding, she dismounted and pulled her rifle. "No, I'll go along."

His gaze met hers. "You're the boss."

Right. But he seemed to keep forgetting that, she thought, as she fell in beside him.

They hiked toward the break in the rocks. Overhead the sky rode clear and blue above the mountaintop. The sun beat down, golden and hot. And yet a chill circled her neck like a noose. Something was terribly wrong.

Then it hit her. The quiet. It choked the summer day, leaving no sounds but the ones she and Cooper were making. No hawk cried overhead as it soared on a thermal. No breeze whispered in the towering pines. Not even a grasshopper rustled in the weeds.

As they followed the slim cut the creek bed had carved through the butte, the sun hammered the silence. Heat ricocheted off the rock. Each step echoed along the narrow canyon. It was hard to imagine the creek rushing with water during spring runoff just three months earlier. The dry stones reminded Delaney of the skeletal remains of something that died with summer, its bones bleached and dried from the sun.

Delaney glanced up, unconsciously searching for the familiar protected feeling the big sky over the ranch had always given her. Her heart thudded at the sight of ravens overhead.

"I don't mean to be buttin' into your business, but Kincaid mentioned you've been having some bad luck," Cooper said, glancing back at her.

She smiled to herself, doubting this man could ever keep from butting into anyone's business. But at the same time, she was thankful to him for breaking the stifling quiet, even if it was to talk about her misfortune. "A half-dozen head of my horses got tangled up in some barbed wire during a thunderstorm. The brakes went out in the stock truck. Then some more of my horses turned up missing. And now they may be dead."

He shot her a look. "Sounds to me like you'd better put a horseshoe over your door, and quick."

Delaney rolled her eyes at his broad back as he continued up the creek bed. A horseshoe over her door! Leave it to a rodeo cowboy to come up with *that* solution. With her luck, the horseshoe would fall on her head.

But she had to admit, she was getting more than her share of bad luck. And now she had a rodeo cowboy working for her—just when she thought things couldn't get any worse. Maybe Kincaid would hire Cooper out from under her the way he had some of her other hands over the years. She smiled to herself. That would sure serve Jared Kincaid right.

They reached a short wall of boulders smoothed by years of spring runoffs. Cooper stopped, turning back to offer Delaney a hand as he started to climb up. She took it, anxious to get out of the rocks. Jared was right; she had a deathly fear of snakes. But she was also anxious to get to the meadow. And at the same time, afraid of what they'd find. With surprise, she noticed that his hand was callused from hard work. A large, strong hand that had done its share of posthole digging. She frowned, wondering if she'd been wrong about him, then saw he was limping.

"Don't tell me you've already hurt yourself," she said, remembering another rodeo cowboy she'd hired. He'd fallen off his horse the first day and slapped her with workmen's

compensation for an alleged injury that laid him up for two
weeks.

Cooper rubbed his left thigh. "No, ma'am. The truth is
there are some broncs in Texas a sane man shouldn't try to
ride." He looked up at her, his eyes bottomless, and smiled.
"It makes me limp a little, but it doesn't hurt anymore."

She nodded, realizing that must be why he'd come to
work for her. And that as soon as he was healed enough to
ride rodeo again, he'd be gone.

The smell of death grew stronger, the sun hotter. Birds
now circled overhead. As she and Cooper topped the boulder field and started across the meadow, Delaney spotted the
first horse sprawled in the tall grass. Her heart sank. Del
Rio, one of her prized mares. Off to her right she spotted
another carcass in the grass. A deer lay covered with flies.

Delaney shook off a chill and hurried toward Del Rio,
wondering how many more she'd find dead in the grass.
Suddenly the mare stumbled to its feet. Delaney let out a
startled cry. She watched in horror as the mare fought to
stand. Tears rushed her eyes as the mare, eyes wild, took a
few awkward steps toward her, stumbled and fell over into
the grass again.

Delaney stared at the horse, as fear colder than a Montana winter day settled in her bones. Other horses lay in the
tall grass. Some tried to get to their feet as she approached,
but fell back after a few futile attempts. When she looked
up, she realized that Cooper was standing at the edge of the
meadow, studying her.

"They got into something," she said. "Locoweed or...
something."

"Obviously." He eyed her in a way that implied she
wasn't as smart as she appeared.

Delaney stuck the butt of the rifle into the soft earth, settled her other hand on her hip and glared at him. "Something bothering you, McLeod?"

"Aren't these some of your best mares?" he asked, almost angry with her.

"As a matter of fact—" She stopped. "How do you know that?"

"I know good horses." He pushed his Stetson back from his face. His eyes bored into her. "So what are they doing here?"

She focused on the horse nearest her. The Rockin' L was an old-fashioned horse ranch. She didn't keep her stock in fancy arenas or barns. This was a working Morgan horse ranch. But these mares wouldn't have left the rest of the herd. And they hadn't just wandered up here by themselves. "My guess is someone tried to steal them."

He glanced around the meadow. "How were the rustlers going to get them out of here? By helicopter? There's not a road within miles. And why drug them up?"

She didn't like his tone or his attitude. And how did he know there wasn't a road within miles of here? It hit her that he wasn't lost at all when she'd found him sleeping on the rocks.

"What makes you think there isn't a road near here?" she asked, studying him.

He smiled. "If there was, wouldn't we have taken it to get here?"

She flipped a lock of errant hair back from her face. He always had an answer for everything, didn't he? So why didn't she trust him? "I suppose you have a theory on why my horses are here?"

"Maybe."

She watched him circle the meadow studying the ground as he walked, and couldn't help thinking there was more to Cooper McLeod than just some saddle-worn rodeo cowboy.

After a moment he knelt in the grass, then motioned for her to join him. "Seems that someone made a portable corral to keep the horses in. And look at this." He stuck three fingers of wet soil under her nose. She jerked back from the awful smell.

"I'd say a mixture of oats and astragalus—heavy on the locoweed," Cooper said.

Delaney swore as she looked around the meadow at her mares. "They corraled my horses, drugged them and let them loose. Why? What did that accomplish?"

She turned, surprised when Cooper didn't throw in his two-cents' worth.

He was still hunkered in the grass. She noticed he had a handful of rank soil that he was slowly letting spill through his fingers. "Oh, I think they accomplished what they set out to do." He leaned back on his haunches and squinted up at her.

"Spit it out, McLeod."

A smile turned up the corners of his mouth, setting off those dimples. His eyes burned like blue flames, but there was no humor in his look, just a deadly seriousness that froze her blood.

"It scared you, didn't it?"

She swallowed and turned away, surprised by his insight. She *did* believe that's exactly what the recent accidents were about—someone was trying to scare her. But she hadn't even admitted it to herself.

She glanced over her shoulder at Cooper, realizing he was much more dangerous than she'd first thought. He had intelligence along with all that charm and good looks. "Why would someone go to all this trouble just to... try to scare me?" she asked.

"That's a good question." He picked up a small, flat stone from the ground, his thumb making slow circles on the weather-worn surface. She remembered the feel of his hand earlier. The hand of a working cowboy, suntanned and weathered, strong and callused. She dragged her gaze away.

"Or it could be someone's out to get you," he said. "But I suppose you'd know better than I would about that."

She met his gaze. The intensity of his look startled her. Not much got past those blue eyes of his. She'd have to remember that.

Cooper dropped the stone and dusted his hands on his jeans. "Well, there's not much we can do here now. The veterinarian should be able to tell you what they were drugged with. I would imagine they weren't given enough to kill them and that this should wear off."

"Really?" she said, looking at him. While she agreed with his appraisal of the situation, she wondered where he'd learned so much about horses. And locoweed. Not on any rodeo circuit.

"You want me to help draw the blood?" he asked.

She nodded as she opened her bag, wondering why she felt Cooper McLeod knew more about her troubles than he was letting on. What did she know about the man anyway? She promised herself she'd run a check on him when she got back to the ranch. If she didn't fire him before the end of the day.

COOPER WATCHED Delaney closely as they started back down the mountain. All her bad luck sounded a little too familiar; minor accidents that frightened ranch owners but didn't devalue the stock or the land. It was the same kind of thing he'd done on other ranches. What the hell was happening on the Rockin' L? And what was the story with Delaney? Was she really as much in the dark as she pretended to be? Not that it mattered. It was obvious this job had more complications than his employers had anticipated. He needed to get to a phone and call them. And of course there was that little matter of the mixed-up information. But worse were the so-called accidents at the Rockin' L. His employers needed to know just what they'd gotten him into. And then they could damn well get him out of it.

He let her lead the way back down. He liked following her, but not just because of the view. He felt she'd be safer with him bringing up the rear. The feeling surprised him. He hadn't felt protective toward a woman in a long time. Especially one as capable as Delaney Lawson. But it also meant he thought she needed protecting. And that worried him.

They were almost out of the narrow canyon of rock, almost to their horses, when he heard the splatter of small stones, like raindrops overhead. He glanced up, caught a blur of color and lunged for Delaney. Catching her around the waist, he took her down into the gravel at the edge of the rock wall. They hit hard, Cooper absorbing most of the impact as he pulled her back under the overhang, drawing her tight against his body.

"What the—" Delaney's words were drowned out by the rock slide that whirred in front of them as loud as helicopters. Rocks hammered the creek bed in a meteorlike shower. Delaney pressed into him and he held her tighter.

"McLeod?"

It took him a moment to realize the rocks had quit falling. It took another to realize the thudding of his heart was only partially due to the near accident. He lay with Delaney spooned against him, his arms wrapped around her, his forearms against her soft, full breasts, his face buried in her hair. At every point where Delaney's body pressed against his, he felt the heat of desire. She turned in his arms, and without thinking, he sought her lips—

"McLeod." Her lips barely brushed his and were quickly gone as she slipped out of his embrace, leaving him with nothing but her hat in his hands. Fast on her feet, he decided, looking up at her standing over him.

He'd thought he might see at least a little fire of longing burning in her eyes. There was a fire, all right. But this one could have been set by an arsonist—a very mad one. Forget longing. Forget desire. Only anger burned in those dark eyes. A whole lot of anger. And all of it directed at him. She stood with her hands on her hips, eyes blazing.

"And just what was all that about?" she demanded.

Realizing he still held her hat in his hands, he got to his feet and picked up his rifle. "Ma'am?"

Angrily she dusted herself off as if she could erase the feel of him against her and picked up her own rifle from the ground. "Don't 'ma'am' me, you...you..." She waved her hand through the air.

He joined her in the rock-strewn creek bed. "You don't have to thank me for saving your life—"

"Saving my life! Is that what you were doing?"

Her ebony hair spilled around her shoulders. She threw it back as she narrowed eyes as dark as midnight at him.

"And here I thought you were just taking advantage of the situation."

He looked down at her hat in his free hand. What was wrong with him? He'd charmed his way into enough women's hearts to know better than to overplay his hand. Why in God's name had he tried to kiss her? He met her gaze. Because at that moment all he'd wanted was to kiss her. Great. "Pardon me, ma'am—I don't know what I was thinking," he answered honestly. "It was just a crazy impulse."

She took the hat he offered her, her fingers shaking. "McLeod, I have enough problems without you—"

"I'd say you're right about that. But before you fire me, there's something you might want to know. That rock slide wasn't an accident."

She glared at him. "And how do you know that?

He studied her, realizing he had nothing to lose. She planned to can him, and he couldn't say he blamed her. "I think there's something you'd better see."

They hiked back up the mountain, then across the top of the rock butte. The sun slipped toward the mountains to the west, stealing across the sky, taking the heat with it.

"See those?" He pointed to the boot tracks in the dust where he'd seen the flash of clothing. The rocks had been disturbed where someone had started the rock slide. "Right before the slide, I saw someone up here."

DELANEY FELT her legs turn liquid beneath her. She plopped down on a large boulder at the edge of the steep bluff, all her strength suddenly gone. Cooper was right. Someone had purposely started the rock slide. She rubbed the back of her neck, trying to make sense of everything that was happening, slowly realizing that like it or not, Cooper had saved her life. She looked up to find him silhouetted against the sinking sun. She didn't need to see his face to know he was watching her.

"I'm sorry. I thought you'd somehow orchestrated the rock slide just to—" She bit down on her lower lip, realizing how crazy that must sound. Almost as crazy as that split second when she'd wanted to kiss him.

He grinned. "I usually don't have to pull off such elaborate feats to get a kiss from a woman."

"I'm sure you don't." She tried to laugh, but it came out a whisper. "Thank you."

"Forget it," he said, seeming to study the dusty toes of his boots.

Delaney pushed herself up and walked toward a stand of pines, fear mixing with anger as she thought about the person who'd drugged her horses, who'd no doubt caused her other "accidents," who'd just tried to kill her. She stopped at the sight of a horse's tracks in the dirt and squatted to study them. One of the horse's shoes had been barred across the back, a corrective measure for a broken hoof, and just as individualized as a fingerprint.

She looked up to find Cooper standing over her.

"Recognize the horse?" he asked, nodding at the print.

She shook her head. "It could even be one of mine." The shoer had just been to the ranch. Buck hadn't mentioned a horse with a broken hoof, but she hadn't seen much of Buck lately. She pushed herself to her feet, fighting tears of anger, fear and growing frustration.

"Maybe I'm out of line again, boss, but I can't help thinking you know who's doing this. And why."

She took a deep breath and let it out slowly as she turned. Her first impulse was to tell him to mind his own business. But he'd just saved her life, hadn't he? Her gaze wandered across the land, then settled on Cooper. "I knew he wanted the ranch," she said quietly. "I just never believed he'd try to kill me to get it."

Chapter Three

Delaney found she was shaking by the time they reached their horses. A delayed reaction. From her near escape in the rock slide. Her near escape from kissing Cooper McLeod. She didn't know what had possessed her. She blamed it on fear, on all the bad luck she'd been having, on this cowboy's unexpected insight on the mountain.

"Is it Jared Kincaid?" Cooper asked as he put his rifle back into his scabbard.

It was a question she knew he'd been dying to ask, but she hadn't given him a chance.

She sheathed her own weapon and swung up into the saddle. "Jared? Why would you think that?"

"He seems to have an interest in your bad luck," Cooper said as he mounted Crazy Jack.

Delaney watched him, thinking the same could be said of Cooper McLeod. But Cooper had almost been caught in the rock slide with her, she reminded herself. If it hadn't been for him— "Jared's made no secret of the fact that he'd like the Rockin' L. But this isn't his style." She hesitated, having never voiced her fears before. "A man claiming to be my half brother showed up at the ranch about a month ago, about the time my so-called bad luck started."

"A half brother you didn't know about?" Cooper asked, incredulous.

Delaney looked toward the mountains, debating how much to confide in McLeod. He'd just saved her life; she owed him at least the truth. "It seems he's the son of an old . . . girlfriend of my father's."

"You don't sound surprised. Or convinced he's your brother."

They rode toward the ranch house, the sun melting behind the peaks. "Surprised that my father had mistresses?" She shook her head, but couldn't meet McLeod's gaze. "Hank Lawson required more attention that any one woman could give a man, not even my mother, who adored him. Ty's mother was one of many. I guess that's why I don't believe Ty Drummond is my half brother."

Cooper pulled off his hat and ran his fingers through his sandy blond hair. It was a gesture Delaney had seen her father do a hundred times.

"I heard about Hank's death while I was riding the circuit. I'm sorry."

She shook her head at the memory. "He was still riding bulls in small exhibition rodeos, even though he was too old for it and had been hurt too many times. He just couldn't quit." She glanced over at Cooper. "And I'm sure you also heard about the bull that killed him. Its name was Death Wish. How appropriate, huh?"

"Riding bulls is dangerous no matter what the bull's name. It's just something some men have to do."

"So my father told me." She couldn't help sounding disgusted. What was wrong with grown men who had to ride wild bulls or broncs? Was it the thrill? The challenge? Or did they have to continue proving themselves? Her father had never been able to explain it to her. And she doubted Cooper McLeod could, either.

They were almost to the ranch. It sat just over the next rise. Delaney quickened her pace. It was a sight she never tired of. Her grandfather, Del Henry Lawson, had built the two-story ranch house. It had weathered many storms over the years—from the worst blizzards to the loss of her mother and finally the death of her father. She hoped the house had the strength to weather more storms, because she knew it was going to have to, and soon.

As the home place came into view, she watched Cooper take it in. He nodded with appreciation.

The house seemed to fill the open landscape, stone glistening, logs glowing warm in the failing sun. Shadows lounged in the shade of a wide porch that ran the width of the house. Behind it all, ponderosas glistened like dark silk against the rocky bluffs. A small creek wound its way through the pines. Off to the side, an old barn hunkered, its horse weather vane reflecting the last of the sun. Another, newer, barn and corrals stretched to the south.

"It's beautiful," Cooper said.

She could feel his gaze on her. It warmed her face the way the sun had.

"It means a lot to you, doesn't it?"

She smiled at that. "It means *everything* to me, Mr. McLeod. I'd die before I'd let anyone take it from me."

He frowned as if suddenly hit by a sharp stab of pain, and she wondered if his leg bothered him more than he let on.

Her smile faded as they rode nearer and she saw the beat-up pickup parked off to the side of the house. "Damn," she swore under her breath. "It looks like you're going to get to meet my alleged half brother, Ty."

COOPER SPOTTED a lanky young cowboy in the shade of the porch, his feet up on the railing, his hat tipped back. His look, as well as his demeanor, oozed defiance.

"I can take care of your horse if you want to go on up," Cooper offered.

But Delaney shook her head. "Let Ty wait. It will be good for him. And I'd just as soon you not take off yet."

She seemed a little rattled. He figured Ty was to blame.

"I have some tax forms I need you to fill out, so you might as well come on up to the house."

They unsaddled the horses and Cooper cut Crazy Jack out with the others. One of the horses in the corral was still lathered up, as if it had just been run hard, he noted, hoping it wasn't Buck's horse. For a while, Cooper had forgotten about the lie he was living. But Buck Taylor would certainly take care of that once they met. Cooper wondered also when the *real* ranch hand would turn up.

"I suppose that's Buck's horse in the corral?" Cooper said, pointing at the freshly ridden dark bay.

Delaney frowned. "No, he keeps his horse, Sugarfoot, down at his place. And Buck's out of town for a few days, so he couldn't have ridden any of these horses." She glanced toward the lathered bay. "I've got a couple of college kids helping with the haying while Buck's gone. Maybe one of them took the horse out." She wasn't convinced.

Cooper climbed into the corral and checked the prints the bay was making in the dirt. No barred horseshoe.

Delaney seemed lost in thought as they walked toward the ranch house. Ty hadn't moved from his spot on the porch, but Cooper detected an agitation that belied the cowboy's apparent calm. His age surprised Cooper. Ty looked to be in his late twenties, like Delaney.

Yet there wasn't much real resemblance between the two. Ty was dark like Delaney, but lacked the striking features that made her beautiful. His eyes were a lighter version of hers, but there was no kindness in them, no compassion, no passion at all. Just an icy darkness that seemed bottomless.

"I heard about the horses," Ty Drummond snarled before Delaney reached the porch.

He sounded accusing and belligerent and Cooper suspected he'd been drinking.

"Jared said—"

"Jared?" Delaney asked, pushing back her hat to look up at him as she leaned against the porch railing.

Cooper watched the two of them from the yard.

"I ran into him in town," Ty said, avoiding her gaze.

"You didn't by any chance borrow one of my horses this afternoon, did you?"

He jerked around to glare at her. "*Your* horses?" Then he gave the idea a dismissive shrug. "What would I need with a horse?"

"I was wondering that myself," Delaney said.

Ty glanced around the ranch yard, pretending a nonchalance he wasn't pulling off. His gaze fell on Cooper. He eyed Delaney questioningly.

"Cooper McLeod is my new hand," she said with more force than she had earlier with Jared. It made Cooper feel a little better. "This is Ty Drummond."

Ty glared at her, then tipped his hat at Cooper. "I'm her brother."

"Half brother," Delaney corrected as she climbed the steps and pushed open the screen door. "Maybe." She glanced over her shoulder. "Cooper, come in and I'll get those forms for you to fill out."

He liked the way she called him "Cooper," even though he figured she only did it to make him sound more important than he was to needle Ty. Nor was he fooled by her asking him inside the house to fill out some tax forms. He figured she didn't want to be alone with Ty. He couldn't blame her. Ty made him nervous, too, but for a different reason.

Cooper followed her into the house. He'd seen photographs of the inside, but none had done it justice. A huge rock fireplace dominated the room. Pine floors gleamed golden beneath a scattering of rich-colored Native American rugs. The furniture, while rustic, looked comfortable, the cushions colorful and inviting.

Behind him, he heard Ty's boot soles slap the floor with angry thuds. The cowboy shoved past him and into the kitchen.

"You can't keep ignoring me," Ty called, stomping after Delaney. "I have our father's will, naming me heir. The Rockin' L is mine and you know it."

Cooper swore under his breath. A will naming Ty heir to the ranch? This was worse than he'd thought. How many more surprises were going to turn up like dead bodies on this ranch? Cooper wondered.

"All I know is what my father told me a week before he died," Delaney said, her voice carrying into the living room. "He said he'd made out a will, leaving me the ranch and everything else, including his bills."

"So where is *this* will?" Ty demanded. "Show it to me."

"It will turn up, don't worry."

Delaney sounded worried, but she wasn't half as worried as Cooper. He had to call his employers—and soon. This job was starting to go sour just like the last one, he thought as he trailed Ty and Delaney into the kitchen.

Like the living room, the kitchen had the same warm and cozy feel to it. Pots hung from the ceiling. A checked red-and-white tablecloth draped the long wooden table. Wild flowers sat in the middle in an old white porcelain vase. Cooper frowned, realizing they must have been from an admirer, because Delaney Lawson seemed too busy a ranch woman to stop to pick flowers.

Ty stomped over to the table and dropped a bundle of letters tied with a ragged purple ribbon onto the tablecloth. "You wanted proof that I'm your brother—there it is."

Cooper watched Delaney pour two glasses of lemonade. She handed one to him, then looked at Ty.

"I don't want any lemonade," he said impatiently. "Well, aren't you even going to look at them?"

Cooper watched her glance toward the package of worn letters, but she didn't reach for them.

"They're love letters," he said smiling, obviously enjoying her discomfort. "From *our* father to *my* mother. I was his son. And he wanted me to have this ranch."

Delaney laughed. "Too bad you weren't around to help pay the bills when he was alive."

Anger rose up Ty's neck like a deep red rash. "I didn't know I was his son. No one bothered to tell me."

Delaney studied him for a moment, then opened the fridge and began to rummage around inside it as if she were searching for something. Cooper figured she just didn't want to deal with this and he couldn't blame her.

"The courts will decide . . ." Delaney said from inside the refrigerator.

"You're just trying to drag this out."

He glared at Cooper, probably since his glares at Delaney were going unnoticed.

"I'll have this ranch, and sooner than you think." He picked up the bundle of love letters, bumping the table and spilling the vase of flowers. "You can have the *copies* of the letters," he said, dropping some papers on the table before he stomped out. Cooper heard the front door slam and, a moment later, a rough-sounding engine start, then a rattling pickup sped off down the road, gears grinding.

Delaney slammed the refrigerator door and leaned against it. "So what do you think of Ty?" she asked sarcastically.

"As charming as Jared Kincaid," Cooper said, picking up the copies of the love letters and spilled flowers and mopping up the water with the towel Delaney tossed him. "But I can't help thinking he's not the one behind your accidents—or the rock slide today."

"McLeod, didn't you hear what he just said about getting the ranch, and soon?"

Cooper wished she hadn't gone back to calling him "McLeod" so soon. "I just wonder why he's trying too hard to prove to you that he's your brother, especially if he has a will."

"Because he's not my brother, nor is his will any more legitimate than he is," she said angrily. "My father died six months ago, the ranch is tied up in probate and I haven't been able to find the will he told me he wrote, leaving everything to me."

"He didn't leave it with his attorney?"

Delaney looked at him askance. "His attorney?" She laughed. "Hank Lawson was a rodeo cowboy. He didn't have an attorney. Or an accountant. Or even a safety-deposit box at the bank. He lived out of a travel trailer he dragged around the country with an old pickup truck. But I'm sure you, if anyone, would understand that."

"Me?"

She brushed her hair from her face and looked away. "I'm sorry. It's just that you remind me a lot of my father."

He wasn't sure he wanted to hear this. "Because we both rodeo?"

She studied him for a moment, her eyes dark and troubled. "He was handsome like you." She smiled. "Don't act as though you're surprised to hear that you're handsome." She narrowed her gaze at him as she searched his face. "And Hank was charming, and funny, and . . . sexy like you." She laughed when he raised an eyebrow at the last. Then she looked away. "Unfortunately, he broke my mother's heart and didn't do a half-bad job on mine."

"I'm sorry to hear that." He leaned toward her and heard her breath catch in her throat. As he handed her the photocopies of the letters, he noticed a slight tremble to her fingers as she took them. It struck him that she was afraid of him. He frowned. "You know not every cowboy who rides the rodeo abandons his family for the sport."

She almost looked as if she wanted to believe that.

He glanced around the homey kitchen, thinking about Ty Drummond. "A bastard son who can prove paternity could get a portion of the estate," he said quietly. "Or even if he isn't your brother, Ty could get everything if the will he has from your father is legitimate. Unless you can come up with a more recent will your father had witnessed and dated."

"You almost sound like a lawyer."

Those dark eyes of hers seemed to penetrate him.

"Who are you really, Cooper McLeod?"

He shook his head and summoned up a grin, hoping it would mollify her. "Isn't it bad enough I'm a rodeo cowboy? Now you think I'm a lawyer?"

She laughed. "What I don't think you are is a ranch hand."

He tried to appear crushed. "I guess I'll just have to work harder at it," he answered truthfully.

A movement caught his eye outside the kitchen window. "Looks like you have another visitor."

Delaney moaned and moved over to the window to see. A frown creased her brow and real worry etched itself in her expression. "Oh, no, it's Tess." Delaney bolted for the front door. Cooper ran after her. They reached the ranch yard as an old mule came trotting up.

Delaney hurried to it, running her hand along its neck, hugging the animal to her. "Oh, God." Delaney scanned the empty road and Cooper saw the same worry and fear he'd witnessed earlier when they'd found the drugged horses. "We have to find Digger."

"Digger?" He followed after her as she took the mule into the barn, gave it food and water, then grabbed her rifle from the tack room and her doctoring bag.

"I suppose you're coming with me." She didn't wait for an answer.

He pulled his rifle from the scabbard, wondering what kind of trouble hunting for Digger was going to get them in and limped after her.

"If anything has happened to Digger..." Delaney muttered as she headed for a pickup parked by the barn.

They were in the truck tearing down the dirt road, when Cooper asked, "Who's Digger?"

Delaney glanced over at him as if she'd forgotten he'd come along. "Digger O'Donnel. His camp is up near Hogback Mountain." She stared ahead at the road. Beyond it the horizon had turned lavender in the twilight. "Digger and Tess are inseparable. For Tess to come home like that—"

Home? Cooper heard the break in Delaney's voice. Whoever Digger was, he meant a great deal to her. How many men did this woman have in her life anyway? Cooper wondered.

"Digger has to be in trouble," she said quietly, not even trying to hide her fear. Or the tears that brimmed in her eyes.

Cooper watched the road ahead, worried that whoever this Digger was, he'd met with one of the Rockin' L's notorious accidents.

Chapter Four

A cool darkness had settled in the pines by the time Delaney stopped the pickup in the middle of the mountain road. Without a word, she jumped out, turned the hubs into four-wheel drive and slid back into the cab. Then she pulled onto what could only be called a Jeep trail.

Dark pine boughs closed around the pickup, reminding Cooper of the close confines of a car wash. He squirmed uneasily. "Just exactly who is this Digger we're looking for?" he asked, unable to take his eyes off the patch of road he could see in the headlights, for fear of what would appear around the next curve. His claustrophobia and Delaney's anxiety were making him jumpy. That and the feeling that they were riding into something nasty just, as they had the drugged horses on the mountain earlier.

The pickup climbed at a crawl, bumping over large boulders that formed the roadbed. Delaney gripped the wheel, all her concentration on the road. Worry made her eyes darker than the coming night and her expression bleak.

"Digger O'Donnel is a prospector," she said after a moment. She seemed to loosen her grip on the wheel a little. "He pans for gold, but mostly just wanders the mountains with Tess."

"Gold?" Cooper asked, trying not to let his surprise show.

"Digger used to work one of my grandfather's claims with a friend of his, Gus Halbrook. They were in their early twenties when they met my grandfather, Del Henry Lawson. It was the 1930s and some of the mines around here had been reopened. My grandfather, who was by then in his late fifties, hired Digger and Gus to work the Golden Dream."

"Did they strike it rich?" Cooper asked, more than a little curious.

Delaney carefully eased the pickup over two large boulders before she answered. "To hear Digger tell it. He swears they found the mother lode." She glanced over at Cooper. "But then, Digger has no money to show for it if they did."

"What about your grandfather?" Cooper asked. "He must have found some gold originally to buy this ranch."

Delaney laughed. "My grandfather married a young woman with money. Grandmother helped him start the Rockin' L after his mining claims on the land proved to be near worthless."

"But Digger says they found the mother lode?"

She turned her attention back to the road. "You see Digger is... well, his mind kind of... snapped when his friend Gus was killed in a cave-in long before I was born."

"This mine that caved in is the one Digger said was the mother lode?" Cooper asked. "The Golden Dream?"

She nodded. "I think that's the only way Digger can accept what happened. My grandfather said they found a small vein of gold but it quickly petered out. Unfortunately Gus kept working the mine on his own time, obsessed with the belief that it was the elusive mother lode. Gus didn't take the time to shore up the walls adequately and was killed in a cave-in."

She let out a sigh. "After that my grandfather closed the mine, blasting the entrance so no one else would get killed in it. The Golden Dream is gone in more ways than one. I doubt even Digger remembers where it was."

Cooper turned to stare at her. "*You* don't know where the mine is?"

She shook her head. "There are so many mines on the ranch. None of them is worth anything."

"That's interesting," Cooper said, without thinking. He tried to remember what he'd heard about the area. It had been gold country, that was for sure. Confederate Gulch and its tributaries weren't far from the Rockin' L, and they'd produced millions of dollars in gold back in the 1800s.

Delaney must have heard interest in his tone. They'd just topped a small rise, the pines dense and dark, the road nothing but rocks.

"You're not getting any romantic ideas about finding the missing mother lode, are you?"

Suspicion put an edge on her words. She sounded as if she'd expect just about anything from him, as long as it was bad.

Cooper laughed. "I'm a cowboy, not a gold miner. Anyway, there is no mother lode, right?"

"Right."

He could feel her watching him out of the corner of her eye.

"We're almost there."

Cooper stared ahead, thinking about gold, missing mines and an old prospector who swore he'd found the mother lode—and was now maybe missing himself. Everything about the Rockin' L was turning out to be a surprise, Cooper realized with growing concern.

They dropped into a ravine and Delaney slowed as the truck's headlights illuminated a makeshift lean-to built of tarps and log poles. An iron skillet hung from a nail on one of the poles. Near it a cracked mirror reflected the light from the headlights.

"My grandfather built Digger a cabin not far from here, but he prefers *this* except in the dead of winter," Delaney lamented, obviously unable to understand.

Cooper stared at the camp. It resembled many he'd spent time in. "There is nothing like being able to see the stars at night," he said as Delaney brought the pickup to a stop.

She reached under the seat for a flashlight. Her fingers shook as she fumbled to turn it on. Cooper took it from her. His hand brushed her wrist and he could feel her pulse pounding. "If he's around here, we'll find him."

She nodded and swallowed. He opened his door and heard her do the same. They walked into the sparse camp. It appeared as if its occupant had just left for a moment. A worn bedroll was spread in the pine needles beneath the tarp. A striped pillow lay on top of it beside a dog-eared gold-mining book.

Cooper checked the fire pit. It was cold.

"Did you hear that?" Delaney whispered.

He listened. Night had dropped into the ravine and Digger O'Donnel's camp. The air felt cold and brittle, as if warning that fall wasn't far away.

"Over there." Delaney pointed into the dense pines. "I heard something, over there."

Cooper started to shine the flashlight into the trees, when he heard it, too. A moan. He flicked the beam across the dark boughs, then brought it back to what looked like a bundle of clothing piled next to a tree trunk.

"Digger!" Delaney cried, and scrambled toward the heap.

Cooper hurried after her, pointing the way with the light. She dropped to the ground beside the ragged bundle, speaking in a hushed tone.

Cooper shone the flashlight for her, afraid they'd arrived too late. A weathered old man lay against the tree trunk, his eyes closed. He wore a hunting cap and overalls beneath a ragged coat. His head was tilted at a strange angle, his mouth drooped open.

"Oh, Digger," Cooper heard Delaney cry as she cupped the man's ancient face in her hands. Cooper noted with shock that there were tracks in the pine needles where he'd dragged himself for some distance, obviously trying to get back to his camp.

Cooper knelt beside the pair. He was sure the old prospector was headed for the Pearly Gates, when Digger opened his eyes. His startling brown-eyed gaze fought to focus on Cooper, then Delaney. A smile worked at his lips.

"I knew you'd come, sweet Winnie."

Cooper shot Delaney a look. Who the devil was Winnie?

"Yes, Digger, I'm here now," she said softly.

The old man lifted his hand to pat Delaney's cheek. "In the lake. Damnedest thing you've ever seen." His voice dropped to a whisper; his eyelids drooped. "Space aliens, Winnie. In the lake." His eyes closed, his breathing grew more ragged. Suddenly his eyes flew open again. "Tess!" he cried. "Where's Tess?"

"She's fine, Digger," Delaney assured him. "She came to the ranch, so I knew you were in trouble. I put her in the barn with some oats."

He smiled, then his eyes widened with fear. "He's back from the grave, Winnie. Back for revenge. Gus. He tried to kill me."

"We have to get him to a doctor," Delaney said, motioning for Cooper to help her lift him.

"Easy," Cooper said as he noticed the blood-encrusted lump on the back of Digger O'Donnel's head.

"He must have taken a fall," she said, swearing under her breath. "He's too old to be wandering the woods like this."

Cooper started to argue that confining him to a cabin would probably kill him. He'd seen what could happen to a man who'd lost his freedom. Instead he handed Delaney the flashlight and lifted the old man into his arms. "We can put him in the middle. You drive and I'll try to keep him as stationary as I can."

Delaney shivered and mumbled, "Space aliens. I wonder where he got that?"

As Cooper carefully laid Digger on the seat, his old eyes flickered open. "Del," he said, his voice weak. He smiled and fumbled for Cooper's hand. He pressed a piece of crumbled paper into Cooper's fingers, then closed his eyes again. Cooper shoved the paper into his pocket as Delaney climbed behind the wheel and Cooper slid in beside Digger.

WHILE THEY WAITED at the hospital for word on Digger's condition, Delaney paced. Cooper brought her coffee and a sandwich, but she'd taken only a few bites. Like her, he was worried—just not for the same reasons.

"Digger called you 'Winnie,'" he said, trying to distract her from staring down the hallway toward Digger's room.

Delaney glanced at the sandwich in her hand, then at Cooper. "Winifred Lawson. My grandmother. I've always suspected Digger was in love with her. They were about the same age."

"If this Winnie was anything like her granddaughter, I can understand why," Cooper said.

She rolled her eyes. "I'd say thank you, but I know charm is second to breathing for men like you."

He laughed, not even bothering to deny it, and shoved his hands into the pockets of his jeans. That's when he remembered the crumpled paper and dug it out. "Digger thought I was you as I was loading him into the pickup. He called me 'Del' and gave me this." He pressed what appeared to be a piece of paper bag flat on the waiting-room coffee table.

"More than likely he thought you were my grandfather, Del Henry." She stepped closer.

Cooper stared at the crude drawing on the paper bag, then up at Delaney. He let out a low whistle. "Correct me if I'm wrong, but that looks like a space alien, complete with space ship."

Delaney contemplated the drawing for a moment. "I don't understand this."

"Digger said he saw space aliens on the ranch. In the lake. There isn't a lake on the ranch, is there?"

She frowned. "Not really. We call it Johnson Gulch Lake, but it's just a place where Johnson Gulch Creek pools in the rocks."

"And it's near Digger's camp?"

"Just over the ridge. But he can't have seen…" She waved her hand at the drawing.

"Extraterrestrials?" Cooper asked, then shook his head. "Who was this Gus he was talking about?"

"Gus Halbrook, I assume."

"Oh, the old prospector who died in the cave-in."

Delaney nodded. "Obviously Gus hasn't come back from the dead, nor did Gus try to kill him. But do you think someone did attack him?"

Cooper avoided her gaze, but not quickly enough.

"You think it has something to do with my problems on the ranch?"

Cooper shrugged. "It just crossed my mind that Digger might have seen something he wasn't supposed to."

"Like what?" she asked, her gaze drilling him.

He felt cornered. "Space aliens. Or maybe someone in the process of causing one of the accidents at the ranch."

Delaney put the sandwich down and rubbed her arms as if suddenly cold. "I just assumed he'd taken a fall. But after everything that's been happening on the ranch—"

They both turned as the doctor came down the hall. Cooper folded the drawing and pushed it back into his pocket. "You might want to keep this space-alien stuff just between the two of us," he whispered as the doctor approached.

She glanced at him indignantly. She seemed to have that look down when it came to him. "How's Digger?" she asked the doctor.

"He's resting quietly," the doctor assured her.

Delaney pressed her fingers to her lips, tears brimming in her eyes. "He's going to be all right, isn't he?"

The doctor smiled as he laid a hand on Delaney's shoulder. "Digger O'Donnel is one tough old bird. I'd put *my* money on him. You can see him for a moment if you'd like."

She looked over at Cooper.

"I need to make a phone call anyway," he said, happy to finally get a chance to call his employers.

COOPER FOUND a phone booth at the end of the hall, closed the door and dialed the familiar number. Thom Jamison answered on the second ring.

"We've got trouble," Cooper said by way of introduction. "I got the wrong information on my ranch assignment. And that's just the beginning."

"Something's not right," Jamison said after hearing Cooper's story. "All of this should have come up in our preliminary report on the ranch. We couldn't have been that far off."

"I say we pull off this job now and that's what I intend to recommend to the agency." Cooper thought about Delaney and wondered what she would think when he didn't show up the next morning. He felt a twinge of guilt. And regret.

"Wait a minute, Coop. If someone screwed up at the agency, I want to find out before they can hide their mistake. Give me a couple of days before you pull off. I want to find the person responsible for this mess—the person who supplied me, and you, with the wrong information."

Cooper looked up to find Delaney coming down the hall toward him. Just the sight of her made his pulse quicken. He couldn't quite put his finger on what made her so desirable. "Two days. Then I'm out of here." He hung up and opened the door.

"Where are you staying?" Delaney asked as they were leaving the hospital.

It seemed like days since he'd parked his pickup, camper and horse trailer in a wide spot off the county road and saddled up to do a little snooping around. "I'm camped on the west end of the ranch."

Delaney didn't appear surprised to hear he was camping out. In fact, he saw her shake her head and mutter "rodeo cowboys." She was probably comparing him with her father again. One of those damned rodeo cowboys, who'd rather have stars over his head than a roof. No ties. Nothing to hold him down. Always looking to see what was over the next rise.

She wasn't far from from the truth, he realized.

"I need to drop off the blood we took from the mares at the veterinarian's and then I'll take you home," Delaney said.

Home. He liked the image that came to mind when she said it. He told himself that when this job was over he'd finally have enough money to buy himself a real home. He could settle down. But as he looked up the night sky, he wondered if he ever would. Somewhere along the line he'd become hooked on the freedom. The adventure. Even the danger.

Stars brighter than any he thought he'd ever seen sparkled in the soft blue velvet. They drove toward the mountains, now etched deep purple against the sky. As they neared the campsite, the moon rimmed the Big Belt Mountains with its own kind of gold.

"What a night," Cooper said, looking over at Delaney. "But then, it's been quite a day." He couldn't help thinking about earlier in the canyon when he'd held her, when he'd almost kissed her. The sudden, overpowering desire he felt surprised him. What was it about this woman?

He smiled to himself as he realized it was more than physical attraction, more than plain-old lust. He liked her. Liked her spunk. Her determination. Her fire. She reminded him of some of the broncs he'd tried to ride.

He just hoped she was tough enough to protect herself from what was happening on her ranch. Someone was set on hurting her. Maybe Ty Drummond. But Cooper would put his money on Jared Kincaid. There was nothing about the man he liked, and he'd seen the way Kincaid looked at Delaney. Like a predator. And Cooper recognized predators; he'd been one long enough.

Delaney slowed for his campsite. "What in the world?" she cried, and hit the brakes.

Cooper swung his gaze to his camp, expecting for just an instant to see Martians waiting for him beside his weathered camper. Instead, munching grass next to the horse trailer, was Crazy Jack.

Cooper shrugged apologetically. "Crazy Jack's never been wild about being corraled for long."

Delaney laughed, shaking her head. "That's some horse you got there, McLeod. He's a lot like his owner, huh?"

Cooper smiled, opened the pickup door and stepped out. He hesitated in the darkness, thinking about the woman in the truck, wanting suddenly to warn her. But warn her about what? He didn't have the faintest idea who was behind her problems. All he knew for sure was that it wasn't him. Yet. He leaned back into the pickup.

She looked more beautiful than she had earlier that day when she'd interrupted his nap. There was a softness and a strength about her in the lights from the dash that tugged at him in a way no other woman had.

"About tomorrow—"

"We start work at five a.m. There're fences that need mending, hay to get in and those mares to get down out of the high country." She shifted the pickup into Reverse. "Good night, McLeod."

"Good night, Ms. Lawson." He closed the pickup door and stood in the middle of the road, watching the vehicle's taillights disappear over the next rise, until Crazy Jack gave him a good hard nudge.

"Don't say it," he told the horse. "I'm not getting involved."

Crazy Jack let out a snort and wandered off, probably in search of dinner. Cooper stood in the dark, telling himself Delaney's problems were none of his business. In a couple of days he'd be gone. And Delaney Lawson and the Rockin' L would be forgotten—just like other women he'd conned, other ranches he'd acquired.

Chapter Five

Delaney awoke with a start. She lay in bed, listening to the night sounds beyond her second-story window, listening for the one sound that had brought her abruptly from her sleep. The pines along the creek behind the house let out a sigh in the breeze. In the distance, a horse whinnied softly. No other sound disturbed the night. She closed her eyes. Instantly they flew open as she heard the familiar creak of the old barn door. She sat up, slipping out of bed to go to the window. What was someone doing in the barn this time of the night?

Through the glass, Delaney could see the old barn hunkered behind the house. The door stood open. She reached for her robe, but the soft chenille fabric fell from her fingers as the night outside the window exploded and the barn burst into flames. A dark figure hurried along the edge of the burning structure, disappearing into the darkness.

Without thinking, Delaney raced down the stairs and out into the ranch yard. The aged, dried wood of the barn blazed, hot and fiery. Flames licked up the sides. Smoke billowed up into the starlight. She stared in horror, stunned that someone had deliberately set her barn on fire. Anger made her want to chase after the shadowy figure, but common sense held her back. She didn't even have a weapon.

Nor was she dressed, she realized, looking down at her nightgown and bare feet.

She grabbed the garden hose from the side of the house, knowing it would do little to save the barn but afraid the near flames would catch the side of the ranch house on fire. She turned the icy water on the log siding, praying it would do some good. Smoke and sparks showered the darkness.

Delaney wasn't sure if it was the cold spray from the hose or the memory of the figure sneaking into the night that gave her a sudden chill. With a start, she turned to find Cooper standing behind her.

"What are you doing here?" she demanded, startled to realize he'd sneaked up behind her without her hearing him. Like her, he was only half-dressed, his feet bare. Nearby, Crazy Jack stood without a saddle, his flanks sweaty as if he'd just been run hard.

"I SAW THE FIRE," Cooper said, taking the garden hose from her. "There's nothing else you can do," he said softly. The barn was now little more than a black skeleton. Flames ate up the last of the fuel, then began to die back as a portion of the barn collapsed in a pile of charred wood.

He watched her stare at the destruction, her arms at her sides. Her face was flushed from the heat. Her hair fell around her shoulders, free as the night breeze. She wore a flannel nightgown that hung to her ankles. Her muddy bare feet peeked out the bottom. All the fight seemed to have gone out of her. She looked small against the night, small and vulnerable.

He resisted the urge to take her into his arms and try to comfort her.

"I saw someone out here right after the barn went up in flames," she said quietly. "It's not going to stop, is it?"

Cooper watched the fire die away and darkness take back the night. Having orchestrated enough of these kinds of "series of accidents," he knew that once they started happening—

Slowly he dropped the hose and touched Delaney's arm. "I think you'd better call the sheriff."

Under normal circumstances, calling the sheriff would be the last thing he'd suggest. But nothing about this was normal, he realized. This job would have to be handled differently. He'd seen the suspicion in Delaney's eyes. He would have to be careful around her. Very careful.

Delaney looked over at him. Her gaze met his. He groaned softly, amazed how sexy she was even in all that flannel. "I'm not sure calling the sheriff will do any good, McLeod."

"Why is that?"

"Jared Kincaid is the county sheriff."

"WHAT TERRIBLE LUCK," Jared said as he entered the kitchen, the early-morning sun filling the room with warmth. Jared didn't appear much different from the way he had earlier. He still had that hungry look in his eye when his gaze fell on Delaney, and the sheriff's uniform, which did little to hide his growing gut, seemed only to increase his arrogance.

"Someone torched my barn, Jared," Delaney said wearily. She'd dressed in jeans, a western shirt and boots. Her fingers shook as she curled them around her coffee cup. "It had nothing to do with luck. I heard someone in the barn. When I looked out, the barn exploded. I saw a figure running away."

"Now, Del," Jared said as he reached out to pat her hand.

She moved her coffee cup, avoiding his touch. "Dammit, Jared, I don't need your sympathy," she said, her voice full of anger. "I need you to find out who's behind the vandalism on my ranch."

Jared pulled back his hand, rubbed his jaw and turned his gaze on Cooper, who stood against the wall trying to be as invisible as possible. "When did *you* get here?"

"Not until the barn was almost to the ground," Cooper said carefully. Any officer of the law made him nervous. Jared Kincaid scared the hell out of him because Kincaid was too personally involved.

"Is that right? Can you prove it?"

"Jared! It wasn't Cooper I saw out there."

Jared lifted an eyebrow at her. "Then just who was it, Del?"

FEAR PRESSED against her heart as Delaney thought about the figure she'd seen sneaking along the side of the burning barn. She glanced toward the window. She couldn't be sure who she'd seen. So why had she defended McLeod so quickly? Because she didn't want it to be him, she told herself. "The person was smaller than Cooper and didn't move like him," she said with less conviction that she'd hoped for. Cooper moved like a big mountain cat, sure, swift and powerful. She thought of the person she'd seen from her bedroom window. If only she could be sure.

Jared must have heard the hesitation in her voice, seen the doubt in her eyes. A muscle in his jaw twitched.

"Smaller and didn't *move* like your ranch hand. That tells me a lot, Del. What I really want to know is who you think burned down your barn."

Anger bubbled up inside her as hot and fierce as any passion she'd ever felt. "Maybe the same person who's been causing all the accidents on the ranch, including setting off a rock slide yesterday afternoon that could have killed me."

Jared turned a shade of gray that didn't become him. "Why didn't you tell me about this, Del?" he demanded between gritted teeth. "I *am* the sheriff, you know."

Delaney brushed her hair back and looked toward the window again. *Then act like the sheriff,* she wanted to say.

Stop acting as if you want to own me. "I don't have any
proof, but I'm willing to wager Ty Drummond is behind it."
Ty had something to gain by tormenting her. Cooper
McLeod didn't, did he? she wondered, shooting him a quick
glance.

"Your half brother?" Jared asked, surprised.

"Alleged half brother."

"Del, why would your brother want to burn down part of
a ranch he's inherited?" Jared asked, even more incredulous.

How did Jared know about the will? Obviously Ty had
been shooting his mouth off around town. Delaney started
to argue that the will Ty said was from her father hadn't
been proven authentic in a court of law, but decided to save
her breath. "It was an old barn, Jared. We hardly used it for
more than storage. Ty would know that as well as you or
anyone else. And whoever is behind this seems intent on not
costing the ranch too much money—just in driving me out,
or possibly killing me. In my book, that makes Ty a suspect, because he's the only one who'd benefit from my
death."

"Where's Buck?" Jared demanded, sounding more than
a little testy. "What kind of ranch manager is he? Never
around when you need him?"

She stared at Jared. Buck and Jared had always gotten
along well. Where was all this animosity coming from?
"Buck wouldn't have been here anyway." Jared knew her
ranch manager lived in her father's old rodeo trailer down
the road, several miles from the ranch. "He couldn't have
even seen the fire from his place."

Jared glared at her, no longer sympathetic. "That doesn't
really answer my question, Del. Where *is* Buck?"

"Surely you don't think Buck—"

He cut her off with an oath. "Tarnation, woman, *everyone* is a suspect." His gaze glanced over Cooper as if to
make his point. Delaney realized Cooper was being awfully

quiet, and she found that more than a little strange, since he usually couldn't seem to keep his two cents to himself around her. Nor did he seem nervous, which surprised her even more. If Jared considered her a suspect, she'd be as nervous as the devil in the company of angels.

"Buck had some personal business to attend to in Helena," she finally answered. Buck had been acting strange lately and she suspected he had a woman in Helena he was seeing.

"When's he supposed to be back?"

Jared was all business now and she realized she'd hurt his feelings as usual. Probably not a good idea, all things considered.

"Sometime tomorrow." Was it her imagination, or did Cooper finally seem a little worried?

"While you're looking for suspects, Jared, you might add the people who've been trying to buy my ranch," she said.

"What people?" he snapped.

Out of the corner of her eye, she thought she saw Cooper tense. "A man named Jamison, Thomas Jamison, from a company that calls itself Rattlesnake Range. They've made a couple of offers on the place."

"I didn't think your ranch was for sale," Jared said, appearing even more peeved than before. "I believe I've made you a couple of offers myself."

She glared at him. "It *isn't* for sale. That's the point."

With a curse, Jared pushed himself to his feet. "I'll get an arson expert out of Helena to come take a look at your barn. And I'll see if your brother has an alibi. I'll even run a check on this Rattlesnake Range. That's about all I can do, Del, other than come camp outside your house."

"That won't be necessary," Cooper said, making Del turn and stare at him in surprise. "If it's all right with Ms. Lawson, I'll be moving my rig out here."

She gaped at Cooper, amazed and at the same time almost relieved that the outspoken, too-bold cowboy she'd found sleeping on a rock had returned. While his pushiness had irritated her to no end, he made her even more nervous when he was silent.

"And you think that's going to make you feel safe?" Jared asked Delaney quietly as he reached for his western hat, which he'd hooked on the back of her chair. "Well, it's your life, Del. But you know what they say—crawl in a cave with a grizzly and you're liable to get eaten alive." He slammed the door on his way out.

She looked over again at the cowboy leaning against the wall. Jared was right. A grizzly might be far safer than getting too close to this man.

"You realize, McLeod, that was probably the worst thing you could have done," she said, shaking her head at him. "He'll try to hang all this on you now for sure."

Cooper shrugged. "I'm not worried about me." He met her gaze.

She felt the shock, a surge of wild current that rushed through her veins. Something in his blue eyes pulled at her, tempting her with unspoken desires. She dragged her gaze away, fighting the sudden heat that fired her skin. "And don't think that this show of chivalry is going to make any points with the boss."

He laughed. "Never crossed my mind. I just thought it would help me get to work on time."

"Good thinking, McLeod, because we have a lot of work to do."

COOPER CUSSED all the way back to his camping spot. Cussed Rattlesnake Range for going behind his back and making an offer. Several offers. This had never happened before, so why was it happening now?

But mostly he cussed himself for his impulsiveness. What had he been thinking, telling Delaney he'd camp next to the ranch house? Especially with Buck coming back tomorrow.

"You're acting like a damned fool," he told himself. Crazy Jack jerked the reins as if in agreement. "Don't you start in on me, too," he told the horse.

Taking a deep breath, he looked across the Rockin' L and reminded himself how many times he'd done this sort of thing before, and successfully.

The whole idea was to get closer to Delaney, right? That's what he got paid to do. What better way than being camped right outside her door? Also, he could protect Delaney from Jared Kincaid. He didn't trust the man and wasn't convinced Kincaid wasn't behind her problems, sheriff or not. He assured himself keeping Kincaid away from Delaney had nothing to do with anything but business.

And by camping on the ranch, Cooper would have the pickup handy in case he had to make a run for it. By the time Buck got back, he'd be gone anyway. He hoped. He rubbed his thigh, figuring that the way things were going he was apt to get shot again before this was over. And once was enough.

By the time he got his rig loaded and Crazy Jack in the horse trailer, that little voice in his head that had saved his butt numerous times was telling him to hit the road and not look back. He almost had enough money to buy that little place he'd always talked about owning. Almost. All he needed was this last job.

He started the pickup and sat looking out at the valley— and the Rockin' L. He could call Delaney from town and tell her he'd quit. She couldn't expect a hand to stay at a ranch with the kind of problems she had. He'd cut his losses and walk away while he still could. He'd ask Rattlesnake Range for another assignment, one far away from here. Shifting the truck into gear, he headed for York.

At a phone outside the York Bar, he dialed the agency. York was nothing more than a spot in the road that had once been named New York, Montana, before the "New" was dropped sometime in the previous century. The only busi-

ness in town was the York Bar, a quaint little place with log
walls, a couple of pool tables, some poker and Keno ma-
chines and a few tables for eating the burgers the bar served.
Houses dotted the narrow valley along Trout Creek from
York seven miles up to where the road dead-ended.

Jamison answered on the second ring.

"You made two offers on the Rockin' L," Cooper said
without preamble. "Behind my back."

Jamison was silent for a long moment. "It wasn't my doing, Coop. The agency wants that ranch."

Cooper's heart thundered in his ears. "What are you
saying, Thom? That they're willing to do anything to get
it?" It was a question he'd asked before, only back then he'd
been running the scam. He'd been the one who'd decided
just what it would take to acquire a ranch. Now he realized
he was just one of the players on the wrong side of a deadly
game. And he worried how he'd gotten there.

"The Rockin' L is just one of many acquisitions planned
in the agency's overall—"

Cooper knew the agency's standard response by heart.
"Don't give me that crap, Thom. What's going on? The
company's sent in someone else to get this ranch?"

"There was a mix-up, Coop. You were supposed to acquire a cattle ranch in eastern Montana. Someone else was
handling the Rockin' L."

"Someone from the agency?" Cooper demanded. Jamison hesitated a moment too long. "Don't tell me they hired
someone local."

"The agency wants this ranch, Coop. And they plan to get
it."

Cooper glanced over at a war monument someone had
built across the blacktop road and noticed Ty Drummond's pickup, and wondered suddenly where the out-of-
work rodeo cowboy got money to live on. "Why do they
want the Rockin' L so badly that they'd hire an amateur?"

"You know the board doesn't release that kind of information."

Cooper swore. All he knew was that Jamison fronted for a group of men who made up "the agency." "I thought I could trust you."

"You can," Jamison said wearily. "I'd tell you if I knew. It's all very hush-hush. I just do what I'm told. And I was told to tell you that since you're already there, they'd like you to stay on and keep me informed if there are any... problems."

"Problems?" Cooper laughed. "He tried to kill her."

"What?" Jamison demanded in surprise.

"The guy the agency hired to get the ranch. He tried to kill Delaney Lawson in a rock slide yesterday."

"You know we specifically tell our people not to use excessive force—"

"Is attempted murder considered excessive force, Thom? Because that's where he's at. And he's going to take everyone down with him, including you. You're looking at prison, Thom. And you aren't going to like it—I can assure you of that."

"That's why I need you there, Coop."

He heard an urgency in Jamison's voice he'd never heard before.

"Listen, I don't know what's going on. I don't even know who they've hired. Whoever it is reports directly to the board. That's why I need you on the inside, reporting to me."

"You'll try to find out who they hired?" Cooper asked, wondering why he was doing this, knowing it was because Jamison had always been straight with him. Because if there was anyone at Rattlesnake Range he could trust, it was Jamison.

"I'll work on it from this end. You work on it from there. And Coop, I can pull a few strings and double your commission on this one."

Cooper laughed to himself. For a moment there he'd forgotten why he'd become involved with Rattlesnake Range to start with. For the money. And now Jamison was offering him a way out. After this job, he wouldn't have to work for Rattlesnake Range ever again if he didn't want to. And all he had to do was let Jamison know what was happening. Why did it feel too easy?

"Coop, I'm counting on you."

Jamison sounded scared. He should be.

"I'll phone when I've got something. If you need to talk to me before that, call me at the York Bar and leave a message." He read the number off the phone and hung up.

As he stepped away from the phone, he took a couple of deep breaths. Why did Rattlesnake Range want a relatively small horse ranch near Helena, Montana, bad enough that the agency would kill for it? It didn't make any sense. Unless a lot of money was involved. That ruled out raising Morgan horses. It had to be something else, but what? The missing mother lode?

Cooper didn't like anything about this, hadn't from the start. And now he felt double-crossed—no matter what Jamison had said about a mix-up. The agency had hired an amateur from outside, an amateur who'd almost killed Delaney—as well as Cooper himself—in a rock slide. The whole mess brought back his suspicions about Rattlesnake Range from his mishaps on his last job.

His instincts told him to get as far away as fast as he could. When this thing blew—

He got into his pickup. *It's not your problem, McLeod. You don't owe Jamison anything. Let him get himself out of this. You don't need this kind of trouble.*

Yet Cooper found himself headed for the Rockin' L, right into the heart of trouble. He told himself he couldn't leave until he found out what Rattlesnake Range wanted. And who they'd hired to do their dirty work. And of course there was the money. Going back had nothing to do with Delaney, he assured himself. Nothing to do with all that temptation in blue jeans or his fears for her life if Rattlesnake Range decided to make any more offers on her ranch. No, he was just going back to finish the job he'd started.

As he pulled his rig under some pines, not far from the house, he noticed a dark green pickup parked in front. Rockin' L Ranch, it read on the door. He got out and started toward the ranch house, then saw Delaney sitting on the porch with a man. Cooper swore under his breath as he realized who the man had to be.

"Speak of the devil," Delaney said. "Buck, you remember Cooper McLeod, that rodeo cowboy you hired?"

Chapter Six

Buck frowned and stumbled to his feet. "Rodeo cowboy?" he repeated, sounding more than a little surprised.

But he wasn't as surprised as Cooper was to see him back a day early. Buck stood a solid six feet of hard-boned cowpuncher. Cooper had seen his kind before. The kind who could pick up a half-grown calf and toss it in the air like a cowpie. And right now he looked big *and* mean.

As Cooper mounted the porch steps, his mind raced for a way out of this. He'd been so busy with all the other problems that came with this job, he hadn't really given much thought to how to handle the little problem of his hiring. Not that he usually planned things. He'd just always talked his way out of trouble. Until the last job, he reminded himself.

"I have to tell you the truth, Ms. Lawson," Cooper said before Buck could say anything more. "I wasn't entirely on the up-and-up with your ranch manager here." He shot Buck his best smile and held out his hand. "Buck, it's nice to see you again."

The cowboy hesitated, then with almost resignation took Cooper's hand in a killer grip. Cooper smiled in acknowledgment of the not-so subtle warning, withdrew his aching fingers and quickly turned his attention again to Delaney.

He was about to tell her some cock-and-bull story, but didn't get the chance.

"Buck?" a honey-filled female voice called from inside the house. "Could you come in here a moment?"

"Sure," Buck said, still frowning at Cooper as he pushed back his chair, but a lot of meanness had left his features. "Del, if you'll excuse me?"

"Buck, you aren't getting off that easily," Delaney said.

"I'll be back and we'll get this straightened out," Buck said, giving Cooper the evil eye before hurrying into the house.

With relief, Cooper watched him go, then grinned over at Delaney. "Nice day, isn't it?"

"Save the charm, McLeod," she said, shaking her head. "Buck might have bought it, but I'm not."

The phone rang. She groaned. "Don't move," she ordered as she got up to go in to answer it.

Cooper let out a relieved sigh and glanced around the empty porch. Just what had Buck already told her? Did Buck's surprise indicate that he hadn't told her anything yet? Cooper sure wished he knew. Now more than ever he didn't want to get fired—let alone shot.

Voices from inside the house drifted on the afternoon breeze. Buck's. And the honey-sweet one. Cooper tiptoed over to the screen door and, standing in the shadows, peeked in. Buck and a young blond woman were standing by the couch. A bunch of photo albums were strewn across the cushions, where the woman had obviously been sitting just a few moments ago. Cooper could catch only a few words, but Buck sounded upset. Sneaking across the porch, Cooper planted himself next to the open window near the two.

"What are you saying?" the blonde asked.

She was young, only about half Buck's age, with wide green eyes and a button of a nose. Cute. But the oddest thing was that Cooper knew he'd seen her somewhere before. He just couldn't put his finger on where. He swore under his breath. This could be trouble if she remembered him from one of his other jobs.

Buck motioned for her to keep her voice down, as he looked over his shoulder. Delaney must have been in the office off the other end of the living room.

"She thinks I hired this cowboy."

"So tell her you didn't," the woman snapped.

"The point is, I was *supposed* to hire someone." He brushed his fingers down the tumbled length of her bottle-blond hair, coming to a halt just above her right breast. "I forgot because I was with you."

She giggled, wiggling a little under his touch, just enough to make Buck suck in his breath and pull back his fingers as if burned. She sobered. "You're not going to lose your job, are you? She won't give me that interview."

He looked pained. "Don't worry, I'll think of something."

"Can't you tell her you were helping me with my research?" she suggested.

"I don't think that would necessarily make her happy. I've missed a lot of work *helping* you with your...*research*."

"Then come up with a better lie or something. Surely getting blamed for hiring a rodeo cowboy isn't as bad as forgetting to do your job."

"You don't understand—"

Delaney came out of the office and they both turned. Cooper made a quick trip down the porch to lean against the railing and pretend to study the horizon. A moment later, the screen door creaked open.

"Now, where were we?" Delaney asked.

The look she gave Cooper made it clear she remembered exactly where they were.

"Something about you not telling the truth, I believe?"

"Why, hello," said honey-sweet as she stepped through the open screen door past Buck to extend her hand to Cooper.

Cooper gazed into her baby dark greens, looking for any sign of recognition. Zip. Either she didn't know him, didn't remember him or wasn't letting on. He took her out-stretched hand. She wasn't as cute as he'd first thought. Or maybe his taste in women was changing.

"I'm Angel," she said, squeezing his hand.

"Of course you are," he answered, flashing her a grin. He knew her game. She was just hoping to save Buck. And Cooper didn't mind playing; he was just trying to save his own neck.

She giggled. "Angel Danvers. The writer."

"Cooper McLeod. The ranch hand."

Delaney let out a low oath. "Angel, if you could excuse us for a moment longer..."

Angel turned, fingers going to her painted lips. "Oh, I'm so sorry. Of course you have things you must talk to Buck about."

She shot Buck a heart-melting smile that had the desired effect. Cooper had never seen a man look more smitten.

"I'll just go back in and look at the photos until you're through."

"Yes, we need to clear up a couple of things," Delaney said.

"Then perhaps we can talk about that interview," Angel said. "It just won't be any kind of book without the history of *your* ranch in it."

"Ranch history?" Cooper asked, watching Angel's swing, trying to remember that old expression... if I had a swing like that... And at the same time, trying to place where he'd seen it—and her—before.

"Angel is a historian," Buck said with a note of pride. "She's doing a book on old ranches and I've been helping her do her..." His words died off as he realized Delaney was glaring at him. "Research."

"Okay, what's going on here?" Delaney demanded the moment Angel was out of earshot. "And don't tell me 'nothing.'"

"Well, the truth is..." Cooper said. He looked at Buck meaningfully, hoping the old fool would go along with him. "I might have oversold myself just a little to Buck."

Delaney let out a knowing chuckle. "I can just imagine."

"And I might have told him I was damned good with horses, but I might have failed to mention I'd done a little rodeoing." He shrugged and glanced over at the ranch manager. "I needed the work."

Out of the corner of his eye, he watched Delaney. She studied him as though she'd be able to spot the truth if he so much as even moved a wrong muscle.

"And what do you have to say about all this, Buck?" she asked finally, shifting her gaze to him.

"Well, Del," Buck said, studying the dusty toes of his boots. "I know how you feel about rodeo cowboys, and under normal circumstances I wouldn't dream of hiring one—" He did a pretty good imitation of Cooper's shrug and gave Delaney a poor-ol'-boy look.

Cooper let out the breath he'd been holding. "Buck did me a favor, Ms. Lawson. And I owe him one."

Delaney searched their faces, her gaze shifting between them. "Is that right? Then why is it I'm having trouble believing either one of you?" She swore when neither responded.

"Buck, tell your...friend I'll consider that interview if it will get your mind back on your work. Have her stop by tonight," she said, heading for the barn. She waved off his gushing gratitude. "McLeod, get saddled up. We're going after those mares." She strode across the yard, stirring up dust in her wake. "And Buck, if you're of a mind to do a little work today, you could see if the haying is finished.

We'll need to get that burned barn cleaned up as soon as the arson expert's done with his investigation."

"You bet, Del," Buck called after her.

The moment she disappeared into the new horse barn, he swung around to face Cooper, all that big and mean back.

"Just what is your story, cowboy?" he demanded. "You and I both know damned well I didn't hire you."

Cooper quickly told him how he'd ridden onto the ranch to look for a job but hadn't found anyone around and had been taking a nap up in the hills on the way back, when Delaney found him and mistakenly thought he was already employed.

"I meant it when I said I owed you," he assured Buck. "I really do need this job." Cooper didn't bother to point out that he had Buck over a barrel now. Cooper doubted Delaney would take kindly to the fact that her ranch manager had just lied about hiring him.

Buck made a good show of looking as if he was considering telling Delaney the truth, then nodded, clearly anxious to go tell Angel the news about the interview, as well as assure her that the new ranch hand was no longer a problem. "Well, you'd better be a damned good hand."

Cooper hustled off to saddle Crazy Jack, wondering what Angel saw in the well-preserved ranch manager. It wasn't Buck's good looks or his money, as far as Cooper could tell. And he wondered about her interest in the Rockin' L. He knew it would drive him crazy until he remembered where he'd seen her before.

DELANEY RODE with Cooper up into the high country, taking the long way around the rocky butte to avoid the narrow canyon and any more rock slides. She tried not to think about all the other recent calamities: her drugged mares, the fire, Buck's infatuation with that Angel creature, and Cooper McLeod. Especially not Cooper McLeod.

"Well, how about that," Cooper said as they topped the ridge line. Below them the horses milled in the tall grass—an idyllic, tranquil setting so different from the one they'd witnessed the day before. "Whatever they were drugged with seems to have worn off."

"That call I got earlier was from the veterinarian." She looked over at him. His face was in shadow, but she could still see a hint of those blue eyes of his. "You were right. The horses were drugged with locoweed. Lucky guess, huh."

"Yeah."

Was it her imagination, or did he avoid her gaze?

He hadn't said much on the ride. Which was just as well, as far as Delaney was concerned. She wasn't sure what had transpired between Buck and this cowboy, but none of it had rung true. She felt angry, and wasn't sure exactly why. It was probably that blamed charm of McLeod's. She'd seen the way he worked it on her. And Buck. And Angel. She grimaced, remembering how Angel and Cooper had hit it off. It was enough to make a grown woman sick.

"I've been meaning to ask you what other ranches you've worked on," she said now, more determined than ever to check up on her new ranch hand.

Cooper shoved back his hat. One eyebrow flicked up as he grinned at her. "I kinda thought you might want a list, so I wrote them down for you." He handed her a piece of paper containing a half-dozen ranch names and phone numbers printed neatly.

"It's amazing the way you anticipate my every need," she said, studying him.

He grinned. "Isn't it, though."

She made a mental note to call a few of them and stuffed the list in her pocket. "You don't stay in one place long, do you, McLeod?"

"Never found a reason to," he said, leaning on his saddle horn as he gave her a long, lazy look.

"Let's get these horses out of here," she said, spurring her mare and swearing under her breath. Why did she let him get to her?

"Whatever you say, boss."

But as she rode away she had to admit the man had a way with horses. And women, she thought.

After they got the mares back down into the valley, Delaney sent McLeod off to mend fence, having had more than enough of his charm for one day.

The sun was falling by the time she finished making calls to the ranches where McLeod had worked. Each gave her the same kind of response to her questions. Yes, he'd worked for them. No, they hadn't had any problems with him. They'd found him to be a good worker. Cheerful and cooperative. They'd wanted him to stay.

By the time she hung up from the last one, she wondered if maybe she'd misjudged McLeod.

Delaney showered and took the mail she'd dropped on the kitchen table the day before and a hot cup of coffee out to the porch. When she sat down in her rocker, she realized she'd also picked up the copies of the love letters Ty had left for her.

Slowly she put the mail down beside her chair and began to read the letters.

Neither the coffee nor the late-afternoon sun could chase away the hurt the letters left. Or the fear that settled itself around her heart.

The letters were damning evidence of her father's betrayal. They left little doubt Hank Lawson had had an affair with Ty's mother, Marguerite Drummond. The letters appeared to have been written in her father's scrawled handwriting and many of the phrases sounded just like him. What hurt her was the depth of emotion behind the words he'd written. He'd actually seemed to care for this woman. But who knows where Hank's charm ended and true feelings began? He'd certainly charmed Delaney's mother into

an early grave. And, Delaney thought bitterly, he'd done a
pretty good job on her, as well.

Delaney reread the letters, feeling all the more betrayed by
the man who'd had an affair at the same time he'd had a
young wife and new baby girl at home. Why? It was something she would never be able to understand.

The letters made her wonder if Ty might be telling the
truth. Not only could he be her brother, but he could be the
legal heir to the ranch. Her father could have left him everything, just as Ty contended. Hank had never made a secret of his disappointment in not having a son. What would
he have done if he'd discovered he had a son right before
he'd died?

The love letters were all old, dating back to before Ty was
born. There was no mention of Marguerite's pregnancy or
Ty's birth, or any acknowledgment from Hank that he was
about to become a father.

Ty hadn't known Hank was his father. Why had Marguerite waited so long to tell Ty? Had Hank known about
his son? It didn't make any sense, unless of course she was
lying about Ty's parentage in the hope that her son might be
able to get her former lover's ranch. But if the will Ty had
was legal, he wouldn't need to prove paternity. So why was
he trying so hard, as McLeod had pointed out?

As unpleasant as the thought was, Delaney knew she had
to meet her father's mistress and make her own appraisal of
the situation. The Rockin' L was at stake and she had to
have all the facts to fight Ty.

She folded the letters and put them in her jacket pocket
as she spotted Jared Kincaid's pickup coming up the road.
Now what? she wondered.

"'Afternoon, Del," Kincaid said as he got out of his
truck.

Delaney groaned when she saw the wildflowers he
clutched in his left hand. She couldn't believe the man's de-

termination to get her ranch. And she wondered with a chill what lengths he would go to.

"Thought these might cheer you up," he said, handing her the bouquet.

"Thank you," she said, taking the flowers, "but the only thing that will cheer me up is information on who's behind my problems on the ranch."

He dragged a chair around so he could face her and sat down heavily as if she'd added several years to his age. She saw the disappointment in his expression. And the suppressed anger.

"I brought that, too, Del," he said.

She placed the flowers beside her chair, realizing she might have something to fear from Jared. In the past, she'd always figured she could handle him. But now she wasn't so sure. He seemed far more angry at what he saw as her rejections. Could McLeod be right? Could Jared be responsible for the accidents on her ranch?

"I called the state arson department," he said slowly, as if pained by this whole conversation. "They're sending a man out here this afternoon."

"And Ty Drummond?" she asked.

"He was at the York Bar until closing, then spent some time with one of the local gals before returning to his room down at Lakeside."

"Alone?" Delaney asked.

He shook his head. "The girl confirms his story."

"And gives him the perfect alibi. How handy."

Kincaid studied her, making her slightly uncomfortable. "I know you're determined he's behind this, but you have no proof. You bring me some hard evidence, Del. Otherwise I'm just wasting the taxpayers' money trying to run down your suspicions."

"I'll keep that in mind, Jared." She took a sip of her coffee. It had grown cold and bitter, but she drank it anyway, too stubborn to get more from the kitchen because she'd have to offer Jared a cup. "What about Rattlesnake Range?"

"That's the bad news, Del," Jared said. He leaned back in his chair with an I-told-you-so look that concerned her. What had he learned?

"Seems Rattlesnake Range is a company that buys up ranches. I did a little checking." He shook his head. "Buys 'em up at reduced rates after the ranches experience some 'bad luck.'"

She met his gaze. "You know this for certain?"

"If you mean, can I prove it?" He shook his head. "These guys are good. But the word is that if Rattlesnake Range wants your land, sell before someone gets hurt."

"That's ridiculous." She looked out across her land, anger and fear mixing in lethal proportions. "Why would they want my ranch? And even if they do, if Rattlesnake Range is behind my bad luck, they're wasting their time. I have no intention of selling."

Kincaid shook his head at her. "That was the attitude of some other ranchers, but they ended up selling for less than they were first offered. It seems Rattlesnake Range tries friendly persuasion first, but if that doesn't work, they're not above strong-arm tactics. At least that's what I hear."

She glared at him. "You're the sheriff and you can't do anything about this?"

He puffed up like a field mushroom that had gone sour in the sun. "Dammit, Del, these guys get away with it because they're good. They don't get caught. They don't leave evidence lying around. I'm trying to warn you for your own good. If Rattlesnake Range wants your property, then you'd better sell it to them."

"Why don't you try to find out who might be working for them, instead?" she demanded. "Or maybe I should call the county attorney in Helena?"

Jared stroked his jaw for a moment, eyes squinted in anger. "I'm looking into Rattlesnake Range and who they might have sent to your ranch." He let out a long sigh. "What do you know about this new hand you hired, this McLeod character?"

Delaney had warned McLeod that the sheriff would try to pin this on him. "Forget it, Jared. I checked out McLeod myself."

"Then you won't mind if I do a little checking on my own," he said, pushing himself out of the chair.

"I'm sure you will anyway," she said as she followed Kincaid's gaze to a state truck coming up the ranch road.

Delaney hung around, watching the arson expert and Jared dig in what remained of her barn. It didn't take long before Jared came over to the edge of the porch with the news.

"Someone set the fire," he said. "Made a gasoline bomb out of a pop bottle. Looks like arson."

"I already knew that," she said. "The question is who?"

Jared shrugged. "Anyone can get a book at the library to learn how to make a gas bomb, for crying out loud." He stomped off in a huff.

Delaney waited until the dust died behind his pickup before she drove into town to visit Digger. She found him arguing with the doctor about when he could be released from the hospital.

"That's a nasty gash on your head, Digger," the doctor told him. "But if you're still feeling good by this time tomorrow, we'll talk about you leaving." The doctor stopped beside Delaney. "See me before you leave, all right?"

"Got to talk to you," Digger whispered the moment the doctor closed the door behind him.

For a moment, Del thought he knew who she was and might be able to tell her what had really happened to him up on the mountain.

"Gus tried to kill me again," Digger said in a conspiratorial whisper as he motioned her closer to the bed. "He blames me for the cave-in. He thinks Del Henry and I killed him."

"Digger, Gus is dead," she said gently. "Remember?"

He nodded gravely. "I thought that, too, Winnie, but I seen him. No one has eyes like Gus. The damnedest color ever. I looked into those eyes, Winnie. Right before he tried to kill me."

Delaney took his weathered old hand in hers, sorry he was calling her by her grandmother's name again. It only made her doubt his story all the more. "How could that be, Digger?"

"I know it sounds crazy, but I think those space aliens have something to do with it. However Gus did it, he's come back from the grave." His rheumy old gaze met hers. "He was here last night, in this very room. Tried to smother me with my pillow."

Delaney blinked back the tears that rushed to her eyes. No wonder the doctor had said he needed to talk to her. Digger was much worse than she'd thought. "Are you sure it wasn't just a bad nightmare?"

Digger shook his head. "He would have killed me for sure if the nurse hadn't come in and scared him away."

"Where did he go?" Delaney asked, looking around the tiny room. There was only one way out other than the window—the door in.

"He went out the window," Digger said.

Delaney stared at the open second-story window. No screen. And the window was large enough. There was even a wide windowsill with flower boxes. She went to look out, gauging the distance between the flower boxes at the next window. She supposed someone could have escaped that way. Digger's story was feasible. It just wasn't credible. Was it?

"Did the nurse see . . . your attacker?" she asked, hoping for Digger's sake she had.

He shook his head. "She pushed open the door, but was talking to someone in the hall and didn't come in until Gus had gone out the window." Doubt clouded his eyes. "It was real, Winnie. The space aliens on the lake. Gus." He closed his eyes. "I know it was real. I need a little rest now."

She squeezed his hand, silently promising to call Jared and ask him to put a deputy outside Digger's room. Just in case. "I'm going to ride up to Johnson Gulch Lake and check it out, Digger." He opened his eyes in pleased surprise. She smiled at him. "I'll let you know what I find."

"Be careful, Delaney," he said quietly. "There's evil on the Rockin' L. A terrible, dark evil."

"Don't worry," she assured him, chilled by his use of her name. She agreed some terrible evil had come to the ranch. She just didn't believe it was space aliens. Or Gus Halbrook back from the grave. "I'll be careful. You be careful, too."

Chapter Seven

Cooper finished the last of the fence and went back to the ranch house to find no one around. He knocked several times before trying the front door. It opened, and he cussed Delaney for not locking her doors. Who knew what kind of scumbag would just walk in and take a look around?

He wasn't sure exactly what he was trying to find. Something that might give him a clue about who Rattlesnake Range had hired. And why. Starting upstairs, he made a quick search, keeping an eye out in case Delaney or Buck returned.

The ranch house was exactly like the plans and photographs he'd been given for the job. He found Delaney's bedroom and carefully opened the door. The room looked just the way he'd imagined it would: rich hardwoods from floors to furniture, soft cool-colored linens and drapes. The scent of her lingered on the air, making him ache in a way that confused him. With women, it had always been physical—*that* ache he understood; this was something entirely different, so different it was foreign to him.

He stepped in to examine a photograph on one wall. Delaney was about eight years old at the time of the photo. She stood beside her father and a Morgan colt. Cooper had to admit Hank Lawson was what most women would consider a very handsome man. Delaney had his good looks.

And his smile. But what Hank lacked in character, Delaney seemed to have gotten in spades. Even back then she'd had that fierce independence and determination in her dark eyes. Almost defiance.

He smiled, realizing how much he liked that about her. Yet there was something else about Delaney that drew him to her. He wasn't even sure what it was, but it scared the hell out of him.

Downstairs, he made a cursory search, ending up in the office. It took only a few moments to find the letters from Rattlesnake Range. Standard offer proposals. Both signed by Thom Jamison. Both dated within the past three weeks. Nothing unusual about either.

At the sound of a pickup coming up the road, he hurried out the back door and circled around to the horse barn, where he'd left Crazy Jack eating oats.

"McLeod?" Delaney came through the barn door moments later.

He looked up to find her in the doorway. Something about the way she stood, her hands on her hips, her jean jacket open, her western hat tipped back slightly. He felt a pull toward her that was so strong it staggered him. It was followed quickly by another alien sensation: guilt.

"You're finished mending the fence?" She was surprised.

"Piece of cake," he said, trying to shake off the strange feelings.

"Then I guess you're through for the day," she said, leaning into a stall to check one of the new colts.

"Yeah, I guess so." He studied her, wondering what was up. He'd seen the list of ranches he'd given her beside the phone and figured she'd called. But he also knew the response she'd get from each. He didn't think that could be the problem. It had to be something else. "The barbed wire was deliberately cut, you know."

"I know." She looked around the barn as if making up her mind about something. Had Buck told her the truth? Not likely. Or maybe Angel had remembered him—and it *was* from some Rattlesnake Range operation.

"I thought I'd drive up to Johnson Gulch tomorrow and look around," she said after a moment.

He didn't say anything, relieved his fears weren't warranted. "I'm sure it's all just Digger's imagination but..." She looked up at Cooper. "He thinks someone tried to kill him last night in the hospital. Maybe there's something at the lake to—"

"Prove his story?" Cooper asked.

She smiled. "Yea, I don't want to believe Digger's as loco as everyone thinks."

"Yet you don't want to believe Digger's life is in danger either, huh," he said.

She nodded and smiled. "That's about it."

"Would you like me to come along just in case...you might need me?" He told himself he planned to go up there anyway to check it. Going with Delaney just made it easier. But that little voice of reason inside his head argued he was making a mistake. Because when he was around her, he tended to screw up and forget he was only her hired help. He tended to think about things that a ranch hand had no right even to think about with the boss. About kissing her. About holding her in his arms. About making love to her. *And it's going to get you shot again and this time you might not be so lucky.*

Delaney seemed to be having a battle of her own. She obviously didn't want to go alone, but she didn't seem so sure about Cooper going with her.

"I suppose it wouldn't hurt if you came along."

She didn't sound all that convinced, as if she had something to fear from him. Or as if she wasn't quite sure she trusted him. He smiled to himself; she was a very perceptive woman.

THE NEXT MORNING, Buck drove up in a cloud of dust. Delaney came out on the porch to see what was going on.

"Someone's cut a stretch of fence and a bunch of the two-year-olds are out on the country road," Buck said, his face flushed from anger.

She glanced over at Cooper's camp. He'd heard and was already saddling up Crazy Jack. "McLeod and I will round up the horses. You get the fence fixed, then ride the perimeter and see if there are any other problems."

"I just can't figure who'd do such a thing," Buck said, his face etched with worry.

"Yeah, me, neither," she said, staring at Cooper's broad back. She watched her new ranch hand for a moment, his movements sure and smooth, then she turned and headed for the barn.

THEY SPENT the morning and part of the afternoon rounding up the young Morgans and herding them to a large, fenced pasture nearer to the ranch house.

Cooper found himself studying his boss as she rode, surprised at her skills not only in riding and roping, but in doctoring the horses that had got caught up in the barbed wire. He'd known women ranchers before. But none as at home in the saddle as Delaney Lawson. She seemed as much a part of this land as the rocky buttes and the tall ponderosas. He was just as startled by her attachment to the land. It showed not only in the way she didn't overgraze her horses, but in the way she'd rein in just to look across it—the way a woman looked at the man she loved. Cooper wondered if Delaney would ever look at a man like that. He felt a twinge of remorse at the thought of her losing her ranch, but shook it off as they headed back to the house. Sentiment had no place in this business.

"I was thinking we should drive up to Johnson Gulch Lake," Delaney said, after making them both a late lunch.

"Whatever you say, boss," he answered distractedly.

"You all right?" she asked, intent on his face. "You've been awful quiet today."

He'd been quiet, thinking. A dangerous thing for a man like him to do, he realized. He grinned at her, wishing she weren't so beautiful, so intriguing. "Don't tell me you miss me minding your business?"

She laughed and shook her head. "Actually, you seem pretty capable of running your own life."

She smiled. "Why, McLeod, I do believe that was a compliment."

DELANEY NOTICED the temperature had dropped, making the warm summer evening near perfect. A slight breeze stirred the ponderosas. They shimmered, the color of green silk. She felt oddly at ease riding in the pickup with Cooper. The scent of pine and fresh water from Johnson Gulch Creek grew stronger as they drove, the windows down, a warm wind blowing in.

She reached over to turn up the country-and-western song on the radio. McLeod tapped his boot in time to the tune. She found herself drumming on the steering wheel and feeling a strange sort of contentment, which surprised her.

She took the same road they'd taken the night before to look for Digger. And Delaney noticed a change in Cooper the moment she pulled onto the Jeep trail.

"What's wrong?" she asked, suddenly worried he might know something she didn't and that was why he'd offered to come along.

He looked over at her and grinned sheepishly. "Claustrophobia. I can't stand being in tight places."

She laughed, relieved. "Then how can you sleep in that camper?"

"I don't." He met her gaze and held it for a moment. "I sleep outside under the stars unless it's pouring rain or freezing cold."

She raised an eyebrow. Under the stars. "You never cease to amaze me, McLeod," she said as she pulled off into a clearing and drove up to the top of the ridge.

Below them Johnson Gulch Creek wound through a small, rocky canyon. The last of the sun rimmed the mountains and turned the horizon to liquid fire. The warmth filled the cab of the pickup.

"That's Johnson Gulch Lake," Delaney said, pointing across Cooper to a place in the creek where the water pooled among the boulders.

"And Digger's camp is on up the road not far, right?" he asked.

She smiled to herself, remembering why she'd brought him along. True, she hadn't wanted to come alone, but she also trusted McLeod's instincts. He seemed to notice things other people didn't. She liked that about him. She told herself she didn't care that he was a drifter and would be gone before the first snowfall. Or that when she was with him sometimes she felt reckless, as if just being around him was dangerous.

"You saw Digger today?" Cooper asked as they headed down a path between the rocks to the natural lake. "Is he all right?"

"He's better physically." Delaney bit her lip, almost afraid to repeat Digger's story for fear the truth was even worse. "His doctor's worried about him. Digger still thinks his old prospector friend Gus Halbrook tried to kill him and that the space aliens he saw in the lake somehow brought Gus back from the dead." She glanced over at Cooper, expecting him to laugh.

"What do you think?" he asked as he walked down the shoreline to a pile of small rocks and sand and bent to inspect them.

What *did* she think? "I want to believe that he fell down, hit his head and that in his confusion—" Cooper turned and the afternoon light ricocheted off the water to catch his face in sunlight. He hadn't shaved for several days and she could see the blond stubble of his beard, rough as the land around them—and just as appealing.

"Come here," he said softly.

His words stirred something she'd buried long ago—desire. She walked toward him, her limbs weak, pulse fast and erratic. When was the last time she'd felt like this around a man? She laughed to herself as she realized the truth. There'd never been another man who tempted her the way Cooper did, who made her want to let go and forget all the reasons he was wrong for her.

She met his gaze. His eyes, as blue as the summer sky, filled her with sunshine, warming her in places no man had ever been able to touch.

He looked away first, breaking the spell. The breeze stirred the loose hair at her temples and cooled her skin. She brushed the hair back from her face, chastising herself. Feeling anything for this cowboy was foolish, and she wasn't a woman who could afford to be foolish. Especially now.

As she joined him at the edge of the lake, he pointed to a series of indentations in the sand.

She mocked her racing heart: *all he wanted was to show you some tracks in the sand, fool woman.* "It almost looks like . . . giant ducks."

Cooper laughed and pushed back his hat. The devil was back in all that blue just dancing up a storm as Cooper settled his gaze on her again.

"Or swim fins."

"Fins?" She did a couple of fast two-steps with the devil, then dragged her gaze away to stare at the tracks. "Why would anyone swim here?" The lake wasn't large or very deep; this was private property and so near the high mountains the water was ice-cold.

"You got me." He glanced over at her, a faint grin playing at his lips.

He knew his effect on women, she told herself. He knew exactly what he was doing to her and was enjoying her discomfort. She moved away from him, swearing to herself. At herself.

Cooper picked up a rock and chucked it out into the center of the pool. The waves circled, widening toward them. "Digger said he saw a spaceship floating on the surface, right?"

Delaney watched the ripples come closer. "What are you getting at, McLeod?"

"What if Digger is telling the truth? What if he saw something? Just not what he thought he saw. And it put his life in danger?"

She nodded, remembering that Cooper had suggested this same theory at the hospital. And that very night, someone had tried to kill Digger. Or at least, Digger thought someone had. "After what's been happening on the ranch, I'm not sure what to believe. But I can't take a chance with Digger's life. I asked Jared to put a deputy outside Digger's hospital room."

Delaney walked out on the rocks to the deeper water and scooped up a handful. It felt cold. She splashed a little on her face, chasing away all the crazy thoughts she'd had earlier about Cooper.

"But what could he have seen that would make someone want to kill him?" she asked. "There haven't been any accidents up here except Digger getting hurt."

"I don't know," Cooper said from the shore.

As she straightened, she spotted an object glistening in the lake a few yards out. "There's something in the water." She stepped closer, balancing on the bare boulders that trailed out into the water. A small piece of gray metal was wedged in the rocks. In the metal was a bright blue stone. She moved closer.

"Here, let me," Cooper said from the shore. She turned to find him pulling off his boots.

"I can get it," she said, stepping to another rock, this one just under the water. Her boot slipped as she leaned out. She tried to catch herself, but the rocks were slippery and she fell headlong into the pool. The icy water made her gasp with shock. She struggled to find her footing in the chest deep water.

"If you had just waited, I would have gotten it for you," Cooper said, standing over her, grinning. He'd rolled up his jeans, left his hat and boots on the beach and tiptoed out to balance barefoot on one of the larger rocks.

She glared up at him, shivering from the icy cold, feeling like a drowned rat, wanting to wipe that smug look off his face.

"Here, give me your hand," he said, shaking his head at her.

She handed him her hat, the felt wet and dripping. Pure stubbornness made her try to climb out over the slippery rocks by herself. After several futile attempts under his knowing grin, she gave up and reached for his hand.

In that instant, she met Cooper's gaze and glimpsed a wistfulness she recognized.

He pulled her up onto the rocks—and straight into his arms. She forgot about the cold water, forgot everything but his touch.

He groaned softly as he pulled her into him and kissed her.

She tried to resist at first, pushing against his hard chest with her palms. Then she lost herself completely in his lips, in the sweet gentleness of his kiss, in the heated hunger he tried so hard to contain. When he raised his lips from hers, she found herself trembling as she looked up into his eyes.

Then she felt something that made her heart pound even harder, that made her pulse thunder in her ears. A longing that she thought she recognized. For love. For the kind they wrote songs about. The kind she'd never let herself even dream existed.

Then Cooper seemed to back off as if he'd made a mistake. He grinned and the devil danced again in his gaze. And she wished she hadn't enjoyed kissing him, wished she'd never met him.

"Sorry, boss," he said with a shrug as he tried to move past her.

She didn't even resist the idea for a moment. Her palms were still pressed against his chest, where only moments earlier she had felt his heart beating beneath them. She took her hat with one hand and shoved him with the other. He teetered for a moment on the edge of the boulders, then toppled into the lake.

She heard him gasp as he hit the icy water, heard him swear, saw him come up dripping wet. "All you had to say is that you didn't like the kiss."

She stomped up the hill to the truck, pretending to look for something dry to put on, using the time to catch her breath, to get her balance again and run down that list of reasons she should keep her distance from Cooper McLeod. He knew damned well she liked his kiss!

It wasn't bad enough that the rodeo cowboy was her ranch hand and she his boss, but now he'd sparked something in her that she could feel starting a slow burn. Maybe Jared was right. She needed a man. But not this man, not this cowboy with the killer grin and enough charm to change the weather. Cooper McLeod was nothing but a drifter. She couldn't let herself forget that. She wasn't looking for a one-night stand.

A few moments later Cooper came up to the pickup, wringing wet, still dripping water. "Here, I guess this is what you saw in the water."

She turned to find him holding an old handmade spur. He appeared as wet and cold as she felt. She fought a smile. "It looks like an antique," she said, taking the spur from him.

The silver had darkened from age and probably years in the water. She rubbed the star sapphire embedded in the shank with her finger. "I've seen one like it somewhere," she said, gazing up at Cooper. "I wonder how long it's been in the water?"

"What is the stone?" Cooper asked.

"A sapphire. They mine them at the Eldorado Bar just down the road. You passed it on your way to the ranch."

He nodded distractedly, as if he'd lost interest in the stone. She saw him glance up the creek to where it ran down out of the mountains. She followed his gaze, wondering what he was thinking, that maybe the spur had washed down from the high country?

"We'd better get back," she said, still chastising herself for allowing the kiss. For not just allowing it. For wanting it. "About what happened down by the lake. It better not happen again. Do we understand each other?"

He looked up at her, innocence making his eyes a pale, pale blue in the dying light. "You mean the kiss or you pushing me into the water?"

She felt her breath catch in her throat as his gaze brushed her lips, sparking the memory of the kiss, of being in his arms, of feeling him pressed against her. He knew. He knew how badly she'd wanted him to kiss her. And he knew the effect he had on her!

"You know damned well what I mean," she said as she jerked open the pickup door.

"That's too bad," he said behind her.

She turned about to make a remark she'd have probably regretted, when suddenly the pickup side window next to her exploded. In the instant it took her to realize that the sound echoing through the canyon was a rifle shot, Cooper McLeod grabbed her and shoved her into the cab of the pickup.

"Stay here. Keep down," he barked. And he was gone.

Chapter Eight

Delaney lay on the seat, listening. A pine bough creaked in the evening breeze. Overhead, a hawk let out a cry. Silence. Delaney reached up and pulled her rifle down from the rack above her head. Holding it against her chest, she listened for footfalls on the dried ground outside the truck, knowing they could be Cooper's. Or the person who'd taken a shot at her. Slowly she slipped out of the pickup and crouched beside the truck.

The sun had disappeared, leaving the mountaintop cloaked in cool evening shade. Delaney looked up at the shattered window. From the angle the bullet had struck the glass, she assumed the shot had come from the other side of the creek.

But that didn't mean that whoever had fired it wasn't now headed this way. She glanced around, wondering where Cooper had gone. Darkness huddled under the pines. The trees swayed in the light breeze throwing shadows onto the forest floor.

"Damn you, McLeod, where are you?" she whispered.

Carefully she moved to a stand of pines beyond the pickup to get a better view of the creek and the opposite hillside. She knelt beneath the boughs, alert to any movement. The light had gone out of the day and the water. The lake pooled among the rocks, dark and foreboding. Delaney shivered. From her cold, wet clothing. From fear. She moved closer to the base of the tree, hoping to make herself less of a target. She couldn't believe someone was trying to kill her. It didn't make any sense. Ty was the only one who would benefit from her death. But that would also make him the number-one suspect. Was he that foolish, or that desperate, he'd try to kill her for the ranch?

Delaney glanced down at the ground by her feet. Her heart thundered in her ears as she recognized the tracks. Boot and mule prints. Digger and Tess had stood in this very spot overlooking the lake.

What had Digger seen? He'd said someone had tried to kill him after he'd spotted space aliens in the lake. And she'd come to investigate, only to have someone take a shot at her. She stared at the lake, which was now bathed in twilight. It looked no different than it ever had to her. No space ships. No aliens. But was she seeing something she didn't realize was important?

At the sound of a twig breaking behind her, Delaney spun around, bringing the rifle with her, her finger sliding onto the trigger with practiced speed. But instead of a dangerous killer, she found McLeod in her sights.

"Whoa!" He held up both hands in surrender. An uneasiness flickered across his face as he realized just how close he'd come to getting himself shot. "Take it easy. It's only me."

Delaney tried to settle her heart down as she slipped her finger from the trigger and fought to still her trembling limbs. "Where have you been?"

"Chasing whoever shot at you," he said, sounding a little indignant. "They're gone."

She stepped out of the shelter of the trees and cocked her head at him as a thought struck her. "How do you know the person was shooting at *me?*"

"What?"

He shoved back his hat to stare at her. Even in the dying light she could see the blue of his eyes.

"You were standing right next to me. Just as you were yesterday before the rock slide. Maybe it's not me they're after. Maybe it's *you.*"

COOPER STARED at Delaney as her words sank in. Why hadn't he thought of that? No one had actually tried to kill her before he came to the ranch. All her trouble had been pretty much incidental and no one had been hurt. Then, within a couple of days, there had been two attempts on her life. Or had there?

He rubbed his thigh, remembering the searing pain of the bullet when it tore through his flesh after the last job had gone bad. He'd just assumed he'd been shot by an angry rancher. Now he wasn't so sure. The incident had never been investigated. Rattlesnake Range had seen to that, just as it had found a doctor who wouldn't report the gunshot wound.

He looked up at Delaney and didn't like what he recognized in her eyes. Suspicion. Fear. Two things he couldn't afford if he hoped to keep her confidence.

"Why would anyone want to kill *me?*" he asked. "I don't have anything. And I've always tried real hard not to make enemies." He gave her his best innocent look, but all the time his heart was pounding and his brain racing. Why *would* anyone want to kill him? And who? He figured it would only be someone from an old job. Or this job. Or…someone from Rattlesnake Range set on seeing he took early retirement. But why? "No one's burned *my* barn," he added.

"That could be because you don't have a barn, McLeod."

"Exactly."

Delaney shook her head at him. "But I'm sure there's a woman out there somewhere who'd like to have you in her sights right now."

He laughed softly. "I do my level best to leave women happy." He gave her a shrug and a grin. "So far I haven't had any complaints."

Delaney swore under her breath and headed for the pickup, the rifle riding easily in the crook of her arm. "I don't know about you, McLeod. But you'd better be telling me the truth."

The truth? He didn't even know what that was anymore. But if she found out that he was in any way connected with Rattlesnake Range… And worse yet if she found out about the rest of his past.

"Stay there," she called over her shoulder. "I want to show you something."

She came back with a flashlight and shone the beam on the ground by the pines. "The tracks are fresh—in the past couple of days. And they have to be Digger's and Tess's."

Cooper leaned down and ran his fingers along the impressions in the dirt. "You're right," he said after a moment. "And look at these," he said, following the tracks away from the tree. I'd say Tess was balking. See how she dug in?"

"You mean as if she was scared?" She shook her head at him as he got to his feet. "McLeod, you amaze me," she said. "I can't help wondering *why* you're so perceptive. If I didn't know better I'd suspect you were either running *from* the law—or maybe were the law himself."

Cooper gave her a shrug. "I just notice things." He grinned. "Like your hair. It's the same color as obsidian in sunlight. And your eyes. They're like late-summer thunderstorms, dark, dangerous, mesmerizing."

She laughed and shook her head as she headed for the pickup. "I take it back. I'm more amazed that someone hasn't shot you."

He sighed, relieved to see that they were back on their usual footing. He'd deflected her curiosity about him. For the time being anyway.

Taking one final look at Johnson Gulch Lake, he went to join her in the cab of the pickup.

"So, this person you chased, I assume you didn't get close enough to see who it was?" she asked as she turned the pickup around and started back toward the ranch.

"No. But I can tell you this—he rode in by horseback this time."

She glanced over at him. "*This* time?"

"I found an old road on the other side of the creek that someone's been using."

She hit a bump, almost sending him flying through the windshield. "That old mining road? They couldn't have driven down that. It's been closed for years."

"Not anymore. Someone took a chain saw to the downed trees, widened it in a couple of places."

Delaney frowned. "Why would anyone go to so much trouble to open a road that doesn't go anywhere?"

He glanced over at her. "But it does go somewhere. Johnson Gulch Lake. In fact, *that* road runs right up to the lake."

"But why not use *this* road, the one we're on?" She narrowed her gaze at him. "Okay, let's hear it. I know you have a theory."

He picked up the spur from the seat between them. "Not far past the road I found tracks that led up the creek to an old abandoned mine. All I can figure is that someone was using the road to bring in equipment to work the mine."

She stared over at him. "I don't understand. The gold ran out years ago."

He shrugged. "Who has the mineral rights on the ranch?"

"I do." She stared at the road ahead. "Wait a minute. Didn't Digger say he saw lights near the lake?"

Cooper grinned. "I believe he said he saw lights *in* the lake."

"It could have been a reflection," Delaney said, sounding excited. "It makes sense. He *did* see something. Someone working that old mine. And maybe he's right. Maybe someone did try to kill him to keep him quiet. And for the same reason, tried to scare us away by taking that potshot at us."

Cooper had to agree. He just wasn't as convinced as she was. "By the way, whoever took that shot was riding the same horse as the guy who started the rock slide. The horse with the barred shoe."

She drove the rest of the way back to the ranch in silence. He figured she was scared. He damned sure was. He couldn't throw off the notion that maybe she was right. Someone was after him instead of her. But with Rattlesnake Range trying to buy her ranch, Ty trying to inherit it and Jared trying to marry it, Cooper still thought Delaney was more apt to be the target. It just made sense for them *both* to be careful until they could sort it out.

Delaney stopped the pickup beside his camp. "I'd like you to ride fence tomorrow." She avoided his gaze. "Then I need you to help bring in more of the two-year-olds. I'm going to start working with them in the morning."

He nodded. Business as usual. Did she really think she could just ignore what was happening on the ranch and it would go away? "It isn't going to work."

"McLeod—"

"Your troubles aren't going to stop until you find out who's behind them."

"How do you know that?" she asked, shifting her gaze to his.

"I know."

She stared at him. He expected her to ask how he knew. He debated telling her and decided it was too risky. If she knew about him and Rattlesnake Range, she'd run him off the ranch. And he wouldn't blame her. But he also couldn't let her do that for reasons even he didn't understand anymore. He just knew it didn't have anything to do with his job.

"The sheriff's looking into it and I'm sure—" She bit her lip. "You still think Jared's behind this, don't you?"

"I've seen men do foolish things for money." He looked into her eyes, feeling warmer even in his wet clothing. "And even more foolish things for a woman. Jared wants more than just your ranch, Ms. Lawson."

"Good night, McLeod," she said shifting into gear again and ending any more conversation on the subject.

He opened the door and got out. "'Night, boss."

She drove off a little too fast. He watched her park in front of the ranch house. Then he turned to find Crazy Jack dragging his oat bag around the yard beside the camper.

"Give me a minute to change clothes and I'll make us both dinner," he told the horse as he heard an engine and saw the lights of a vehicle coming up the road.

A pickup pulled up in front of the house. Buck and Angel got out. Cooper could hear Angel's laugh on the night breeze. It grated on him; he still hadn't been able to place her. Buck knocked at the front door and a moment later Delaney invited them inside.

DELANEY HESITATED in the kitchen doorway to watch Buck with Angel. He hovered over the woman, looking nervous. Now that Delaney thought about it, he'd been acting nervous for weeks. He jumped every time she said something to him; it was obvious that he didn't have his mind on his work.

The poor old fool was besotted with the woman. She felt sorry for him because he was just as obviously headed for heartbreak. Angel was much too young for him. Or maybe Buck was just too old for Angel. Delaney felt a pang of guilt as she realized she was hoping this thing with Angel wouldn't last much longer; she needed her ranch manager back.

She sighed as she carried the tray of coffee into the living room and placed it on the table in front of them. Angel had pulled a notebook out of her purse. She tapped a pen on her slim thigh as she looked around the room with appreciation, clearly anxious to get the interview over. Not as much as Delaney. It had been a long day and she couldn't quit thinking about what Cooper had said.

"This is quite the place you have here," Angel said. "You really lucked out, huh?"

"It's more hard work than luck," Buck said quickly. "Ms. Lawson saved this ranch after her father pretty near ran it into the ground."

Delaney smiled at him, knowing he was just coming to her defense and didn't realize he was telling something she would rather keep private. "I believe Angel wants to know the history of the ranch," she said tactfully. "What exactly is your book about?"

"Ranching in gold country," Angel said quickly. "Your grandfather was a gold miner, right?" she asked, flipping open her notebook.

"He was a horse breeder like his father," Delaney corrected. "My great-grandfather came west during the gold rush in 1865, hoping to make his fortune and start a horse ranch. But it was my grandfather, Del Henry, who started the Rockin' L after he met my grandmother, Winnie. It was in the early 1930s. Winnie was twenty-two. My grandfather was fifty-eight."

"Phew!" Angel said, shaking her head. "That's *old.*"

Buck looked at the floor uncomfortably. Delaney knew he was fifty-two. Surely Angel realized that.

"So your grandfather's the one who struck it rich."

Delaney shook her head. "Rich? No, he quit mining when he met my grandmother. They bought this place with her dowry, built a house and started the horse ranch."

"But there were so many gold strikes back in the 1800s," Angel said. "In Helena, buildings were paid for with the gold found in just digging the foundation. Confederate Gulch and Last Chance Gulch. Men got rich overnight. And they say the mother lode was never even found."

Delaney laughed. "My great-grandfather got enough gold together to start a small horse ranch in Helena, but he lost it in a poker game. My grandfather had a couple of younger friends who worked his mining claims when he got too old to work them himself. One of the prospectors still roams the ranch looking for that elusive mother lode." She thought of Digger with a note of sadness.

"It *does* exist?" Angel asked in total innocence.

"With today's technology, a mining company would have found it if it did," Delaney said.

"But aren't there still small pockets of gold around that are worth something?"

Delaney thought about the old mining road someone had opened to one of her grandfather's mines. "I suppose so. But with thousands of miners scouring this country for gold in the 1860s and again in the 1930s, any real gold is gone."

Angel frowned down at her notes. When she looked up, Delaney realized the woman was disappointed.

"I'm sorry it isn't more...romantic," Delaney told her. "The only thing we do here at the Rockin' L that might interest you is we raise Morgan horses the way my grandfather did. No fancy barns and stalls. We put them out to pasture. As a matter of fact, I'm going to be working with some two-year-olds tomorrow if you'd like to come out and watch."

Angel closed her notebook and put her pen in her purse. "I have research to do tomorrow." She looked up and seemed to remember her manners. "But thanks anyway."

AFTER COOPER FED Crazy Jack, he built a campfire and started dinner, his favorite, beans. He'd had a lot of time to think since Delaney had dropped him off. Two things kept coming back into his thoughts: their kiss—and Delaney.

The kiss had been stupid and impulsive. But as he watched the beans begin to bubble, he found himself grinning just thinking about it.

It had been one hell of a kiss. And not one that he'd soon forget. Nor would he forget her pushing him into the lake. The woman had spunk. More than was advisable in any woman.

He shook his head as he glanced up toward the ranch house. Lights spilled out onto the porch. He could hear faint music stealing out the windows. She'd turned on the music not long after Buck and Angel had left. He wondered if she was thinking about their kiss. And if she was, whether it just made her more angry with him.

The kiss had been the kind of thing he'd never done on a job before. Not that he hadn't kissed a lot of women as part of his job. But the women had come to him. They'd wanted him more than he'd wanted them. He considered it a bonus.

Delaney was different. He'd *wanted* to kiss her. He let out a laugh. No, it was much more than want. He *had* to kiss her. And he told himself at the time, it was worth it. But now he acknowledged that the kiss probably hadn't helped his standing as her ranch hand. Probably not at all, he thought, as he recalled how mad she'd been. The good news was that she hadn't fired him. Yet, he thought, as he saw her come out on the porch and look in his direction.

DELANEY STOOD on the porch, listening to the sounds of the night. She'd been antsy since they'd returned from Johnson Gulch Lake. And worried. The worry made the night feel cold. She hugged herself and looked out at the pines and Cooper's camp, remembering his kiss. She could see him silhouetted against his camp fire and felt a longing that made her ache. Who was this man who had the power to make her desire him even when she knew how wrong he was for her?

It struck her that he didn't act like anyone's ranch hand, certainly not hers. He was much too cocky and sure of himself to have been anyone's hand for long. Maybe that's why he never stayed in one place. Or maybe he was running from something, hiding from something—here on her ranch. He'd convinced her that the rock slide and the rifle shot were more than likely meant for her. And yet, standing here now, she wondered. The feeling that Cooper McLeod wasn't who he seemed to be nagged at her.

So did the memory of Digger's and Tess's tracks beside the pines overlooking Johnson Gulch Lake. There could be something to Digger's story. Not that she believed Gus Halbrook had come back from the dead. But maybe there was an explanation for all of it. She just couldn't think of what it could be.

Nor could she explain what drew her to McLeod, she thought with a curse. It had been so long since she'd been interested in any man. Her preoccupation with McLeod had nothing to do with his good looks or that infuriating charm of his, she assured herself. It was something else, something she couldn't quite put her finger on.

In the distance, coyotes yelped. Overhead, the moon was a mere sliver among the stars. Millions of stars. She smiled as she remembered Cooper sleeping under the stars instead of in his camper. Claustrophobia. The man had an Achilles heel.

She glanced back at her house, surprised at how empty it felt tonight, and noticed that someone had put a horseshoe over her door. She smiled, shaking her head. Cooper. For good luck. The man never ceased to amaze her, she thought, as she looked out at his camp again. The tantalizing scent of his campfire beckoned her. She made a dozen excuses for what she was doing as she walked toward his fire. Only one of them was the truth: she didn't want to be alone tonight.

WHEN COOPER SAW Delaney headed in his direction, he shifted his gaze to the fire and realized he'd been so busy watching her surreptitiously, he hadn't noticed his beans were burning. He grabbed for the pot, burned his fingers, swore and dropped it. The beans started to spill out as the pot tipped toward the dirt. He hurriedly righted it with the toe of his boot.

"I hope that's not your dinner," Delaney said across the fire from him. She took a whiff and made a face.

He sucked one blistered finger as he looked up at her. Something was on her mind. He wondered what it was. He couldn't let her fire him. Not yet. "I *like* my beans a little charred."

"How about a lot burned?" she asked, raising an eyebrow at him.

He looked down at the beans, now blackened in the bottom of the pot. "I wasn't all that hungry anyhow," he said, pushing them out of the way with his boot. "I hope you weren't coming over for dinner."

She shook her head and looked around as if unsure why she'd come. "It's been a while since I've eaten over a camp fire." She smiled suddenly. He followed her gaze to where he'd laid out his bedroll near a pine and shrugged, a little embarrassed.

"Haven't you ever wanted a real roof over your head?" she asked as she picked up a stick and knelt to poke it into the coals.

"I have a roof," he said. "Clear blue by day. Black velvet by night."

She looked up. She had to admit it was one heck of a roof. "You know that's not what I mean. Haven't you ever wanted to settle down, stay in one place for a while?"

He thought of the ranch he talked about buying, wondering if it was no more than an excuse for continuing to work for Rattlesnake Range. "I'm afraid settling down has always come at a price I couldn't afford."

"You mean your freedom?"

He saw her jaw tighten. She tossed the stick into the fire and watched it burn. In the firelight, her hair was the color of a raven's wing, her eyes as dark as night.

"Freedom was the precious commodity my father revered above everything else—including his family and the ranch."

He could see angry tears in her eyes.

"At what price does *your* freedom come, McLeod?"

Cooper stepped around the fire to take her shoulders in his hands. "I can't change the way your father was," he said roughly. "And I'm not Hank Lawson. If you're thinking you might be able to break me like one of your horses, you'd best be sure you've got the right horse."

He let her go and started to turn, but she grabbed his arm. "Cooper." The sound of his name on her lips held both pleading and desire. She urged him closer. Her kiss was brazen. Fevered with abandon. Knowing what she was offering him gave him both pleasure and pain. Pleasure because he wanted her. Pain because he couldn't take her like this, knowing how he was deceiving her. It had never mattered before, with other women he'd known. But did now.

He pulled back, holding her at arm's length. "You don't know what kind of man I've been." He gently thumbed her cheek. "I've done things...."

"I don't care about the past," she whispered.

He smiled. "But I do. I can't do this, not now."

She pulled away from him; tears stung her eyes. "Damn you, McLeod." He watched her turn and walk away, realizing he'd lost a part of himself when he went to work for Rattlesnake Range—his integrity—and he wasn't sure he could get it back. Without it, he could never have the one thing he now so desperately wanted. Delaney.

Chapter Nine

Delaney was in the round corral working with one of the two-year-olds when Jared Kincaid drove up. She was still stinging from making a fool of herself with Cooper the night before. She couldn't believe she'd made a play for her ranch hand, which made his turning her down even worse. All day she'd been trying to see the humor in it. And couldn't. She'd invested more of her heart last night than she wanted to admit. She certainly wasn't in any mood to deal with the sheriff.

She finished, then cut the young Morgan out with the others.

"'Afternoon, Del," Jared said, tipping his hat. He'd taken a seat on the top rail of the fence. Now he jumped down to join her outside the corral.

"Jared."

"Del, we've got to talk about Digger. The doctor says he can leave the hospital soon and Digger is anxious as hell to get back to his camp."

She knew what was coming.

"I'm not going to be able to keep a deputy on him once he leaves the hospital. The only reason I have this long—" he looked up and met her gaze "—was as a personal favor to you."

"So you don't believe anyone's trying to kill him?" she asked, already knowing the answer.

He pulled off his Stetson and ran a hand through his graying hair. "Dammit, Del, how can I believe Martians dug up some dead prospector named Gus Halbrook and took him by spaceship to Johnson Gulch Lake?"

"Is that what Digger told you?" Maybe the sheriff was more responsible than she'd thought. At least he'd talked to Digger about it.

Jared shook his head. "My deputy told me all about it. I'm not sure what you're going to do with that crazy old man, Del, but it's just a matter of time before the county is going to catch him and put him in a home."

She gritted her teeth and fought back the series of oaths that came to her tongue. "He's not crazy, Jared. Just a little confused sometimes. It comes with age." She looked pointedly at the sheriff's graying head.

Jared stuffed his hat back on his head, covering his hair. "And we're all getting old, right, Del?"

She'd ruffled his feathers, as usual. "I just think there might be something to Digger's story." She told Jared about the tracks and Cooper's theory that Digger had seen something because of the balking mule prints on the mountainside above the lake.

"Digger and that damned stubborn mule have been all over that country. I can't see that some balking mule prints in the dirt near Johnson Gulch Lake prove anything." He held up his hand before she could protest. "And even if the craz—senile old coot had seen something, no one in this county would believe him. He thinks the mother lode is still out there and that he's going to find it. So why try to kill him? What would be the point?"

Delaney grudgingly had to admit Jared had something there. Digger was generally thought of as crazy and this latest episode certainly wasn't helping his credibility. "What if it was someone who didn't know Digger and considered him a threat? A stranger to these parts of the country?''

Jared laughed. "Like space aliens?" He turned to look back at her pickup, parked in front of the house. "Which reminds me. What happened to your side window?"

She followed his gaze to her truck. The window was a web of broken glass with a hole almost at dead center. "While I was up at Johnson Gulch Lake, looking into Digger's so-called hallucinations, someone took a potshot at me."

Jared swore, jerked his hat from his head and slammed it against his leg. "Dammit, Del, if someone's taking shots at you, don't you think you ought to at least let the sheriff know?" He wagged his head at her. "I'm worried about you. This can't go on." His gaze softened. "Have you ever thought about getting out of ranching? Maybe go to some island and sip fancy drinks in the shade beside the ocean?"

She laughed. "No, Jared, I never have."

"Maybe you should." His grave expression made her uncomfortable. He *was* serious.

"Are you warning me to sell before something worse happens?"

He chewed at his lip and squinted at the horizon for a moment. "There's only so much I can do to protect you, Del. I just don't want to see you get hurt. Or worse yet, killed."

"Jared, you almost sound like you know something I don't," she said, shaking from the worried look in his eyes.

"Dammit, Del, how do you expect me to take the news that now you've got someone shooting at you?"

"I expect you to investigate," she snapped. "Because I'm not selling, Jared. And I won't be run out. They'll have to kill me to get the ranch. And then as sheriff, you'll have to arrest them. You make this sound like it's my fault."

He stomped over to his pickup and came back with a notebook and pen. "Where did this shooting occur?"

She described it for him, stopping short of telling him about the barred-shoe tracks. If he investigated the incident, he'd find the tracks himself. And if Cooper was right and the horse belonged to Jared...

She watched the sheriff scribble down the information she gave him. He'd left little doubt in her mind that he knew a lot more than he was telling her. Her uneasiness about him jumped from misgivings to downright suspicion. Could Cooper be right about Jared?

When Jared finished, he stuffed the notebook into his pocket and shoved his hat back on his head. He seemed calmer than he had earlier, more in control again. But it was a cold kind of control that made her all the more concerned. "You know, Del, I was thinking that you and I should have dinner and talk about some things—" He stopped as Cooper came out of the barn.

The two men scowled at each other and she wondered how much of the conversation Cooper had overheard, or if it was just his general dislike for Jared coming out.

"'Afternoon, Sheriff," Cooper said. He turned to Delaney and tipped his hat. "Boss."

Just seeing him brought back the anger, embarrassment and hurt she'd been fighting all day. "Find any more fence down on your ride?" she asked. She'd just about convinced herself her behavior last night was nothing more than a moment of weakness. But as she met Cooper's gaze she knew that wasn't true. All those feelings she'd blamed last night on—everything from the scent of his campfire to the lonesome coyote's call—were just as strong in broad daylight. Damn this man for making her feel this way.

"Didn't find any problems," he said. "Any trouble here?"

Delaney knew he meant Jared, and she resented his protective tone. "No, Jared was just about to ask me out for dinner. And I was just about to accept." Cooper's shocked expression gave her some satisfaction. "How about to-night? Six sound all right to you?"

Jared broke into a smile. He was even more surprised than Cooper, she thought. "Six sounds just fine with me, Del." He gave Cooper a smug look, tipped his hat to Delaney and headed for his pickup.

"I don't think that was a good idea," Cooper said as the sheriff drove away.

"It's a good thing it's none of your business then, isn't it?" Delaney didn't think it was a good idea, either. As a matter of fact, it probably ranked as one of the stupidest things she'd ever done. But she wasn't about to admit that to Cooper. When she'd sent him out at daybreak to ride fence, he'd acted as if nothing had happened the night before, which was smart of him. She hoped he had the good sense not to bring it up now.

"You're right, boss. It's none of my business."

She told herself that wasn't hurt she saw in his eyes, nor was that guilt that pierced her heart with doubts. The man had saved her life. And he seemed to be trying to help her. But why? What did he want? It certainly wasn't her. He'd made that clear last night. And yet her heart argued that she'd witnessed her own desires reflected in his eyes. She'd felt it in his kisses. He'd wanted her as badly as she wanted him. So what had stopped him last night?

She cussed herself for making a date with Jared just to get back at Cooper. But that wasn't the only reason she'd done it, she assured herself. Jared had said they needed to talk. Maybe he'd tell her what he knew, because nothing could convince her that Jared Kincaid was telling her everything. Men! Maybe he thought he was protecting her by not telling her everything. Or, she realized with worry, maybe he was behind her problems and only protecting himself.

Either way, she intended to find out tonight.

"Should I go help Buck with the rest of the haying?" Cooper asked. "Or bring in some more of the two-year-olds?"

He was all business now, generating coolness like a hint of fall. She fought the urge to reach out to him, already missing the closeness they'd shared over the past few days. "Why don't you bring in the colts. Buck can finish the haying." He started to walk away. "McLeod." He turned, his gaze lifting to hers.

Her heartbeat did a little double time. She fought the urge to drown herself in the blue of his eyes. She dragged her gaze away, remembering what he'd said the night before. *"You don't know what kind of man I've been. I've done things...."* What kind of things? she wondered now. "Nothing. Just be careful."

He nodded. "You, too." He turned and walked away.

COOPER WAITED until Jared and Delaney had left on their date before he rode down into the ranch yard. He cussed, kicked and stomped around for a while, until he finally gave up and went down to the creek behind the house to try to drown his bad mood. The bath did little to soothe his frustration or his worry. He couldn't get his mind off Delaney. Why would she accept a date with Jared? Especially after the man had pretty much told her to sell out or else.

The mind of a woman! Cooper wasn't sure he'd *ever* understand this one. He figured she'd done it out of orneriness, something he was more than familiar with. But it had been a fool thing to do, considering who she was with tonight. He swore. Angry with himself, as well. He'd felt like a heel last night. He'd never before turned down a woman he'd wanted. And he'd regretted it all day. Now Delaney had gone and done something reckless. Jared Kincaid wasn't a man to mess with. If he was behind her bad luck—

Cooper had considered following them in his pickup, but tailing his boss and the county sheriff seemed downright foolish. And if Delaney got wind of it, she'd can his butt for sure. No, anything he did could only make things worse. Delaney had called this tune; now she was going to have to dance to the music. He just hoped the sheriff wasn't as deep in her troubles as Cooper suspected he was.

Cooper waded out of the creek, dried off and dressed in the pines that sheltered his bathing hole. He wasn't sure what he was going to do tonight, but he'd be damned if he was going to sit around the campfire, eating beans and being reminded of how foolish he'd been the previous night!

As he was saddling up Crazy Jack, Buck drove up. "She's not home," Cooper called as Buck started for the house.

"Where is she?" the ranch manager asked, disappointed he'd missed her. He walked over to Cooper, frowning.

"Out to dinner with Jared Kincaid," Cooper told him, trying hard not to sound angry. Or worried.

"Jared?" Buck raised an eyebrow. "Kinda late for a ride, isn't it?"

"Thought I'd go over to the York Bar for a beer. It's a lot shorter by horseback than pickup." It was just over the hill, a few minutes' ride. "Wanna come along?"

Buck shook his head. "I'm picking up Angel." He glanced toward the house again and Cooper had the distinct impression that Buck wanted to talk to Delaney about something important. "You think Delaney will be late?"

Cooper swore to himself. He certainly hoped not. "She didn't say. You know, I meant to ask the other night. Angel didn't mention where she was from."

"California originally," Buck said. "But she's been living in Great Falls. Why?"

Great Falls. The home of Rattlesnake Range. Cooper shrugged. "Nothing, just curious."

Buck gave him an I'm-not-sure-I-like-you look. Cooper didn't feel the least bit intimidated. In fact, he kind of wished Buck would throw the first punch. A knockdown, drag-out fight might make him feel a little better.

Buck must have recognized the challenge in Cooper's expression, because he turned and headed for his pickup. "Have a nice ride," he said, making sure it sounded just the opposite.

Cooper swung up into the saddle, disappointed. Tonight he thought he could whip Buck. He felt ornerier than hell. "Have a nice time with Angel," he called to Buck, trying to match Buck's insincerity.

The ranch manager peeled out in a cloud of dust. Cooper laughed as he rode off into the night.

DELANEY REALIZED her mistake immediately. Jared had insisted they drive into Helena for dinner instead of grabbing a burger at the York Bar. He'd complained until she changed out of Levi's and boots into a dress and pumps. Then he wanted to take her to some quiet, intimate little place in Last Chance Gulch. She couldn't stand the thought of a romantic dinner for two. She'd asked him to take her to her favorite Mexican restaurant, Rose's Cantina, saying she hadn't been there in years.

"Jared, I can't help thinking about what you said earlier," she began when they reached the restaurant. "I got the impression you know who might be behind the trouble at my ranch."

He shot her a look. "Del, I told you, I don't know."

She wasn't buying it and wondered why he wasn't being straight with her. "Jared, I'm at my wit's end," she said, trying a damsel-in-distress tack. "I need your help. As a friend. If you have any idea—"

"You're too trusting, Del," he said, shaking his head. "Things could be going on right under your nose. People you trust could be hurting you and you wouldn't even notice. You need a man around to look after you."

Oh, no, not this again. She took a breath. He was telling her something was going on, damn him. Something she was too trusting to see. "What *are* you saying?"

He smiled sadly. "That I wish you didn't have to be so darned independent. That if you opened up to a man—" He looked at his menu with a heavy sigh. "I'm starved. Let's not talk sheriff business tonight, Del. This is the first time we've gone out. Let's just enjoy it."

Delaney figured she'd just have dinner and then call it an early night. She didn't think things could get worse. She was wrong.

"Delaney, you have the prettiest eyes I think I've ever seen," Jared said after his second margarita. He pressed his knee against hers under the table.

She moved her leg, bit her tongue, determined not to make a scene in the restaurant. This had been really stupid. She'd thought she might get some information out of Jared—

He leaned toward her. "And your lips—"

"Excuse me, Jared, would you pass me the salsa?"

"DAMMIT, THOM." Cooper lowered his voice and turned to look out of the ancient phone booth at the back of the York Bar. The jukebox cranked out a twangy western tune and no one in the place seemed interested in his conversation, but he knew better than to take a chance. He spoke more softly into the phone, more than a little worried and suspicious of Rattlesnake Range. "You said you'd try to find out who the agency had hired."

"I have tried, Coop." Jamison let out a weary sigh. "But you know how the board operates. They don't tell me a damned thing. It's supposed to be for my own protection. And yours."

And the board's protection, Cooper thought. "Well, their *agent* is taking potshots at her now."

"I'm telling you, Coop, the board has assured me it's not our agent on the Rockin' L job who's doing those things. There has been no attempt on Delaney Lawson's life. None."

"They're lying." Cooper pulled off his hat and ran a hand through his hair in frustration. "How do you explain what's going on?"

"I can't. Unless someone else is involved. Someone other than Rattlesnake Range."

Ty, Cooper thought as he shoved his hat back. Or Jared. Or Buck. Or someone he didn't even know. Or— "Maybe they aren't after Delaney. Maybe it's me they want."

"What?"

Cooper laughed. "Surely you know working for the agency is a little risky."

"I'm aware of that." Jamison didn't sound happy about the fact. "There's a risk on both ends."

Cooper smiled to himself ruefully. He remembered the first time he'd met Thom. Cooper had been riding the rodeo circuit, at odds with his family and down on his luck, when Thom Jamison had come into his life with a proposition. All Cooper had had then were his saddle, his looks and the family charm. And he'd already been in trouble with the law. But Jamison had given him the job anyway. At the time, he thought Thom was doing him a favor. Now he realized his trouble with the law had been a glowing recommendation to Rattlesnake Range.

Becoming a con man for the agency had been relatively easy. He used that charm, his looks and a little friendly persuasion to talk people into selling. When necessary he was forced to use a different sort of persuasion, a little less legal one. But nothing serious or felonious. He'd convinced himself he was just making a living. If he didn't do it, someone else would. He hadn't asked any questions, hadn't wanted to know what happened to the ranches after he'd acquired them. Until recently. And he realized belatedly that the questions he'd been asking Thom weren't the kind Rattlesnake Range would appreciate.

"It could be someone from the agency who thinks it's time for me to retire," Cooper said, testing the waters. "Permanently."

"You aren't serious?" Thom was shocked. "You make the board sound like underworld thugs. They're just businessmen. I can assure you when the day comes that you want to quit, you can."

"Oh, yeah? What if I quit right now? What would the board do?"

"Nothing." He didn't sound very convincing, Cooper thought. And he wondered if Thom Jamison was also having some second thoughts about his employers.

Cooper turned in the phone booth to look at the half-empty bar. *Tread softly,* he warned himself. *They might have already gotten to Thom. And if they think you're having second thoughts or bouts of conscience, who knows what they'll do.*

"Hell, Thom, what would I do if I quit? You know me. I'd be bored to death." It struck him that he knew an awful lot about the agency's methods and might make a pretty good witness in court. The businessmen at Rattlesnake Range had to know that. "I'm just a little paranoid. Everything about this job has gone sour."

"I can't blame you. It seems this one has a lot of complications."

Jamison sounded calm, convincing. Cooper wondered again if the agency had gotten to him. If that was true, then Cooper had already told Jamison too much.

"It's got to be someone who wants the Rockin' L other than the agency," Jamison continued.

He was so reasonable, so assured. Cooper almost felt himself being drawn back into the web. "I'm sure you're right," he said, relenting. "I'm just a little jumpy, that's all. Have you heard anything about what the agency wants with the ranch?"

"No, Coop. Nothing." The background silence changed just a little and Cooper realized Jamison had put his hand over the phone. "You know, Coop, maybe you should get out of there," Jamison said.

His voice was different and Cooper suspected one of the board members had joined Thom in his office. "Everything is under control now on that job."

Right.

"You wanted a vacation before this assignment. Why don't you take it now? We won't be needing your help there anymore."

Cooper smiled to himself. Was the board worried about him getting a conscience and maybe doing something like turning state's evidence? Or did they just want him out now that things were really going to get crazy? "Maybe you're right. A vacation sounds tempting."

"Good," Jamison said, clearly relieved. "Call me when you're ready to work again."

Count on it, Cooper thought. He knew it was just a matter of time before the board found out he hadn't left on vacation. He wondered what the agency would do, and decided he'd find out just what businessmen did in a case like that.

"I hope you get this one figured out, Thom."

"You know Rattlesnake Range. They always get what they want. And this job is near completion."

Really? Cooper hung up, shaking his head. Near completion. Did the board really believe that? Maybe they were banking on Ty Drummond. But even then, the ranch would be tied up for years in litigation, if Cooper knew Delaney. And he felt he'd come to know her pretty well. Maybe the person the agency hired was lying to them about more than just the alleged murder attempts. Maybe that person was telling Jamison he had Delaney ready to give up. Or— Or maybe Rattlesnake Range had something up its sleeve that Cooper didn't know about.

He sat back down at the bar. The jukebox was wringing out a sad country song. Cooper stared into his draft-beer mug. What a mess, he thought. He was on the wrong job with the wrong information. He couldn't get Rattlesnake Range to back off and he wasn't any closer to finding out who was behind the attempted murders, his or Delaney's or maybe both. Now Jamison was trying to get him off the Rockin' L. And on top of that, there was Delaney. And the way he'd been feeling toward her.

He swore at the thought of her with Jared. He'd replayed last night over and over in his head, trying to get it to end differently. It always ended the same. He groaned.

"Let me guess," Ty Drummond said, joining him at the bar. "Working for my sister has put you in this mood, right? Let me buy you a drink."

Cooper watched Ty pull out a pocketful of twenties and toss one on the bar. He wondered again where the cowboy got his money.

"So, how *are* things going at the Rockin' L?" Ty asked, ordering them both an expensive import.

"All right," Cooper said, wondering what Ty wanted. Something, that was for sure. "How's life treating you?"

Ty swore. "But it'll be better when I get my inheritance." He took a sip of his beer. "It's just that I can't wait forever—you know what I mean?"

Cooper was afraid he did. He turned the import in his fingers, liking the feel of the sweat on the bottle, more interested in what Delaney was doing right now than her alleged brother's problems. "So you're planning to settle down and ranch, huh?" he asked, already knowing the answer.

Ty snorted. "I don't know anything about raising horses. And I sure as hell have no plans to raise cattle. I've done my share of cowpunching, thank you."

Cooper thought of Delaney and the ranch. Her love for the land and his captivation with her. A small fit of conscience, Jamison would have said. It will pass.

"You know the Rockin' L's been in Ms. Lawson's family for years," Cooper said, not so sure the pang of conscience was going to pass. "But I guess you're part of that family now."

Ty made a rude noise. "They're not my family. I'm Hank's son by accident. Nothing more." He took a swallow of his beer. Bitterness distorted his features. "I would think Delaney would be sick of ranching and be looking for a way out."

Cooper wanted to laugh. Ty didn't have a clue. "I get the impression that ranch is her life."

"A substitute for a man, no doubt," Ty said with a curse.

Cooper didn't like the turn this conversation was taking. As much as the thought of punching Ty in the face appealed to him, Cooper was no longer in the mood for a fight. "What's a ranch like that worth, do you think?" he asked, hoping he could get some information out of Ty. If Ty got his hands on the ranch, he'd sell it in a heartbeat. But to Rattlesnake Range. Or someone else?

Ty smiled smugly in the mirror over the back of the bar but didn't say anything.

Cooper had wondered what was so special about the Rockin' L that Rattlesnake Range would hire someone outside the agency, something he knew was unheard of. But now another thought struck him. Maybe it wasn't the ranch that was special, but the person they'd hired. A person who was in a position to get them the ranch easier than an agent. Rattlesnake Range had to know about Ty and his claim that he was the beneficiary. Would the board hire him to get the ranch for them?

He looked over at Ty and wasn't so sure about his latest theory. He personally wouldn't hire Ty to feed his pigs, if he had pigs. It dawned on Cooper that even if Ty was dealing with Rattlesnake Range, Ty probably didn't know what the agency had planned for the ranch. But it was worth a shot.

"The Rockin' L isn't very big," Cooper said, almost thinking out loud. "And it's not like it's in prime ranching country."

Ty played with his change on the bar. "Look, McLeod, my sister seems to like you. I was thinking—"

"Can't see that it would be very good for subdividing into lots, either," Cooper continued, ignoring Ty's attempt to change the subject. "It's too far from anything." What *did* Rattlesnake Range want with the Rockin' L? It didn't make any sense.

"Let's just say I'm going to do all right when the time comes." Ty finished off his beer. "The thing is, I thought maybe you could talk to her, tell her how stupid it would be to drag this thing out in court, tell her—"

"I'm just a hired hand," Cooper interrupted. "She wouldn't listen to any advice I had to offer. Believe me." He thought about the wisdom he'd given her on Jared. Look how she'd paid attention to that!

"Yeah, I guess you're right." Ty picked up his money, failing to leave a tip for the bartender, and stuffed it into his pocket.

"Maybe you're Hank's son," Cooper said, disliking Ty more than he originally thought he could. "But all you have to do is prove that the will you have is legit." Cooper smiled, unable to hide his satisfaction in needling the cocky fool. "But you're right. You probably won't see any money for years while the ranch is tied up in court."

Ty adjusted his hat in the mirror. "Mister, if I were you, I'd start looking for another job," he said, sliding off his barstool. "And soon. Because when that ranch is mine, you won't be needed there anymore."

As Ty left, he tipped his hat to a blond woman coming through the door. Angel Danvers. The writer. And her boyfriend, Buck Taylor. Cooper let out an oath as she made a beeline for the bar—and him.

Chapter Ten

In an angry silence Delaney knew was directed at her, Jared drove the pickup out of Helena. They left behind the houses and businesses that dotted the countryside from Helena to Hauser Lake, crossing the dam and turning onto Trout Creek Road. Tall ponderosas lined the narrow road, darker than the sky. Delaney could make out starlight above the trees and thought of Cooper. Was he lying under those same stars right now? He was probably thinking what a fool she'd been to go out with Jared. And he'd be right, she thought with annoyance. But it wasn't as if she hadn't known that from the beginning. She just hadn't expected things to go this badly.

"So, did you enjoy your dinner, Del?" Jared asked.

He sounded more than a little testy. Jared had become testy not far into the meal and hadn't improved by dessert.

"Why did you agree to have dinner with me anyway?" he demanded.

"So we could talk." Not that it had done any good. He hadn't told her anything she didn't already know.

"Talk?" he snapped. "But not about anything important."

She glanced at him, recognizing for the first time that being on the isolated road with Jared unnerved her. They hadn't seen a car for several miles now. She felt alone and a little frightened. And told herself she was just being silly. She was with the county sheriff, for cryin' out loud.

"I think what's happening on my ranch is important, Jared, but you refused to talk about *that.*"

The muscle in his jaw jumped. His hands tightened around the steering wheel in a death grip. "Dammit, Del, you know what I wanted to talk about tonight. Us."

Her fear level rose like a rocket. She and Jared had been over this before. He just didn't seem to want to accept it. "Jared, you and I are neighbors. There's never been an us."

He looked over at her, anger making his eyes dark beneath his Stetson. Suddenly he brought the pickup to a rattling stop in the middle of the road. The night seemed to close in instantly.

"Del, you know what I want."

She stared at him, pretty sure she did, but equally sure he wasn't going to get it. "Jared," she said cautiously, hoping the three margaritas he'd had would help loosen his tongue and not make him actually dangerous. "You want my ranch."

He looked surprised. "No, all I've ever wanted was you."

That surprised her. She'd just assumed that the attraction was her ranch because it ran adjacent to his. "But I don't feel the same way and you know it."

"Yeah. Well, that's a problem, isn't it?" He turned off the engine.

"Jared, let's not do anything here you're going to regret," she said more reasonably than she felt. Normally Delaney felt she could take care of herself. But that was on her ranch, where she wore something more than a dress and a pair of pumps. And on the ranch she carried a rifle in her truck or in her scabbard. Right now she had nothing but a quarter in her shoe to call for a ride home, a trick her mother had taught her after meeting Hank Lawson.

Jared lunged for her. She elbowed him in the chest. That took the wind out of him long enough for her to jump from the pickup and slam the door in his face.

IT WAS PROVING to be quite the night at the York Bar, Cooper thought as Angel moseyed up beside him, fingered the neck of his beer bottle and whispered, "I've seen you somewhere before, haven't I?"

Cooper smiled sweetly, figuring she'd had too much to drink, and said, "I believe we met at the Rockin' L the other day, ma'am."

She laughed, filling the bar with a sound that did everything but shatter glass. "No, I've seen you somewhere before that. I never forget a face. Especially one like yours."

Cooper glanced over his shoulder to see Buck standing behind her, looking mean. "Can I buy the two of you a drink?" Cooper asked, sliding off the stool to put a little distance between Angel and him.

"No, thanks," Buck said with a snarl.

Angel bumped Cooper's beer as Buck tried to steer her away. It splashed on the bar. Buck and Angel both grabbed for the bottle, making Buck swear and Angel giggle as they finally saved it from tipping over.

"Come on, Angel, it's time to call it a night," Buck said firmly.

"Oh, Buck, you're such a party pooper," she whined.

To Cooper's relief, she went willingly enough. But at the door she stopped to call back to him.

"Don't worry, I'll remember. I always do."

That's what Cooper was afraid of.

STANDING IN THE middle of the road, a half-dozen yards in front of the pickup, Delaney felt like a scared teenager, not sure what to do next. Couldn't Jared see the foolhardiness of this? She heard his side of the pickup open. Surely the night air would bring him to his senses.

"Dammit, Del, get back here." He stood silhouetted against the lights of the truck. "This day's been coming for a long time."

Delaney pulled off her pumps, ready to run.

"Oh, come on, Del. I'm not going to hurt you."

He took a step toward her. She took two back, stepping on a sharp rock that she felt go right through her stocking.

"You going to walk all the way home?"

"If I have to," she said. "You're half-drunk, Jared. And you're acting like a damned fool."

"I'm not drunk, and fool or not, I'm in love with you, Del." He took a step closer. "I know what you need. I can make you happy, if you'd just give me a chance."

"Jared—"

"Let me finish!" he snapped. "Del, don't you see, this is an opportunity for us. We don't have to get up in the middle of the night and check calves or foals in thirty-below-zero weather. We can put all of this behind us."

"What are you talking about?" she asked, backing up.

"Leaving ranching altogether. I'm talking about selling and going away together. We'll be rich, Del. We can go anywhere we want."

Leaving ranching? Going away together? "How long have you been thinking about this, Jared?" she asked. Maybe Cooper was right. Jared was behind her problems, but not for the reason Cooper had thought. Jared didn't want her ranch; he wanted her to sell it and take off with him.

Jared shook his head. "What does it matter?" he asked belligerently. "You're not interested, right?"

She took two more steps back, hoping she could outrun him if it came to that. "And who are we going to sell our ranches to?"

He looked down at his boots. "What difference does it make?"

She had a feeling it made a big difference. He said they'd be rich. Neither of their ranches was worth *that* much. Was he just exaggerating?

"I'm sorry, Jared, but I'm not selling my ranch. Not to anyone."

"But what if you can't keep it, Del?" His voice had dropped dangerously low. He moved closer. She got ready to run. "What if you don't have a choice?"

The roar of an engine and a set of lights came up over the rise in the road. Jared swore and hurried back to move his pickup off to the side. The lights came around Jared's pickup at a snail's pace. Delaney moved to the center of the road to flag down the driver. Anyone was safer than riding with Jared Kincaid.

"Del?" Buck asked as he rolled down his window.

She got a whiff of Angel's perfume from the passenger side of the pickup. It hadn't been empty long, Delaney figured.

"Buck, boy is it good to see you. I sure could use a ride home."

He glanced back at Jared's pickup, now pulled over to the side of the road, engine running. "Jump in."

She started around the front of Buck's pickup, when Jared came roaring up beside her. As he rolled down his window, she saw that his face was an angry red, his eyes wild.

"Get in this truck right now, woman," he said through gritted teeth. "Don't you embarrass me in front of your ranch manager."

She felt her own anger simmering just below the surface. "Jared, I'm going to forget this night ever happened. But don't you ever make the mistake of trying something like this with me again."

He glared at her. "You're crossing the wrong man, Del. You could live to regret this."

She hoped it was just the booze talking, as she walked around to the passenger door of Buck's rig. She heard Jared gun his engine and roar off.

COOPER STILL HADN'T finished the beer Ty had bought him, when Jared walked into the York Bar. The couple of beers Cooper had had before to dampen his sorrows if not drown them had left him feeling even more out of sorts and a little woozy.

But when Jared slammed into the bar and ordered the bartender to pour him a Black Velvet ditch and make it a double, Cooper's mood improved considerably. Jared looked anything but happy. The date must not have gone well, Cooper thought with a grin.

"Let me buy you a drink," he said, moving down the bar with his now-warm beer to pull up a stool by the sheriff.

Jared glared at him, scooped up his ditch the instant the bartender, a guy named Dude, set it in front of him, and drained it. "Give me another one, but this time put some booze in it." Jared turned to face Cooper. "You got a problem, cowboy?"

Cooper shook his head and grinned. "Just wondering how your date went." He thought for a moment Jared was going to take a swing at him. The idea appealed to him, until he remembered Jared was the sheriff, which reminded Cooper how much he hated being behind bars.

"Better than yours," Jared said, looking around the now-empty bar.

Cooper laughed. "Yeah. You got me there. It's been pretty lonesome here."

Jared seemed to calm down by the second drink. He took a buck from the bar where the bartender had left his change and went over to the jukebox. He punched a couple of numbers, then came back and told Cooper to finish the selection off. Cooper didn't have any real interest in listening to music, let alone picking songs, but he did it because he got the idea Jared was trying to be nice to him. And that made him *real* suspicious.

He punched "Pretty Woman" and "Your Cheating Heart," then joined Jared back at the bar.

"Delaney tells me you're not a bad hand," Jared said after a moment.

Cooper doubted Delaney had told him that. Or that the two had talked about him at all.

"I could use a decent hand. And I pay more than Del."

Jared was offering him a job? Cooper wanted to laugh in the man's face. "I'm flattered, but I kind of like working for Ms. Lawson."

That didn't seem to please the sheriff. "Well, you won't be there long."

Funny, that's the same thing Ty had said. "How's that?" Cooper asked.

Jared took a long sip of his drink. "I mean I figure a man like you will be moving on pretty soon. I would imagine you'd be missing the rodeo. Am I right?"

"You sure got me pegged." He could feel Jared studying him in the mirror above the bar.

"So, were you any good?" Jared asked.

Cooper tried not to be insulted. "Good enough not to starve."

Jared chuckled and finished his drink. Cooper pushed some money across the bar and motioned for Dude to freshen the sheriff's drink. Cooper caught a look of something stronger than dislike that passed between the bartender and Jared.

"You know, I've got a horse that no one can ride," Jared said to Cooper after a moment. "He's called Hell's Fire. The meanest bronc I've ever seen. I bet even you couldn't ride him."

"How much would you bet?" Cooper asked, taking the bait.

Jared smiled. "You've probably heard about the little rodeo I put on each year at my place. It's Saturday. I'd make a substantial wager personally, if you were interested. Then there is always the prize money."

"Let me think about." Cooper excused himself to take a trip to the men's room. He didn't doubt for a moment that Hell's Fire was a mean horse or that Jared was hoping he'd get himself killed riding it. But the idea of going to Jared's ranch for the rodeo appealed to him. He told himself it was just because it would give him a chance to look for the barred-shoe horse. He'd had a strong feeling for some time that he was going to find the horse on the Kincaid ranch. He assured himself riding Hell's Fire had nothing to do with the thrill of rodeoing or personal pride, although he had to admit he'd love to ride the bronc to show Jared.

On the way back to the bar, Cooper realized he hadn't eaten since breakfast. That probably explained why he felt a little light-headed. He took a sip of his imported beer, which was now more than a little warm and flat, and told Jared he'd see him Saturday at the rodeo.

The sheriff seemed too pleased, Cooper thought as he went out to find Crazy Jack waiting for him in a grassy spot by the parking lot. He let out a piercing whistle and the horse came running over to him, almost knocking him down.

"Let's go home, boy," he told Crazy Jack as he mounted the animal and headed for the ranch. Home? When had he started thinking of the Rockin' L as home? He shook his head at just the thought of Delaney and her determination to hang on to the ranch. She was going to get herself killed over nothing more than a piece of land and a few horses. It wasn't worth it. Didn't she realize that?

Chapter Eleven

"Buck?" Delaney looked over at him as he drove toward the ranch. He seemed more distracted than ever tonight, almost agitated. From the strong scent of perfume inside the cab of the truck, Delaney knew whom he'd been with and had a pretty good idea what he'd been up to.

He pulled himself out of his thoughts with a jerk. "Sorry, what?"

"Are you all right?" she asked, worried that after an amorous evening, Angel had decided to break it off.

"Just thinkin'." Buck darted a look at her. "I stopped by your place earlier."

"Something you wanted to talk about?"

He ran his hand over the top of the steering wheel. He couldn't seem to hold still. "You know I was married once."

She'd heard the scuttlebutt about his fateful marriage. Buck had married a Helena woman when Delaney was in junior high school, and after about six months, she'd taken off to become a showgirl in Vegas.

"It didn't work out," he said. "She didn't like living way out of town on a ranch. Wanted to live in a city and wear fancy clothes and go out a lot."

Just like Angel, Delaney thought. "Well, some women need that, Buck."

"I suppose." He glanced over at her. "But you don't seem to. Don't you ever wish you lived in town?"

She laughed. "No, Buck. Nor do I want to go live on an island." He frowned at her in puzzlement. "Jared offered to take me to an island."

"Seems your date didn't work out so well," Buck said.

Buck, the king of understatement. "You could say that." She looked over at him. "What makes you think it was a *date?*"

"That's what McLeod said when I stopped by the ranch."

McLeod. She should have known. And to make matters worse, he'd been right about Jared being dangerous. Delaney just hadn't realized how much until tonight. Not that she planned to admit that to Cooper.

"I've been doing some thinking," Buck said.

She studied him out of the corner of her eye. They'd never been what she'd call friends. While almost a permanent fixture on the ranch, he was a lot older and tended to keep to himself. A loner, her grandfather would have called him.

"You thinking about getting married again, Buck?" she asked, hoping he wouldn't feel she was prying. Also hoping he'd say no.

He looked surprised, then sheepish. "It crosses a man's mind sometimes, you know? It's not like I'm getting any younger."

"But this woman you're thinking about wouldn't want to live on a ranch, right?"

He eyed her as if she had ESP.

"Buck, I have to assume it's Angel."

He laughed nervously as he turned off onto her ranch road. "I'm not even sure she'd have me, mind you, and I'd have to do a powerful lot of changing to make her happy."

Delaney started to argue that if you loved someone, you didn't require them to change for you, but she realized if she were to fall for a rodeo cowboy like Cooper—not that something like that would ever happen—she would want him to quit rodeoing. "You thinking about moving into town?"

He swallowed. "That and getting a better job that pays more." He realized what he'd said. His eyes widened. "No offense."

"None taken. Buck, you've got to do what's right for you. If it's moving into town and getting a different kind of job, then I wish you the best of luck. I'd miss you and you'd be damned hard to replace, but I wouldn't stand in your way if it's what you wanted."

He felt relieved. And a little guilty. "Thank you, Del," he said, avoiding her gaze.

And she realized he'd been doing that a lot lately. Angel certainly had put this man into a tailspin.

As Buck pulled into the ranch yard, Delaney automatically looked over at Cooper's camp. No campfire lit the night. No light at all except the stars overhead. Nor did she see Crazy Jack around anywhere.

"I wonder where Cooper is?" she asked, thinking out loud.

"Angel and I saw him at the York Bar," Buck told her.

She tried not to show her disappointment as she climbed out. "Thanks for the ride."

"Are you going to be all right here by yourself?" Buck asked.

"Of course," she said with a laugh. "I've lived here for years alone." But no one has been taking potshots at her back then, she reminded herself. "I'll be fine," she assured Buck and herself.

He bade her good-night and drove away.

Delaney walked up the steps, her pumps making a completely foreign sound on the steps. She hugged herself, feeling a little cool although the night was warm. It struck her that Buck was right. She didn't feel safe here anymore. It didn't help that Cooper was gone.

Well, you'd best get used to it, because it's only a matter of time before he takes off for good, she told herself as she locked the front door.

Going through the house she turned the lights on and off as she went, feeling like a scared kid. But she had to admit, her encounter with Jared had spooked her a little. Everything else that had happened had spooked her a lot.

And what Jared had said about her selling out before she got herself killed left little doubt in her mind that whoever was after her ranch meant business. Someone out there was determined to get the Rockin' L. Someone, it seemed, who would even kill her for it.

Delaney shook her head, fighting back tears. It was becoming harder and harder not to give in to the fear.

Cooper was right. She had to do something. She was tired of feeling helpless, of waiting for the next rock slide or rifle shot. She couldn't wait for the next time the brakes went out in one of her trucks. And that meant starting with Rattlesnake Range.

She flipped on the lights in her office and dug through the papers until she found the offers Thomas Jamison had made on their behalf. She scribbled a note to herself to call the attorney probating her father's estate and ask him to check on Rattlesnake Range for her, and felt a little better. It was time she found out what was going on.

As she turned out the office lights, she decided she'd drive over to Butte and talk to Marguerite Drummond the next day. She needed to know everything she could about Ty. His mother seemed like a good place to start.

Heading up the stairs, Delaney felt her bit of confidence disappear. She'd never been afraid in this house, but she was tonight. She wished Cooper were at his camp sleeping under the stars. Maybe she *should* have had Buck stay on the couch. With some nut case out there—

A loud thump outside stopped Delaney in midmotion. She clutched the stair railing and tried to hear over the pounding of her heart. Just the wind. Except there was no wind tonight. Maybe it was some small critter.

She heard the noise again. Louder this time. Someone was on the porch! And it wasn't a small critter! At least she'd been smart enough to lock the front door. Not that whoever it was couldn't come through a window if determined enough. Hurriedly she reached over and hit the light switch, plunging the house into darkness.

For what seemed an eternity, she stood paralyzed on the stairs, listening. There was the sound again! Whoever it was was moving around the house, possibly looking in the windows!

Shaking, Delaney moved cautiously back down the stairs and edged along the wall to the gun cabinet. The door creaked as she reached in. She felt around until she found her father's old revolver, which she kept for chasing off coyotes.

Feeling her way to the front of the house, she crept up to the edge of the window casing and peeked out. The ranch yard lay in a warm bath of yellow from the yard light. She stared out, straining to see into the edge of darkness that circled the ranch. Nothing moved in the quiet summer night.

She inched her way to a window at the side of the house and peered out, telling herself the sounds had just been her imagination. Right.

Suddenly a face appeared in the glass. Huge. Ugly. Horrible. Delaney let out a scream and fell back into an end table. The large western lamp toppled with a thud, along with Delaney. She lay on the floor, her heart hammering to get out of her chest. Gulping down a breath, she braced herself and looked toward the window. The face was gone. But not the memory of those eyes looking in at her. Crazy Jack's wild eyes.

"Damn that horse," she cried, stumbling to her feet. "I'm going to shoot him *and* Cooper." It did little to still her anger at that stupid horse for scaring her half to death.

She slammed out the front door, ready to give Cooper and his horse a piece of her mind. "McLeod!" He didn't answer. She looked toward his camp and saw nothing but darkness. "Damn your hide, McLeod!" She started toward his camper but stopped, suddenly feeling vulnerable in the middle of the yard. Alone. She'd left the revolver on the living room floor where she'd dropped it. Behind her she heard the shuffled steps of the horse. He'd picked up his oat bag, which he'd been dragging around. She smiled at the horse, her pulse slowing. What a horse! As unique as his owner.

"Come on, I'll get you some oats," she said, motioning toward McLeod's rig.

Crazy Jack trotted toward the camper and truck. Delaney followed, wondering where Cooper was. Surely the horse hadn't come home without Cooper. A sliver of worry worked its way under her skin. With all the accidents that had been happening on the ranch, what if Cooper— She hurried toward his camp.

COOPER AWOKE WITH A start to find Crazy Jack leaning over him in the dark, whinnying softly. He pushed aside the horse's muzzle and reached for the .45 he kept tucked under his pillow. Sitting up in the sleeping bag he'd rolled out near a large old pine, he brought the pistol up with him at the sound of footfalls approaching his camp. He could see boots coming around the end of the camper. Shaking off the last of his deep sleep, he tightened his grip on the pistol, ready for whatever trouble might be coming.

The figure stepped into view. At first he didn't recognize her. Then he saw her dark silhouette against the yard light leaking around the camper. He quickly slipped the pistol back under his pillow, but not before she'd seen it.

"Do you always sleep armed?" Delaney asked.

Her tone was cautious, suspicious, worried, almost angry. Things he didn't want her to be.

He laughed softly, grinning up at her, turning up the charm the same way he turned up the lantern near his sleeping bag. "Like Jared Kincaid said, you never know when some sidewinder will wander into your camp."

She smiled at that, but her body was still rigid, her attitude tense. He studied her face in the lantern light. She wasn't so sure he wasn't a snake who'd wandered into her camp.

He leaned back, trying to put her at ease. "Jared Kincaid seems to have staked a claim on you," he said, surprised he'd said it, since he hadn't meant to. But he was curious what role the rancher played in Delaney Lawson's life. He assured himself he only wanted to know because of business. He had to know everything about Delaney to get his job done here. "Kincaid seems a little old for you."

She laughed. "Don't beat around the bush, McLeod. Why don't you just come out and ask me if Jared and I ever were an item?"

"Were you?" he asked, surprised how much he wanted the answer to be no.

"It's none of your business," she said, shaking her head at him. "Do you always butt into other people's lives this way, or is it just my life you find so fascinating?"

"I believe you're the one who walked into *my* bedroom," he remarked as he sat up, shoving the bedroll down around his waist. Delaney quickly averted her gaze from his naked upper torso and glanced around the camp as if she wasn't sure what to look at. It was the first time he'd seen her uncomfortable, and he smiled, realizing he liked the hint of vulnerability he'd glimpsed.

"I wouldn't have come over here if your damned horse hadn't scared ten years off my life," she said angrily, turning on her heels and stomping toward the ranch house. "Why don't you feed the poor old nag?"

Crazy Jack let out a whinny. "She didn't mean it," Cooper said to the horse loud enough for Delaney to hear. "I think she really likes you."

Delaney let loose an oath right before she slammed the front door of the ranch house.

Cooper leaned back, smiling up at the stars overhead. He was enjoying this job. Then his smile faded. He might be enjoying it too much. He couldn't let Delaney Lawson keep him from doing what he had to do. No matter how intriguing the woman was.

THE NEXT MORNING Cooper went up to the house to invite Delaney over for breakfast.

"I've seen the way you cook, McLeod, and to tell you the truth, burned beans aren't my idea of breakfast."

He grinned. "How do you feel about sausage gravy, biscuits and eggs sunny-side up?"

She studied him for a moment, skepticism written all over her face. "If you can do that over a campfire, why do you eat beans?"

"I like beans."

She smiled. He could tell it was against her will.

"Well?" he asked, raising an eyebrow.

"I guess I'm going to have to see this to believe it," she said, relenting. "I'll bring the coffee."

"You're on."

They sat around the campfire, the sun at their backs, and ate in silence. In the distance, a hawk circled in the clear blue, while a few young Morgans romped playfully in a near pasture. Cooper breathed in the sweet scent of summer— and Delaney—as he ate. Sitting so close to her had made him more aware of everything—from the smooth, warm surface of the log they shared to the feathered edges of the ponderosas etched against the skyline. He felt a longing like none he'd ever known. He told himself it was just simple desire, something he understood.

"Great breakfast," Delaney said, glancing over at him as she set down her empty plate. "I take back what I said about your cooking." She searched his face. "I can't quite figure you out, McLeod. Why is that?"

"I'm a man of many talents," he said, feeling his grin slip a little. He felt his skin prickle at the thought of touching her. Of her touching him. He put down his plate, telling himself the last thing he should do was reach for her.

The phone rang inside the house.

He took a ragged breath and let it out slowly. "I meant to ask you how your date went last night," he said, feeling the need to change directions.

She shot him a look that said volumes and got up to go answer the phone. "I'd better get that. It could be something important."

"I'm going to go take a bath," he said, pointing toward the creek.

"You're welcome to use the shower in the barn," she said over her shoulder.

"I need the fresh air," he said, watching her go, wondering who'd call this early in the morning.

WHEN DELANEY reached the house, the answering machine was just picking up. She started for her office but stopped when she heard the attorney's voice and the defeat in it.

"Delaney, I just received word on the DNA tests," he said.

The tests she'd insisted on. The results she'd asked called to her immediately. She felt her heart fall, her hopes and dreams with it.

"The tests were ninety-five percent conclusive. Ty Drummond is your half brother."

Chapter Twelve

Delaney dropped into her office chair. In a daze, she listened to the rest of the message from the attorney. He explained they could run the tests again if she wanted, although he saw no reason to. With the use of her father's baby teeth, the tests had been fairly decisive. But, he went on, the will Ty claimed was from their father could still prove to be a forgery. And even if it wasn't, they could fight Ty in court for part of the ranch on the grounds that her father hadn't been himself just before he died. Or she could still find a later will, the one her father had said he'd written, leaving her everything.

Delaney couldn't believe it. She'd convinced herself that Ty wasn't her brother, that he'd made up the whole story just for the money, that the will couldn't be real—her father wouldn't have done that to her. Now she worried that she'd been wrong on all counts.

What would Hank Lawson have done if he'd found out just days before his death that he had a son? Would he have left everything, including the ranch, to his only son? It was just the sort of thing a man like Hank Lawson might have done.

She buried her face in her hands and cried, the hurt and pain overwhelming. Her father had betrayed her. All the times he'd hurt her, forgetting her birthdays, missing school events, never being around when she needed him, nothing could compare with now.

"Delaney?"

She looked up to find Cooper standing over her. His hair was still wet, making it dark blond. The cold creek bath had left a glow on his handsome face. He smiled at her, and for a moment all she saw was his irresistible charm, that cocky arrogance that came ready-made with his good looks. Then his eyes darkened with concern as he reached for her. She flew into his arms.

COOPER HELD HER tightly, afraid at first to ask what had happened. "Is it Digger?" He knew how much Delaney cared for the old prospector. He just hoped that if Digger had died, it was in his sleep and not at the hands of a murderer.

She shook her head against Cooper's flannel shirt and hugged him fiercely as if her world had suddenly dropped out from under her. "It's Ty."

She leaned back just enough that he could see her face.

"The DNA tests came back. He *is* my brother." She bit her lip. "And what if he's telling the truth about the will? My father really may have left him the ranch."

Cooper pulled her even closer, rubbing her back with his hand, as he thought about what that would mean to Delaney. If she lost the ranch— He held her, searching for words that would comfort her, knowing there were none. Maybe this was why Jamison thought they were close to getting the ranch. If he'd been in contact with Ty and knew about the DNA results, that meant Jamison also knew about the will Ty had from his father.

After a few minutes Cooper felt her strength coming back. Delaney Lawson wasn't the kind of woman to stay down and he suspected she'd come up fighting. It was a trait he couldn't help but admire. Unfortunately, with her strength would come the wall between them. She was still his boss, he her hired hand. And the other night he'd hurt her, something he regretted.

After a moment, she pulled away and wiped her tears. When she looked up at him, her eyes were clear and dangerously dark. "I'm not sure what's going on, but it's clear to me that as long as you stay around here, your life will be in jeopardy."

He stared at her, suddenly worried. "I hope you're not thinking of firing me because I have to tell you right now, I won't leave." He grinned at her, hoping to lighten up this conversation—and fast. "You'll have to run me off with a gun. And even then I'll still probably come back."

She smiled. "That's good to hear, McLeod. But why is that?"

He met her gaze, then pulled his away. Normally he'd have some quick, response that would appease even the meanest of women. But Delaney wasn't just any woman. "I guess I've gotten involved in your troubles. And I want to see them through."

She nodded. "Good answer, McLeod. Well thought out." She shook her head. "I know I must be nuts, but I realize I can't save this ranch by myself. Buck's gone and fallen in love, and Jared…well I can't depend on the sheriff for any help, that's for sure."

Cooper nodded, seeing where she was headed. "So, since there isn't anyone else—"

"Exactly," she said, narrowing her eyes at him.

"Well, when you put it that way—" He tried to joke about it, but he was hurt that it would come down to this. And he realized with regret how much it had meant to him to have Delaney's confidence in him.

"McLeod, I have a feeling it is only going to get more dangerous from this point on. If you'd rather pass, I'll understand," she said, watching him closely. He started to argue that he couldn't leave, but she held up a hand to stop him. "I just need to know one thing. Can I trust you?"

He almost laughed. He didn't even trust himself. A lie came to his lips as naturally as breathing. And yet the words just wouldn't seem to come out. Instead he stared at her, seeing the strong, hardheaded, determined Delaney Lawson, but remembering the soft, vulnerable, passionate one he'd kissed. The one he'd held in his arms just moments before. He couldn't walk away now. Not the way he felt about her.

He saw her shake her head at his hesitation. "The other night you said you'd done some things," she said. "I don't care what they are or who you used to be. What I need to know, McLeod, is can I trust you *now?*"

He looked into her eyes. "Yes," he answered, hoping that for once in his disreputable life it was true.

"WHERE DO WE BEGIN?" Delaney asked as they drove toward Helena. She was sure Cooper would have an idea. He always did.

"It seems we've got two problems, finding your father's will—"

"If it exists," she added.

"And finding out who's behind the problems on the ranch and why. I thought we should talk to Digger about Johnson Gulch Lake. That's where he saw something that frightened him, where he got hit on the head and where we were shot at," Cooper said. "Do you still have that spur you found?"

She nodded. "What does the spur have to do with it?"

"Nothing, more than likely." He grinned at her. "But you said it looked familiar to you. It's obviously old. Maybe Digger will recognize it." He saw the doubt in her expression. "I thought it might jog his memory, get him talking about what he saw that night. Digger might know more than he thinks he does."

Why did she get the feeling the spur was the least of Cooper's interest in talking to Digger? "Digger thinks there were space aliens," she said.

"True. But when you add it all up—the rifle shot, the swim-fin tracks and an old road reopened—"

"Don't forget the spur." She gave him a smile. "It doesn't add up to anything, does it?"

They drove in silence for a while. In the distance she would see Lake Helena gleaming in the sun. She felt shaky and unsure, and blamed it on all her troubles—not on her feelings for Cooper McLeod.

"Are you all right?" Cooper asked as they passed the capitol building.

She glanced over at him. "I was just thinking. What will happen to Digger if Ty gets the ranch?"

Cooper figured Ty wouldn't have the ranch for long—not with Rattlesnake Range around. The days of the old prospector wandering the Rockin' L were quickly coming to an end.

THE DOCTOR LED them into a small office at the end of the hall.

"Physically, Digger is on the mend," he said. "But mentally, he's very confused. And frightened. I'd like to run some more tests on him."

"For what?" Delaney asked.

"I think this might be more than senility."

"Like what?" Cooper asked.

The doctor sighed. "Digger can't seem to tell reality from his nightmares. He's paranoid. He thinks people are after him. He's extremely agitated. These are symptoms of what could be Alzheimer's."

"Alzheimer's?" Delaney asked, her voice breaking. She looked over at Cooper. He gave her a reassuring smile.

"The tests can't hurt," he said.

"With Alzheimer's," the doctor added, "all we can do is rule out everything else."

The symptoms could also fit a person who thought his life was in danger, Delaney noted.

She looked down the hall. A deputy lounged outside Digger's room. She hoped that as long as Digger was in the hospital, he was safe.

THEY FOUND Digger in his room, sitting up in bed, yelling at a nurse. When the nurse saw her chance to escape, she scampered from the room.

"When am I getting out of here, Winnie?" Digger demanded the moment he saw Delaney.

She went to his side. "It's Delaney, Digger."

He blinked a couple of times, then smiled. "Of course it is. You just remind me so much of your grandmother." Digger motioned for Cooper to close the door. "What did you find at Johnson Gulch Lake?" he whispered conspiratorially. "You don't think I'm losing my mind, too, do you, Winnie?"

Cooper pulled up a chair for Delaney and another for himself beside Digger's bed.

"We did find odd tracks in the sand," Delaney said, trying to give Digger some hope. "They looked like swim fins, as if someone had been swimming there."

The old prospector nodded and smiled. "I told you I saw them in the water. The space aliens. I never noticed their feet, though."

The early-morning sun spilled through the window, warm and bright. Delaney realized the normalcy of it made their discussion all that much more bizarre.

"We definitely think you saw something," Cooper said.

"You remember Cooper McLeod," Delaney said to Digger. "He's my..." She started to say hired hand, but somewhere along the way he'd become much more than that. "Friend."

She saw Cooper smile at that and she looked away. Honestly, the man was incorrigible.

"Did you hear a pickup engine that night?" Cooper asked.

Digger's face wrinkled in a frown. "Can't say as I did. Can't say as I didn't. Tess was kicking up a fuss, noisier than the devil." He looked at Delaney. "How is that old mule of mine doing? Better than me, I suspect."

"Tess is fine." She started to say that the mule missed him, which she knew was probably true, but realized that would only make Digger want out of the hospital sooner.

"Gus came again last night," Digger said after a moment. He stared at the window; worry etched his face. "I told him I didn't steal his gold, but he doesn't believe me. He said he'd come back for revenge. And I imagine he'll have it."

Delaney felt pulled between her loyalty to Digger and fear that these were only the hallucinations of a diseased mind. How could Gus have gotten in with the deputy outside Digger's door? She tried to imagine Gus Halbrook. Gus had died so young. And so violently in the cave-in. It must have been horrible for Digger. She wondered if he felt guilty for what had happened and that was causing some of this.

"It wasn't your fault Gus got killed," Delaney said, taking Digger's old weathered hand.

He smiled at her, tears in his eyes. "He was my friend. I should have been there with him. Maybe—"

"Digger, would Gus go back to the mine?" Cooper asked.

Delaney shot him a look of surprise. Gus? The mine?

Digger turned his rheumy old eyes on McLeod. "You mean the Golden Dream?"

Cooper nodded. "Wouldn't he go back to the place where he died?"

"I suspect he would." He eyed Cooper with respect. "Young man, you're thinkin' that's where we'd catch him, ain't ya?"

Cooper smiled. "That's exactly what I'm thinking. Can you tell me how to find the mine?"

"Excuse me, even if you found it, my grandfather dynamited the entrance years ago," Delaney interjected. Why was Cooper bringing this up now? Surely he didn't believe Gus was back and on his way to the mine. He was beginning to sound like Digger.

"There's evil at that mine, Winnie," Digger said. His gaze flickered around the room. Agitation showed in his features. "Pure hatin' evil. Anyone who goes near there—"

"Don't worry, Digger, I'm not about to let Del—Winnie go there," Cooper said. "The mine's up Johnson Gulch, isn't it?" Digger nodded. "Tell me about the other entrance."

Delaney stared at Cooper. "Another entrance?"

"We got to stop Gus," Digger said, digging in the drawer beside his bed. "What if he tries to hurt Winnie?"

"That's why you have to tell me where it is," Cooper said. Digger handed him a bent-up, worn photograph.

Delaney shook her head but said nothing. She knew it was the photo Digger still carried of his old friend; Gus's face was barely visible anymore. She felt a chill, although the room was unusually hot, even with the air conditioning. What if the doctor was wrong about Digger's delusions? Digger didn't sound confused. If anything, his story had been consistent from the beginning. Space aliens. And Gus Halbrook back from the dead for revenge. Now even Cooper sounded as if he believed Digger. She hugged herself, afraid there might be more truth in Digger's story than any of them had been willing to admit.

"There was a boulder, a huge thing, and a massive old pine tree, as gnarled as my old hands," Digger said hesitantly. "The entrance is small. Used to be covered in brush."

"The entrance is upstream of the lake, right?" Cooper asked.

Digger nodded. "Up on the hillside. But you shouldn't try to find it alone. Not with Gus out there."

Cooper patted Digger's arm and thanked him. "Don't worry." But Delaney could tell Cooper was disappointed. With directions like that, he'd never be able to find the mine.

"We found something else at the lake," she said, rummaging into her bag. "It looks familiar to me." She pulled out the antique spur. "Cooper thought you might—"

Digger let out a gasp. He held up his hands as if to ward off something horrible. She looked down at the spur, the sapphire sparkling, then at Digger. But his gaze was on the window. Shadows waltzed into the room. "Gus."

"Gus?" Delaney actually turned, expecting to see an old prospector still covered with dirt from the grave. She felt a chill.

"No, Gus! Not Winnie." Digger clutched his chest. He seemed to be fighting for breath. His words came out in a hoarse whisper. "Revenge." The alarm on the monitor beside the bed went off and Delaney could hear nurses running down the hall toward them.

"What is it?" she cried.

"I think he's having a heart attack," Cooper said, moving her back as the nurses rolled a cart into the room.

"Oh, Cooper," she cried, turning into the cowboy's embrace. "He can't die."

"It was just an anxiety attack," the doctor told them a half hour later. "He's resting comfortably."

"He scared me," Delaney said. "One minute he was just fine and the next—"

"He's scaring himself," the doctor said. "He's convinced someone is trying to kill him. Someone named Gus. Do you know who that would be?"

Delaney looked down at her boots. "Gus Halbrook. He was a prospector friend. Only, Gus died in the 1930s in a mine cave-in on the Rockin' L."

The doctor nodded. "I suspected it was something like that. Well, don't worry. We'll see that he's taken care of. I'll run those tests." Delaney nodded. "I'll call you when I know something," the doctor added.

COOPER SUGGESTED they stop at the York Bar for a beer and a burger. He wanted to talk to Dude about the night before. He'd noticed a definite animosity between Dude and the sheriff and he was curious why, and having Delaney along might help. She still seemed shaken from what had happened at the hospital, and didn't appear all that anxious to get back to the ranch.

Dude wasn't working. A petite blonde was behind the bar. She gave them a broad smile and a beer and took their orders.

Delaney sipped her beer, worry etching her beautiful face. The bartender went to play some songs on the jukebox before she started their burgers. The place was empty this time of the day. It smelled of beer, worn wood and burgers, not an unpleasant aroma, Cooper thought.

A soft, slow western song filled the barroom.

"Digger's going to be all right," Cooper said, taking Delaney's hand. "There's nothing more we can do. What do you say to a dance?" She started to resist, but he gave her his best grin. "Look, there's only one spot left for us."

She glanced over at the empty dance floor and smiled. "McLeod, you could charm the wind out of the trees."

He laughed as he pulled her into his arms. Holding her was becoming a habit he thought he could get used to. She felt so right. He wondered how he would ever be able to give her up. But he knew his past was eventually going to catch up with him and then ... He looked into her dark eyes and wished he could tell her the truth.

"Why were you asking Digger about the Golden Dream Mine?"

He shrugged. "With Digger going on about Gus and strange happenings at Johnson Gulch Lake, I thought it might all tie up somehow. And that I could put it together and—"

"And solve all my problems." She laughed. "You're a romantic at heart, McLeod."

He grinned. "Yeah. That's me."

They moved slowly to the music, their bodies in unison. He felt her breasts, soft and full, against his chest. Desire spread through him. He saw it reflected in Delaney's dark eyes, in the way she molded her body to his. The music drifted with them, part of them. He kissed her, then traced her lips with the tip of his tongue. She moaned softly as the song ended.

"Well, well, well, isn't this an interesting sight."

Cooper looked up to find Jared standing in the doorway of the bar. The smile on his face couldn't disguise the meanness in his eyes. "Let me buy you two lovebirds a drink."

"Thanks, but we were just about to have lunch," Cooper said as he and Delaney returned to the bar.

"Oh, that's too bad." Jared studied Delaney openly for a moment. Cooper couldn't help but notice the animosity between them. He wondered just how badly their date had gone.

"You haven't forgotten about my rodeo Saturday," Jared said to Delaney. "McLeod told you he's riding saddle bronc, didn't he?"

Cooper saw the look of disbelief on Delaney's face. He groaned under his breath. Damn. He'd never be able to convince her he wasn't just like her father, that rodeoing had been one of the last things on his mind since he'd met her. But he had to admit, just the thought of riding Hell's Fire excited him.

DELANEY COULDN'T believe her ears. She shot Cooper a look, expecting him to deny it. Instead he gave her a shrug and a grin. They never changed! Once they got rodeo in their blood— She kicked at the leg of her barstool and swore to herself.

"It's just a one-time thing," Cooper said, obviously thinking that would calm her down.

"And what if you get hurt?" she demanded. "Or killed? I'll have to find a new hand, won't I."

Jared laughed. "Tarnation, Del, new hands are a dime a dozen, but a man who can ride Hell's Fire, well, that's some kind of man."

"Hell's Fire?" she cried. "Isn't that the wild bronc you bought for this rodeo? The horse no one's been able to ride yet?"

Jared smiled. "That's right, Del."

He was enjoying himself. That only added to her anger with Cooper. Didn't Cooper realize he'd played right into Jared's hand?

"We've got a little wager on it, isn't that right, Mc-Leod?"

Delaney gave them both glares, then stomped over to the jukebox. When the waitress brought their lunch, Delaney motioned for her to leave it at a nearby table. She couldn't bear sitting at the bar with Jared. Actually, the very thought of food sickened her. What was Cooper thinking? Didn't it matter that he was taking his life in his hands riding Hell's Fire?

She punched in four songs, sat down at the table and picked up her burger. No woman can take the rodeo out of a man, she told herself as she took a bite. Look how her mother had tried for all those years. It eventually killed her. She took another bite. Delaney cussed herself for ever lowering her defenses around Cooper. When was she going to learn? She looked down and saw her empty plate, surprised she'd eaten all her lunch.

Cooper sat down across from her and picked up his burger. He seemed about to say something, but probably knew she wasn't going to buy his excuses anyway. He ate in silence. Jared stood with his back to the bar, watching them, a smile on his face. Delaney glared at Cooper over her beer.

"See you Saturday, McLeod," Jared said as they were leaving the bar. "I'm sure you'll want to see him ride, Del. I'll save you a seat."

"I wouldn't count on that, Jared," she said, and slammed out to the pickup.

"Would you like to know why I accepted Jared's bet to ride Saturday?" Cooper asked as he climbed in beside her.

He sounded so rational it made her all the more angry with him. "It's your neck, McLeod." She started the pickup and backed out, sending more gravel flying than she'd meant to. "Why should I care what happens to you? But you did say you'd help me find out who's trying to take my ranch from me. You can't do that if you're dead."

He grinned at her. "It's nice to think you're worried about me." She rolled her eyes. "I agreed to ride because I wanted to get a look at Jared's stock and it seemed like a way to do it without attracting attention," he said calmly. "As one of the participants, I'll have free run of the place."

She glared at him. "You agreed to ride a wild, unridden bronc on the off chance that Jared might have a horse with a barred shoe?"

"I'd bet this month's wages that horse is Jared's."

"You'd better hang on to your money, McLeod. You've already bet Jared you can ride Hell's Fire." She loosened her grip on the steering wheel when she noticed her knuckles had turned white. "You couldn't have come up with a better way to look for the horse than riding in Jared Kincaid's rodeo?" she asked, incredulous.

"It seemed like a good idea at the time," Cooper said sheepishly.

Men! "Jared wouldn't have bet you unless he thought you'd get yourself killed!" She slammed her fist against the steering wheel. "And from what I've heard about Hell's Fire, you probably will."

"You don't have much faith in me, do you?" Cooper asked.

She glanced over at him to see if he was serious. She hit the brakes and skidded to a stop in the middle of the dirt road. "This isn't about barred shoes or finding attempted murderers. This is about the thrill of rodeoing—admit it."

"I quit rodeoing." He met her gaze and held it. "And if I need a thrill...well, I've heard you can find that kind of stimulation in a woman." His eyes darkened. "With the right woman, of course."

An oath came to her lips, but she stifled it and got the pickup going again. He'd quit rodeoing? Then how did he explain that injury to his thigh, the one he said he'd gotten from some bronc just recently? Men. When was she going to learn not to believe anything they told her? Especially one like McLeod.

Not far down the road, Buck passed them in his truck. Angel was cuddled up next to him. Delaney wondered if Buck had popped the question yet. She groaned, thinking about what Cooper had said about stimulation and the right woman. She noticed Cooper had turned to look back at them. "Let's have it," she said. She swore sometimes she could hear the wheels turning in his head.

"What would you say to taking a look around Angel's cabin?"

She stared at him. "Isn't that illegal?"

"Not very," he lied with a grin. "I want to see if she has any reason to want to shoot at me or drop rocks on me."

"Why would a writer want to hurt you?"

He shook his head. "Why would anyone want to?" He grinned. "You seem to be the only person around here who isn't trying to kill me."

"Give me a little time," she said, and headed down the road toward the Meadows Lodge.

A young woman with frizzy brown hair, thick glasses and a mouthful of gum came out of a back room at the Meadows Lodge. She eyed the two of them and smiled knowingly. "Cabin for two? One night? One bed?"

"We're not...together," Delaney snapped, and took a step away from Cooper. She didn't even have to face him to know he was grinning.

"Actually," she heard him say, amusement in his voice, "we're looking for Angel Danvers, the writer."

The woman chewed her gum for a moment. "Cabin twelve." She pointed down the line of cabins to one with a dark-colored van parked outside. "Except she just left with some old cowboy dude."

Delaney bristled at her description of Buck, then realized it was fairly accurate.

"Sor-ree," the woman said, and headed back no doubt to the soap opera on the television in the adjoining room.

"Angel is going to be furious that we missed her," Cooper said to Delaney. "Especially now that she's got a shot at Fabio on the cover."

Delaney blinked at him. Fabio? On the cover of what?

The woman stopped and turned at the mention of Fabio. "Fabio? I thought Angel Danvers wrote dry old history stuff?"

Cooper gave the woman a grin that Delaney recognized only too well. "That's just what she tells people. What she really writes is steamy historical *romances*."

"Steamy" seemed to do it. "No kidding," the woman said.

"But Angel won't be writing anything without her computer," Cooper continued. He looked up at the woman as if a light had suddenly gone off in his head. "Could we leave Ms. Danvers's computer with you?"

The woman shrugged. "Just put it over there." She pointed to a dusty corner.

"I don't think that's a good idea," Delaney said. "It's an expensive laptop. Angel would have a fit."

Cooper nodded his approval. "You're so right."

"I guess you could leave it in her cabin," the young woman said. She reached up and took down the second key for cabin twelve. "You don't suppose she'd sign a book for me, do you?"

"Absolutely," Cooper said, taking the key from her. "Who knows what she'll do when I tell her how helpful you were?"

"FABIO?" Delaney asked as they left. "And what happens when that woman talks to Angel, and Angel then asks us what we were doing searching her cabin?"

"By then we'll have found out what we need and have time to come up with a good cover story."

She shot him a look. "Such as what?"

"Oh, I'll think of something," he said.

She studied his handsome face, remembering the way he'd turned on the charm—and the lies. "Why do I feel you've done this type of thing before, McLeod?"

His grin faltered as he inserted the key and they stepped into the cool, darkness of cabin twelve.

ANGEL WASN'T what anyone would call neat. It looked as if for the past week she'd simply walked into the cabin and stepped out of whatever she'd been wearing. The floor was cluttered with discarded outfits. The bed was unmade and strewn with books and papers. So was the desk in the corner.

"The sign of a creative mind?" Delaney joked.

Cooper went to the desk and thumbed through the piles of papers. Notes. Historical data on gold mines and the York area. He noticed across the creek from the original

townsite of New York was a smaller one that had been
Brooklyn, Montana. Both had been small, but the town of
Trout Creek just down the road, which no longer existed,
had a population of several thousand between 1866-1869.
He glanced through the rest, surprised. It was all the same.
Maybe Angel was who she really said she was.

He left Delaney digging around in the pile on the bed and
went to check the bathroom. Makeup everywhere. Stock-
ings hanging in the shower. Wet towels on the floor where
she'd dropped them.

Her cosmetic case stood open on the toilet tank. He carefully sifted through the case and found nothing of interest.
The medicine cabinet was empty.

As he stepped back into the main part of the cabin, he
noticed the empty clothes rod in the closet. Instead an open
suitcase lay on the closet floor. It looked as if a bomb had
exploded inside it. Angel didn't plan to stay long, it appeared.

Cooper glanced up to find Delaney flipping through a
book. "What did you find?" he asked.

"An old journal," she said, smiling at him as she closed
it. "Sorry, I guess I'm not much help. It was interesting.
Written by a prospector in the late 1930s about the hard-
ships of mining for gold." The swamp cooler behind her let
out a loud bang and she jumped. She gave him a chagrined
smile. "All right, so I'm not cut out for this cloak and dag-
ger stuff."

Cooper smiled back at her. "Actually, I was thinking that
we made quite the team back there in the office." He
glanced at his watch. "We'd better get out of here before
that daytime drama ends."

As he bent to look through the contents of the suitcase,
something caught his eye. With two fingers, he picked up a
little navy blue dress with a white collar from a hanger at the
back of the closet. Memory threw him like a mean bronc.
He knew now where he'd seen Angel. She'd been wearing

this dress, her hair had been pulled up into a no-nonsense style and it had been a different color, a dark auburn. Even her voice had been different. No dumb-blonde routine. No flirting. Strictly business.

"Something wrong?" Delaney asked.

He looked up. The dress slipped from his fingers. He shook his head, too stunned to speak. Angel Danvers had been a different woman the day Cooper had seen her at Rattlesnake Range.

Chapter Thirteen

Cooper had been acting strangely ever since they'd left Angel's cabin. He seemed preoccupied and anxious to get back to the ranch.

"I have a couple of things I need to do in town," he told her vaguely.

"Do they have anything to do with that dress you found in Angel's closet?" Delaney asked.

He laughed and grinned at her. "It just reminded me of someone, that's all."

Her heart tightened. "A woman from your past?" she asked, trying to keep her tone light, hoping the sudden pang of jealousy wasn't audible.

Cooper shook his head. "An old friend I recently lost."

"Oh, I'm sorry." She felt awful for being so nosy and suspicious, let alone jealous. Why did she always jump to the wrong conclusions with him? *Because he's a rodeo cowboy. Because he reminds you of your father.* Both lethal reasons not to get too close to Cooper McLeod.

She stopped the pickup at Cooper's camp. The sun rimmed the mountains to the west. Delaney felt time slipping away. "I've got to get to the bottom of this soon, McLeod. I can't keep playing detective. I have a horse ranch to run."

He nodded. "Maybe I'll find the barred-shoe horse tomorrow at Kincaid's."

She made a face. Momentarily, she'd forgotten about that stupid rodeo.

"Will you be all right here for a while by yourself?" he asked, still awfully anxious to get into town.

"I'll be fine," she answered, trying not to let her suspicious mind run loose.

Cooper nodded as if there were something else he wanted to say but changed his mind. "I won't be gone long."

COOPER STILL couldn't believe it. Angel Danvers at Rattlesnake Range. There was no doubt in his mind; he remembered her now, remembered that walk of hers—something she couldn't disguise even in a business dress.

But why was she in disguise that day? He laughed at his stupidity. She *wasn't* in disguise at Rattlesnake Range. That was the real Angel Danvers. The woman on the Rockin' L was the impostor.

Who was she and what had she been doing at Rattlesnake Range? His mind raced with theories. All of them bad. Maybe she was the person the agency had hired to acquire Delaney's ranch. He rejected that theory almost immediately. Delaney didn't like Angel. And Angel wasn't doing anything to get her to. Nor was Angel even pretending interest in buying the ranch. From what he'd seen in cabin twelve, Angel really was researching a book.

So what was she doing at the agency? he asked himself as he drove into York. Rattlesnake Range kept a very low profile. Few people even knew about it. But if you were interested in acquiring a special property on any terms, at any price, and you had enough money, you'd eventually end up at Rattlesnake Range. Angel didn't appear to have that kind of money. But he'd learned a long time ago not to judge a woman by the color of her lipstick.

He parked beside the phone booth, anxious to talk to Thom Jamison. Cooper was desperate to find some answers before Angel remembered where she'd seen him and blew his cover.

As DELANEY PARKED in front of the house, she noticed her front door. It stood open. Her heart quickened. Maybe the wind had blown it open. Maybe— She pulled the rifle down from the rack behind her and opened the pickup door. Hesitantly she started for the house.

As she mounted the porch steps she could see into the house. Everything looked normal enough.

She stepped in the doorway, rifle ready. And saw them. Boots. Worn, muddy boots. She peeked around the corner of the doorjamb, following the boots up the new denim to find Ty sprawled on her couch. He lay with his head back, his hat partially over his face, appearing to be taking a nap.

Fury ignited her blood—then her tongue. "What the hell do you think you're doing?" she demanded, pointing the rifle at him.

He jumped in surprise, pushing back his hat as he sat up with a start. His gaze focused on the rifle in her hands, and for a moment he looked as if he thought she might shoot him. It wasn't out of the realm of possibility.

"I was waiting on *you*," he said indignantly.

"Do you always just walk into a person's home to wait for her?" He raised an eyebrow and smirked at her. She felt as if she were dealing with a child. "It's not your home yet, Ty. Until it is—"

"I had to talk to you," Ty whined. "There has to be some way we can settle this without dragging it out in court."

She quit listening as she noticed the door to her office was also open. It had definitely been closed when she'd left. Something white lay on the floor. She stared, disbelieving. Someone had ransacked her office.

THOM JAMISON sounded more than a little surprised that Cooper hadn't started his vacation yet.

"You're still at the Rockin' L?" he asked.

Cooper thought about lying, but realized it would serve no purpose. Jamison would find out he hadn't left soon enough from the agent on the job. "Yeah. I was getting ready to leave, when I ran into someone here I had seen at Rattlesnake Range just before I came on this job. Passed her in the lobby. A little too much of a coincidence, you know."

Silence.

"She's going by Angel Danvers. Ring any bells?"

"No."

Jamison answered too quickly.

"I thought you'd be sitting in the shade somewhere by now with your feet up," he continued.

"She's a cute little redhead. Big green eyes. Stacked like a brick outhouse. Smart. And all business. The day I saw her at the agency she was wearing a little navy number with a white collar and had her hair up."

Silence. "You aren't going on vacation, are you?"

Cooper smiled; that Jamison was sharp. "No, I'm seeing this one through."

Jamison swore, something Cooper knew was out of character for him. "The board isn't going to like this."

Cooper laughed. "You don't have to tell them."

Silence.

"Or maybe you do." Maybe he'd been wrong about Thom; maybe he couldn't trust him.

Jamison swore again. "I don't remember her name, but I remember the woman. You're right. She could be trouble. She came in asking about the Rockin' L. It became obvious quickly that she didn't have the resources to buy the ranch. She asked a lot of questions about its ownership, how a person would go about acquiring it if the owner didn't want to sell. I smelled newspaper reporter and got rid of her as fast as possible, but she already knew a lot about the ranch and that the agency was trying to get it.''

''A reporter?'' Cooper asked, still wondering if he could trust Jamison, but at the same time knowing he had to. Jamison needed all the information if Cooper hoped for any help from him. ''Well, she's here pretending to be a blond bimbo historical-book writer. She's hooked up with the ranch manager romantically.''

''I see.''

Jamison sounded concerned.

Cooper shook his head as he considered the latest turn of events. ''You've got an untrained loose cannon on this job, someone else possibly taking potshots at your target, a half brother who's desperate for money and the ranch, and now a reporter who's after Rattlesnake Range.'' Cooper laughed. ''Things get any better, Thom, and you'll be doing time at the state prison in Deer Lodge.''

''You forgot one other problem the agency has,'' Jamison said softly. ''They've got you there.''

''DID YOU FIND the will?'' Delaney demanded as she came out of her ransacked office. Nothing appeared to be missing, but she couldn't tell for sure.

She turned to face her brother. Her brother. As she glared at him, she realized she'd actually accepted the fact that he *was* her brother. For so long she'd resisted any thought that they might be related. But now as she studied him, she admitted there were definitely similarities between Ty and their father. He sounded like Hank. Always making excuses. And he looked a little like Hank. In the eyes. And the cheekbones. And he definitely had that self-serving part down perfectly. ''That was what you were looking for, right, the will?''

''What are you talking about?'' Ty asked irritably. ''I could care less about any will you might have.''

''Then what were you looking for?''

Ty shook his head. "Give me a break. I ransacked your office, then took a nap on your couch to wait for you? Brilliant."

Delaney swore and leaned the rifle against the wall before she shot Ty in simple frustration. He was still standing in the living room, looking lost. "What do you want, Ty?" she asked, noticing the front door was still open as a subtle invitation for him to leave.

"I didn't even notice your office was in a mess," he said, frowning at her. "The front door was open when I got here. I just left it the way I found it." He shook his head as if he couldn't believe she didn't trust him.

Delaney eyed her brother and thought he might be telling the truth. He didn't seem the observant type, she had to admit. "All right, Ty, you didn't search my office," she said. "What did you want to see me about?" As if she couldn't guess.

"You got the results of the test, right?" he asked.

"Right." He appeared ill at ease, and she suddenly realized that maybe he wanted her to welcome him into the family. He had to be kidding. "Ty, I'll concede that we're related. But there is something you have to understand. I've worked this ranch since I was a kid. I've put sweat and blood and heart into it. My grandfather taught me to love the land. He taught me about the satisfaction of hard work over material rewards—" She could tell she was boring him.

"The point is," she said, trying not to raise her voice. "All you seem interested in is money. You don't care about this land, this ranch or this family. You don't want to work the ranch—you don't seem to want to work at all. This ranch has been in the family now for more than sixty years. Doesn't that mean anything to you?"

"I need money. Now."

He sounded scared, but at the same time threatening.

"If you could just give me some money against what you owe me—"

"That's just it, Ty. I don't feel I *owe* you anything," Delaney said carefully. "That's why I intend to fight you as long as it takes. Whatever it takes."

"This ranch is mine," he said angrily. "I have the will, dated three days before Hank died. You have no will, and even if you did find the one you said he wrote leaving you everything, it would be worthless. My lawyer says mine should supersede any others."

His lawyer. Delaney took a deep breath, trying to keep her anger in check.

"You aren't going to drag this out," Ty said, his voice dangerously low as he moved toward her. "I'm our father's only son. And he wanted me to have the ranch." Ty smiled; he knew how much that hurt her. "And I'm through waiting, Delaney." He stepped closer.

"Don't threaten me, Ty," Delaney said, standing her ground. Ty was bluffing. He just didn't strike her as a killer. Too lazy. "You'll never get this ranch by threatening me— I don't scare easily. And even if you killed me, you'd never get away with it. You'd be the number one suspect. Even Jared would know you did it."

Ty swore. "You have it all figured out, don't you? Well, I'm going to take what's mine and you're not going to be able to stop me."

"I think you'd better leave," Cooper said, suddenly filling the open doorway.

Ty looked up in surprise. "Stay out of this, McLeod. It doesn't have anything to do with you."

Cooper stepped into the room. "You're upsetting my boss, so I'm making it my business."

Ty laughed nervously, looking from Delaney to Cooper and back. "Getting involved in this could be fatal, cowboy. For both of you." He stomped past Cooper, slamming the door on his way out.

COOPER PULLED Delaney into his arms, needing to feel her safe in his embrace. On the way back to the ranch, he'd realized just how dangerous this all had become. Rattlesnake Range would push harder now, wanting to get this over with as quickly as possible. He feared what extremes they might go to. Then there was Ty. And Angel in the picture. The Rockin' L had become a powder keg about to blow.

"I'm glad you showed up when you did," Delaney murmured against his shoulder.

"Are you all right?" He pulled back to caress her cheek, his gaze on her face.

"Ty sounded a little too desperate for my liking," she said. "And someone ransacked my office. I guess I'm going to have to start locking my door."

"Delaney," Cooper said, hating what he had to do. He let his gaze run the length of her. His body stirred with desire. But the only thing on his mind was worry. About Delaney's safety. She didn't stand a chance against the people who wanted her ranch. He'd realized that on the way back from town. Ty Drummond was probably the least of her concerns. Cooper just couldn't stand the chance that something might happen to Delaney. "I think you should consider selling the ranch."

She looked up in surprise. "Not you, too."

He'd let her down; it showed in every line of her body, in the bright glint of her eyes as she pulled away from him.

"You can't win," he said quietly. "The odds are too great."

She raised a brow, her gaze locking with his. "How do you know that?"

"I've seen it happen on other ranches. Believe me, I know."

She shook her head at him. "You're a runner, aren't you, McLeod? Things get a little tough and you take off." Her gaze was rock hard and just as steady. "Well, I'm a fighter. And that's what I intend to do. With or without you."

He looked into those dark eyes, seeing a strength that made him feel weak, a determination that more than matched his own stubbornness, a fight that reminded him of himself a long time ago. What a pair we'd have made, he thought with regret.

"You're right," he admitted. "I've always run." He smiled, knowing that's exactly what a smart man would do now. Run. And not look back. Only he didn't want to run anymore. He couldn't run—and leave Delaney alone to fight this battle by herself. "But even us weak-kneed cowards have to take a stand sometime." He shook his head as he realized how good he felt, better than he'd felt in years.

She smiled at him. "I thought you said I don't stand a chance?"

"We don't stand much of one."

"'We'?" She laughed softly. "And with those odds, you're still willing to help me?"

He laughed, thinking how beautiful she looked standing there. Thinking how much he wanted her. "No one ever said I had any sense. See you in the morning."

As Cooper walked into his camp, he spotted Crazy Jack dragging his feed sack around again. "Don't you ever think of anything but food?" he demanded, giving the horse a friendly slap on the rump as he took the sack away. Crazy Jack turned to throw him a look that made Cooper laugh.

"I don't think about women *all* the time," he told the horse, but found himself glancing back at the house as he scooped out some oats. No, he hardly *ever* thought about women anymore, he realized. Just one woman.

He smiled to himself as he made dinner, cold beans right out of the can. Even with rocks and bullets flying, it surprised him how comfortable he felt here. For the first time in his life, he felt at home. The thought came as a shock. The last thing he needed was to feel content here, because it was just a matter of time before he'd have to move on. Settling in was a bad idea. And yet his gaze wandered again to the ranch house. He saw the light come on in Delaney's bedroom as he rolled out his bedroll and lay down. Just the thought of her made him ache in his loins—and his heart. A dangerous place to hurt, he realized with regret, because Delaney Lawson was the one woman he didn't dare believe he could ever have. And he'd never wanted a woman the way he wanted her.

He closed his eyes, letting sleep numb desire, memories of Delaney soothe his growing need for her.

Her scream brought him upright. The gunshot right after the scream brought him to his feet, pistol in hand. He raced toward the house. The light was still on in Delaney's bedroom, the house eerily silent.

He hit the unlocked front door, throwing it open. "Delaney!" No answer. He bounded up the stairs, two at a time, his heart in his throat. Fear made his chest hurt with each ragged breath. Fear of what he'd find. Fear that he'd just lost something he'd never really had, never even tried to have. But desperately wanted. Now more than ever.

Pistol ready, he burst into Delaney's bedroom.

Chapter Fourteen

Delaney stood in her nightgown at the side of the bed, a .45 clutched in her right hand, as she stared down at a huge rattlesnake coiled in the covers.

Cooper lunged forward, ready to kill the rattler, only to find it had already been blown away in one fatal shot. Relief rushed through his veins, making him weak. He fought to still his pounding heart as he tucked his pistol into the back of his jeans. He gently took the .45 from Delaney's trembling hand and pulled her into his arms, realizing as his chest made contact with her thin nightgown that all he wore were his jeans.

"You didn't get bit?"

She shook her head against his bare chest.

"Who—"

"It doesn't matter," he said, holding her tighter. Like hell, it didn't. When he found the person who did this— "All that matters is that you're all right." He held her until her shaking stopped, until her breathing became slow and controlled again. He leaned back to look into her face.

"I hate snakes," she said, her eyes still wide, still full of fright, her face pale.

"I know. Come on. You can't stay here."

Cooper wasn't sure where to take her, but he wasn't about to leave her alone. He led her out to his camp.

"The camper's a mess, but if you wait just a minute—" She shook her head. "Or I could take you into town." Again she shook her head, but this time her gaze came up to meet his.

"Couldn't we just sleep under the stars tonight? Together."

He nodded as he stepped to her. Rubbing his hands along her bare shoulders, he pulled her to him. "Are you cold?" Why hadn't he thought to grab her a robe or some clothes. He hadn't noticed just how sheer her nightgown was until this moment. "I could get you a jacket—"

"Cooper."

He met her gaze. "I can't do this without telling you the truth about me."

"The look on your face when you burst into my bedroom, told me everything I need to know," she said, drawing him to her. "Whatever you have to tell me can wait."

"Delaney." She silenced him with a kiss. He swept her up into his arms and carried her over to his bedroll. Trailing kisses from her lips down her neck to the hollow between her breasts, he lowered her to the sleeping bag. The moon peaked over the mountain, covering them in silver. He pulled back to see that her nipples had hardened into dark tips beneath the thin silk of her nightgown. He covered one and then the other with his mouth, teasing both to hard points with his tongue, nibbling gently with his teeth. Delaney moaned and arched her full breasts against him. He slipped one strap from her shoulder, then the other. As he pulled down her gown to expose her bare breasts to the moonlight, desire coursed through his veins, so strong it stunned him.

"You are the most amazing woman, Delaney Lawson," he said, caressing her cheek. "And the most beautiful." She traced her fingers along his chest, feathering his nipples to hard peaks before she raised her mouth to each. He felt longing ripple through his body. He kissed her, relishing in the sweet lushness of her mouth, the sensuous ripeness of her lips.

"Oh, Cooper," she whispered as he cupped her breast in his hand and lowered his mouth again to its hardened bud. Watching her face, he saw her eyes ignite with a passion that made him groan. She buried her hands in his hair, molding her body to his, then ran her fingers down his bare skin, over his taut nipples to his jeans. He groaned with a desperate need as her fingers sought out the buttons on his Levi's.

THE MOONLIGHT bathed his body in silver as Delaney freed Cooper of his jeans. His body was just as magnificent as she'd envisioned it would be and just as filled with desire as her own. Kneeling over her, he slipped her nightgown down over her hips and tossed it away. For a moment he just explored her body with his eyes, a yearning in his expression that fired her blood and warmed her skin. He ran his fingers over her breasts, through the hollow of her stomach, to gently touch the swollen need between her legs. She reached up to him, aching to feel his bare skin pressed against hers. Aching to feel him inside her, buried deep within her. She opened her thighs to allow his touch to explore her. He groaned as if just the sight of her and her obvious desire for him would be his undoing. His touch brought pleasure. And the desperate craving for more of him.

"Please," she whispered, arching her body up to tempt his.

He smiled as she reached for him. Slowly he lowered himself to her, kissing her, teasing her. She felt his skin, hot and smooth, then the hard fire of his desire. She cupped his buttocks with her hands, urging him deeper inside her. He filled her with heat, fire, strength and power. He looked down at her, wonder in his eyes. And love. Delaney wrapped her arms around him, pressed her breasts to his chest and let him fill her with satisfaction, again and again until the moon reached its zenith and she felt him come to her, hot and sweet and fulfilled. She lay spent in his arms, staring up at the stars overhead, breathing in the sweet night air, smiling.

"That was ... incredible," Cooper said beside her.

She kissed his bare shoulder. "Unbelievable."

He laughed and raised himself up on one elbow. His fingers gently circled her nipple. "Unbelievable." His fingers stopped. His gaze found hers and held it. "I've never felt anything like that. Ever."

She smiled, as shaken as he was by what had happened between them tonight. But equally afraid to admit just what it had meant to her. When she looked away, he turned her, spooning her against him, his arms wrapped around her.

"Sweet dreams, Delaney Lawson," he whispered against her bare neck.

She snuggled against him and closed her eyes, pushing aside any thoughts of the future, savoring instead the happiness she felt just being in his arms in the moonlight.

Delaney awoke in Cooper's arms to find the sun coming up over the Big Belt Mountains. She lay there, looking up at the blue sky through the pine boughs overhead with a contentment she had never felt before.

"Good morning," Cooper said next her.

She smiled over at him. "Good morning."

His kiss was sweet and sensuous, stirring emotions in her like a melting pot. She felt his strength and his tenderness, the smoothness of his naked skin and the roughness of his beard. The breeze stirred her hair, teasing the back of her neck as he had done with his kisses. His lips explored her body. She came to him with a willingness that made him laugh with pleasure. He smiled down at her as he satisfied her fantasies, as well as her desires, in the early-morning sunlight.

"IS THERE ANYTHING I can say to make you change your mind about riding in this rodeo?" Delaney asked later as she leaned on one elbow and looked down into his handsome face. Memories of their lovemaking felt as warm as the morning sun that now streamed through the pines.

"I can't think of anything." He grinned and kissed her nose. "But I wish I *could.*" She thought he wasn't as cocky as he normally was. Maybe he had the sense to be worried about this ride today. But not the sense to cancel it, she reminded herself. She brushed back her hair from her face in frustration.

He gazed up at her. "I hope you won't be there to see me make a fool of myself."

She glanced at the horizon, now golden in the sunlight. "Don't worry, I gave up rodeos years ago. Along with cowboys who ride in them," she said, eyes narrowed.

He raised an eyebrow and pulled her to him. "I thought maybe a good night's sleep would help your disposition."

"You mean the way a good night's sleep helped your good sense? And there's nothing wrong with my disposition, either!" But she gave in to his embrace, letting him mold his body to hers, relishing the feel of him, the scent of his skin, the taste of him.

He grinned at her. Sometimes she forgot how handsome he was, and it startled her that just looking at him could elicit so much feeling within her. His gaze grazed her face as lightly as a kiss. He thumbed her nipple to a hard, throbbing point, then sucked at it for a moment, sending waves of desire racing through her again. Could she ever get enough of this man? She doubted it.

"Delaney, we need to talk," he said, letting go of her to gaze into her eyes.

"Buck could come up the road any minute," she lied as she pulled away from him to pick up his flannel shirt. Turning her back to him, she pulled the shirt on, hugging herself against what he might want to talk about. She'd seen the seriousness in his eyes and knew in her heart, it wasn't going to be good news.

When she glanced over her shoulder, Cooper was watching her, a frown on his face. And that's when she noticed the scar on his thigh. It seemed more like a bull had gored him than a bronc had stomped him. But either way, the scar was just another reminder of who Cooper McLeod really was. A rodeo cowboy.

"And you have to get to the rodeo if you're going to find that barred-shoe horse." She didn't like the edge to her voice but couldn't seem to control it. Just the thought of Cooper riding Hell's Fire brought back memories of the rodeos her mother used to take her to when she was a child.

"I once loved seeing my father ride," she said quietly, not understanding her need to tell him about her secret pain. "Then one day I saw him get gored by a bull. It was the first time I understood why my mother was often sick to her stomach before Hank's rides."

"Is that when you gave up rodeo? And rodeo cowboys?" he asked, shooting her a teasing grin.

"Yes, McLeod. I hated the rodeo after that. It terrifies me." The grin disappeared from his face. His eyes darkened as he realized how serious she was. "My father tried everything to get me to come see him again. But I never did." It opened a fissure between them that the years made into a canyon. And now she'd fallen for a rodeo cowboy, a rodeo cowboy with that same kind of good looks and easy charm and that same need to ride rough stock and risk his fool neck.

"I'm sorry," Cooper said softly. "I didn't know."

She turned away and finished buttoning up the shirt.

"I don't like the idea of you being here alone," he said after a moment.

"I won't be," she said, looking around for her night-gown. "I'm going to Butte to see Marguerite Drummond."

"Ty's mother?"

She nodded as she picked up her gown from where Cooper had tossed it the night before. Her skin warmed with the memory. "If my father's will leaving everything to Ty is a forgery, then I would imagine she's in on it. I need to find out for myself."

He stood up and pulled on his jeans. "And you think Ty's mother is just going to admit that to you?"

She made a face at him. "No, but talking to her should at least give me an idea of what I'm up against."

His look held both sympathy and worry. "You sure you want to meet your father's ex-mistress alone? If you wait, I'd go with you."

She nodded, realizing how much she'd like that but at the same time knowing she needed to do this alone. She couldn't depend on this rodeo cowboy. Thinking she could would be a terrible mistake. He was riding in a rodeo today. Who knows where he'd be tomorrow. Last night and this morning hadn't changed that.

"Thanks, McLeod, but I'll be all right. You'd better worry about your own neck around Jared Kincaid and Hell's Fire." She shook her head at him, fighting sudden tears. "So help me, McLeod, if you go and get yourself killed—"

He grinned and pulled her to him. Carefully he planted a kiss on her lips. "For luck." He held her for a moment longer. "Be careful."

She nodded and broke the physical connection between them as she turned and walked away. When she reached the house she touched her fingers to her lips. She just hoped he was right about the kiss. They both needed luck today.

COOPER DROVE to the Kincaid ranch thinking about Delaney. And their lovemaking. He felt shaky and unsure of himself. This morning he was all set to tell her everything about him. But she'd stopped him. And now he wasn't sure where he stood with her. He'd wanted more after their lovemaking. As much as he couldn't believe it himself, he wanted a relationship. Not some one-night stand under the stars. Yet he'd gotten the impression from Delaney this morning that's all she wanted.

He shook his head, thinking of the times that was all he'd offered a woman. And now the shoe was on the other foot and he didn't like it one bit.

The turnoff to Kincaid Ranches wasn't far past Nelson, Montana, the cribbage capital of the world. Nelson, a town of only two houses, wasn't even a wide spot in the road. Kincaid Ranches ran along the western edge of the Rockin' L. Cooper drove up into the ranch yard, not surprised to see it filled with other rigs. According to Delaney, the annual Kincaid Ranches Rodeo had begun as a little ego thing for Jared, but had grown since he started buying rough stock and inviting circuit cowboys.

Cooper recognized Ty's beat-up old pickup and Buck's rig. Angel was leaning against the front fender, looking bored. As she saw him pull up, recognition in her expression, she pushed herself off the truck and headed into the crowd before Cooper could get out of his pickup. Cooper had to smile. So she'd remembered where she'd seen him before. Maybe Jamison was right. If she was a reporter, investigating Rattlesnake Range on the Rockin' L, then she didn't want her cover blown any more than Cooper did. For the same reason, she wasn't going to say anything about him and Delaney visiting her cabin. "What a tangled web we weave," he thought as he got out of his pickup.

Cooper knew he didn't have a lot of time, so he started with the horse barn—a huge expensive thing with an arena in the center. It appeared Jared Kincaid didn't do anything halfway.

Cowboys wandered in and out of the barn. Cooper checked each stall, pretending just to be admiring the horses, but at the same time keeping an eye out for Jared. As the rodeo got into full swing, the barn emptied out. Cooper hurried, knowing he didn't have much time left.

At the second to last one, he leaned in to check a Pinto mare, when he heard a noise. The shaft of sunlight coming through the barn door at the other end of the building suddenly filled with shadows. Cooper ducked into the stall, squatting next to the Pinto. She stomped restlessly. He spoke softly to her and hoped she didn't kick him before he could get out.

"No more excuses," said a rough male voice.

"I told you—I'll get the money."

Cooper recognized that whine. Ty Drummond.

"You just have to give me a little more time."

"You've had more than enough time," said another deep voice.

Cooper edged his way up the side of the stall to peek over the side. Two large men in western wear had Ty between them. Even at this distance, Cooper recognized the threat in their voices, in their stances. He'd never seen the pair before and got the impression they weren't from around these parts.

"I can give you a little now." Ty dug into his jeans and pulled out a handful of bills. One of the men grabbed them.

Ty stumbled back. "I just need more time. You know I'm good for it."

The one man had finished counting the money. He swore and, without warning, buried his fist in Ty's stomach. Ty folded with a groan to the barn floor. The other kicked Ty in the side with his boot. Ty cried out and curled into a ball.

"Twenty-four hours, Drummond." The two turned and left.

Ty lay on the floor, sucking for breath between sobs. Slowly he pushed himself to his feet with one hand, holding his stomach with the other. He looked around to make sure no one had seen the incident, then straightened a little and walked out into the sunlight.

Gambling debts? Loan sharks? It really didn't make any difference. Ty Drummond had now become desperate and

that made him more dangerous than ever, Cooper thought
as he gave the Pinto a pat on the neck and stepped out of the
stall. He couldn't help wondering where Ty had gotten the
money he'd given the men.

He hurried down the row of stalls after Ty. At the doorway, Cooper hung back to watch Ty head straight for the
ranch house—and Jared Kincaid. At Ty's knock, Jared
came outside in the shade of the back porch. It was clear
that the two were arguing. A moment later, Jared reached
for his wallet, pulled out some bills and practically threw
them at Ty.

Cooper shook his head. At least now he knew where Ty
got his money. The question was, why was Jared giving it to
him? Was Ty working for Kincaid Ranches? Jared always
seemed to know everything that was going on with Delaney. Maybe Ty was being paid for information. Or maybe
Ty was blackmailing the sheriff. But for what?

Cooper could hear the announcer in the outdoor arena as
he started for the last stall. The calf roping was almost over.
That meant Cooper didn't have much time before his ride.
He wondered how Delaney was doing with Marguerite. He
just hoped she'd find out something that would help her
save the ranch from the likes of Ty Drummond.

Just as Cooper reached the stall containing a dark-colored
quarter horse, a male voice asked, "Looking for any kind
of horse in particular?"

"Just admiring yours," Cooper said, turning to flash
Jared a grin. "This one appears fast." Unfortunately, it also
didn't have a barred shoe.

Jared studied him with open suspicion. "I thought maybe
you'd chickened out. You aren't hiding in here to keep from
riding, are you?"

The insult raised Cooper's hackles. He laughed at the
challenge he'd heard in Jared's voice. "If I was going to hide
I can think of better places. The York Bar, for one. There's
cold beer there and the people are friendlier."

Jared actually laughed. "You know, McLeod, I think I could grow to like you."

Cooper doubted that. "So," he said, turning away from the last stall with disappointment. He'd been so sure the horse with the barred shoe would be Jared's. "Where's this bronc that no one can ride?"

Jared slapped him on the back companionably as they headed for the open doorway. "Wait until you see Hell's Fire," he said, chuckling to himself. "Just wait until you see him."

MARGUERITE DRUMMOND worked at a place called Katie's Kut and Kurl on the hill in the center of downtown Butte, not far from the famous mile-deep, five-mile-across open pit mine.

The outside of the beauty shop was old brick much like the rest of the downtown area. But unlike the many empty buildings with their dirty windows and sad-looking interiors, the Kut and Kurl had a festive look.

Delaney stepped through the door, not sure what to expect. The walls were done in bright hot pinks and purples, the stations in striped pastels to match. The place smelled of perm solution and mint shampoo. There were six stations, but only three of them were busy. Delaney had called ahead to be sure Marguerite would be working. She was.

"I'm here to see Marguerite Drummond," Delaney told the young receptionist, eyeing the three women at the stations. She had an idea what Marguerite would look like based on her father's "type." Her gaze stopped on a tall bleached blonde in tight stretch pants who was talking fast as she cut an older woman's hair.

"Marguerite!" the receptionist called back.

A small dark-haired woman in her early fifties turned in the middle of a customer's shampoo. Her hair and dress were understated; her look soft and assured. Her fingers slowed, then stopped, as her gaze settled on Delaney. She turned on the water and rinsed the soap from her hands. She said something to the older woman in the tub, then asked one of the other hairdressers to take over for her.

Marguerite smiled as she approached the counter. "I wondered when I'd finally get to meet you." She extended her hand. "I've heard so much about you, Delaney."

Delaney took the woman's hand, too surprised to speak at first. "You know who I am?"

"Of course. Come on, let's get out of here," she said, taking off her trim white uniform jacket.

They walked down the street to a small café. It wasn't until the waitress had set two cups of coffee in front of them that Delaney asked, "How do you know me?"

Marguerite looked down in her coffee for a moment. "When you were a baby, your father started showing off pictures of you. And he and I kept in touch over the years."

Delaney shook her head. He'd showed pictures of his family to his mistress?

"You were the light of his life," she said, smiling at Delaney.

She'd always thought rodeoing was the only thing that had meant anything to Hank Lawson. She tried to imagine him showing off pictures of her and couldn't. "I can't understand why you waited more than twenty-five years to tell my father he had a son."

Marguerite shook her head. "Hank would have felt compelled to do something honorable like marry me. He was already married and he'd proven he wasn't good at it." A sadness filled her brown eyes. "The truth is, I didn't want Ty coming up like his father, riding rough stock in rodeos. And I knew how much your father wanted a son—" She realized her remark had hurt Delaney. "I'm sorry."

"Everyone knows how disappointed Hank was when he didn't get a son," Delaney said, fighting the familiar anger and hurt. But that wasn't what she'd driven to Butte to talk about. "Based on Ty's age, I assume my father hooked up with you not long after I was born, about the time my mother became ill and couldn't have any more children.''

Marguerite stared down into her coffee. "When I first met Hank, I didn't know about you or your mother." She smiled in memory. "Hank was so handsome and he could turn on the charm like water from a faucet. But that wasn't what appealed to me. It was the sadness in his eyes. A deep hurt that at the time I couldn't explain. It wasn't until later, when he told me about you and your mother, that I understood."

"He killed my mother, you know," Delaney said, unable to hide her anger. "When she got sick, he started staying away from the ranch even longer. My mother blamed herself for his rodeoing, for his infidelities. She believed that if she'd given him a son, he would have stayed on the ranch."

Marguerite shook her head. "Nothing could have kept Hank on the ranch, honey. Not a dozen sons. He was so young when he met your mother and fell in love with her. He thought he could change, that he could be what she needed and wanted. When you were born..." She hesitated. "He said it was the most amazing day of his life. But also the scariest. He just couldn't face the responsibility. I think that's why he wished you were a boy. He felt you wouldn't need him as much."

Delaney thought of all the times she'd needed her father and he hadn't been there. "He dumped the ranch on my mother and me. After my mother died, I almost lost the place and he still didn't care enough to come home."

Marguerite took a sip of her coffee. "He blamed himself for your mother's illness, and just the sight of her made him feel—"

"Guilty?" Delaney asked. "He *should* have felt guilty."

"I was going to say *inadequate*. He couldn't make her well and he didn't know how to make her happy."

Delaney laughed bitterly. "He didn't want to."

Marguerite reached across the table and took her hand. "You're wrong about that, honey. He loved her. He just couldn't live up to what he thought your mother expected of him.''

Delaney freed her hand. "Hank Lawson was a selfish, inconsiderate man who didn't have the backbone to do anything but take the easy way out."

Tears filled the older woman's eyes as she pulled her hand back. "I'm sorry you feel that way about your father. Not that I blame you. But he loved you more than his own life."

"Is that why he left the ranch to Ty?" Delaney demanded, hot, angry tears blurring her vision. "That's how my father showed how much he loved me?" She'd finally voiced her greatest fear. That her father *had* left everything to Ty, that Ty wasn't lying about the will. "My father knew what the ranch meant to me. He knew how hard I've worked to save it. And he left it to a stranger he didn't even know. His *son.*"

Marguerite cradled the cup in her hands, her eyes downcast. "I'd always hoped that Hank would never find out about Ty."

"How did he?" Delaney demanded, trying to still all the years of anger at her father.

"When I found myself pregnant with Ty, I broke it off with your father. I told Ty his father was a rodeo cowboy, a bull rider, but that he'd been killed. When Ty started rodeoing just to spite me, he met Hank and found out that Hank and I used to date. Hank and I have seen each other off and on for years. I think Ty always suspected Hank was his father—he found some old letters. Just recently he got a call from someone who had uncovered the truth."

"Do you know who?" Delaney asked, realizing it didn't really matter.

Marguerite shook her head. "I should have kept lying."

"So Ty went to my father with the truth?" Delaney said, beginning to see what could have happened. "When was this?"

"Just days before Hank was killed."

Delaney felt her heart break as she realized that for Hank, finding out he had a son would be a dream come true. "So Hank changed his will?"

"I guess so. I wasn't there when Hank made the new will, but Ty showed it to me. It was in Hank's writing. I'm sorry. I never wanted anything from Hank."

"But Ty does. He wants everything, but just for the money. I'm sure he plans to sell the ranch as quickly as possible."

Marguerite looked away for a moment as if the truth were too hard to take. "He feels cheated because Hank was never a father to him." She smiled through fresh tears. "I know, Hank was never a father to either of his children." She took a long breath and let it out slowly. "I wish Ty were different. I know now that I spoiled him and that's probably why he's never wanted to work for anything."

"Maybe he just took after his father," Delaney said, getting to her feet. "I'd hoped the will Ty had from my father was a forgery. I know now that my father could have changed his will to leave everything to his newly found son."

"I wish that weren't the case," she said, genuinely sorry. "Ty has no business with your ranch."

Delaney stood for a moment, not knowing what to say to the woman. "Thank you for telling me about my...father."

She smiled, tears in her eyes. "He loved you, Delaney. I know he did things that hurt you, but he never stopped loving you. Or your mother."

Delaney left Marguerite sitting in the café, staring down into her coffee. She'd wanted to hate the woman, but instead she'd ended up liking her. And feeling sorry for her. Marguerite had just been another one of Hank Lawson's casualties.

COOPER CLIMBED UP the side of the chute and swore when he saw the rank horse waiting for him. He'd seen his share of horses like Hell's Fire. Halter-broken rebels with a strong inclination to come apart whenever anyone tried to ride them. They were horses that just plain didn't like to be ridden. And they'd fight from hell to breakfast to throw any rider with the stupidity to get on them. The good news was that very few attempted to attack a thrown rider. But Cooper figured Hell's Fire could prove the exception. This horse was a man killer.

He stared at the horse and felt a shot of pure adrenaline. Bronc riding was one of the most dangerous of rodeo sports. Also one of the most thrilling. He felt that old pull and admitted he hadn't agreed to this just to check Kincaid's horses. He wanted to ride again. Delaney had been right about that, he realized guiltily.

He'd just finished throwing his saddle on Hell's Fire and cinching it down, when a cowboy came by to tell him Jared wanted to see him at the announcer's booth. Cooper wondered why Jared would want to see him now, not long before his ride. Probably just to goad him a little more.

But when he got to the booth, he was told that Jared had left. Cooper heard his number come up to ride. He hurried back to find Jared sitting on the side of the chute above Hell's Fire, smiling. Delaney was right. The bastard was hoping Cooper got himself killed.

"Just wanted to wish you luck," Jared said.

Cooper doubted that, but he shook Jared's outstretched hand anyway. The hand was a little clammy and Cooper wondered what Jared had to be nervous about. Losing the bet? Or having a cowboy he disliked ride his so far unridden horse eight seconds for a win?

As Cooper eased himself down on the saddle, he knew this was going to be the ride of his life. Oblivious to the crowd that had gathered in Jared's covered bandstand, he turned his attention to the horse breathing heavily beneath him. Cooper readied himself. And gave the signal. The chute opened, and just as he'd expected, Hell's Fire came apart like the wild beast he was.

Chapter Fifteen

Delaney hadn't been able to keep Cooper far from her thoughts all morning. As she drove down Beaver Creek Road toward the ranch, she glanced at her watch and realized the rodeo would still be going on. She wondered if Cooper had ridden yet. Her stomach churned at the thought of him on the mean bronc.

"Damn you, McLeod." Against her will, she turned into the Kincaid ranch. The last thing she wanted was to see Cooper ride, but the thought of going home and waiting to hear what happened was too much for her. Her fears about Cooper's welfare outweighed her fears of rodeoing. She had to know he was all right.

She parked and walked toward the rodeo arena. The crowd in the bandstand were on their feet and going wild. She hurried, fear making her heart pound and her breath come at a premium. Delaney went to the end of the arena where the cowboys hung out and climbed the corral railing in time to see Cooper being tossed around on the back of Hell's Fire. The horse twisted and turned, its nostrils flaring.

She closed her eyes, unable to stand it any longer. Then she heard the combined gasp of the crowd and opened her eyes to see Cooper hanging off the side of the horse. Something was wrong with his saddle. It had slipped and Cooper— He was hung up in the saddle. He couldn't get off the bronc! Hell's Fire was dragging him and still bucking, tossing Cooper like a ragged doll.

"Oh, we got a problem here, folks," the announcer said over the screaming crowd. "Let's get that cowboy off that bronc."

Two cowboys on horseback were trying to free Cooper from the bucking bronc. Delaney heard the scream but didn't realize it was coming from her own throat until one of the cowboys riding alongside the bronc finally freed Cooper. He lay on the ground without moving. She stared at his prone body, hating him, loving him, praying he would survive so she could fire him and run him out of the county so she never had to see him again.

"Is he going to be all right, boys?" the announcer asked. Several cowboys had jumped down from the arena fence and run over to kneel beside Cooper.

Suddenly the cowboys stepped back. Cooper moved. First one leg, then the other. He sat up, shaking his head as if to clear it. Then he grinned and got slowly to his feet.

"It looks like he's going to be all right, folks," the announcer said over the loudspeaker. "Let's give Cooper McLeod a big hand. That was one heck of a ride."

Cooper limped toward the fence, banging his hat on his leg as he walked. Dust rose from his boots, from the hat. He spotted Delaney. His eyes widened in surprise. He smiled, then shrugged.

She glared at him, so angry that she'd witnessed him almost getting killed, so relieved he was alive. "McLeod," she said through clenched teeth. "You scared the living— I've a mind to fire you on the spot. Or shoot you."

"I'm glad to see you, too, boss," he said, and pulled her into his arms.

COOPER HELD HER, enjoying the feel of her in his arms but also needing her strength. He was still wobbly and shook-up.

But alive. Alive and unhurt. It had been a close call, one he wouldn't forget for sometime to come.

It took him a moment to realize that Delaney was crying. He held her tighter. "It's all right now," he whispered. "It's all right."

"Oh, Cooper, if you'd been killed, I'd never have forgiven you," she cried against his chest.

"I'm sorry, sweetheart." He realized then that the announcer was calling his name. He turned to listen. Delaney tensed in his arms.

"They're offering you another ride," she said, growing deathly pale. "It looks like your saddle had a weak cinch."

His saddle hadn't had a weak cinch when he'd put it on Hell's Fire. He closed his eyes, cursing his own stupidity. Jared. He'd left his rig to go find the rancher. No wonder Jared had been so nervous when Cooper had found him by the chute. The bastard had done something to his cinch!

"Well, cowboy, do you want another chance at Hell's Fire?" the announcer asked over the loudspeaker.

Cooper knew now he could ride Hell's Fire for a win, and the desire rushed through him. He wanted to show Jared up for the rat he was. But mostly he wanted to prove to himself he could ride the bronc.

Delaney stepped out of his arms. She wiped at the tears streaming down her face as she looked up at him. "You have to do it, don't you?"

He stared into her eyes, suddenly struck by what she'd given him just coming to watch him. She'd admitted to him how deathly frightened she was of rodeo. Yet she'd come to see him ride. And at what price? She'd witnessed him almost get killed on Hell's Fire. He couldn't do it to her again. Not ever. And he realized he'd just ridden in his last rodeo.

He motioned to the announcer's box that he didn't want to ride again, then pulled Delaney back into his arms, hugging her tightly as his heart swelled with love for her. Love. He didn't even put up an argument with himself. Somehow he'd fallen in love with this woman and he was tired of kidding himself that he hadn't.

One of the arena cowboys rode by and placed Cooper's saddle on the top fence rail. "Tough luck," the guy said as he rode off.

Delaney pulled free and reached up to take an end of the broken cinch. "This cinch wasn't weakened. It was cut!" She turned to face Cooper, her eyes blazing. "I knew it. Jared. Jared did this. He tried to kill you!"

"I'd be careful making accusations against the sheriff," Jared said through gritted teeth as he walked up behind them.

"Damn you, Jared. If I can prove you cut that cinch—"

"*If* his cinch was cut, anyone could have done it," Jared said to Delaney calmly. "I think you ought to take another ride," he said, turning to Cooper.

"No, thanks." Cooper circled Delaney's waist with his arm, pulling her to him. He told himself holding her was just so he could keep her quiet, but he knew he was also staking claim to her, just in case Jared had any doubts. "You come to collect on the bet?"

Jared chewed at his cheek as he let his eyes take in the two of them. Like Delaney, he seemed to be trying to contain a lot of anger. "Forget the money, McLeod. I have more important things on my mind right now." He settled his gaze on Delaney. Cooper could feel her trembling with rage.

"I think you'd better calm down, Del," Jared said, his tone condescending as usual.

Cooper felt her tighten like a rubber band about to snap. "Jared, I found out the other night just what kind of man you are, but you've outdone yourself today," she said through gritted teeth. "You could have killed Cooper."

He raised an eyebrow. "'Cooper,' is it now, Del?" He sighed. "Well, that just makes it all the harder for me to tell you what I've found out about your cowhand here."

Cooper felt his gut tighten as Delaney jerked free of his hold and fired herself at Jared.

"I don't know what you've dug up, *Sheriff,* but I don't want to hear it," she said, pointing a finger into his face. "I don't want to hear *anything* you have to say ever again." She stomped toward her pickup.

Jared smiled at Cooper. "Too bad. You didn't ride the horse for a win. And you lost the girl, as well." He turned away to call after Delaney. "I think you'd best hear this, Del," he said, raising his voice to follow her retreating footsteps. "Your boyfriend here is an ex-con. He's got a police record."

Delaney had stopped at her pickup, her hand on the door handle. Cooper saw her stiffen at the news.

"And guess what he was sent up for, Del?" he called after her. "Conspiracy to defraud. He's a con man, Del. A con man and a rodeo bum. So who do you think is behind your problems on the ranch now, Del?"

She jerked open the pickup door. Cooper fought the need to bury his fist in Kincaid's smiling face. Instead he ran after Delaney, grabbing her arm as she started to get into her pickup.

"At least let me explain," he pleaded. "I tried to tell you this morning—"

"McLeod, the best thing you can do right now is to leave me the hell alone." She shook loose of his hold on her arm and climbed in to slam the pickup door in his face.

He stepped back as she started the engine and popped the clutch, leaving him standing in a cloud of dust.

"Like I said, it just hasn't been your day, McLeod," the sheriff said behind him.

Cooper clenched his fists, weighing the options Jared was offering him. Jail time for assaulting a sheriff—but the satisfaction of cramming the bastard's teeth down his throat first.

DELANEY WAS STILL shaking as she started past Buck's place and noticed a strange horse in the corral beside her father's old rodeoing trailer. She stopped, surprised because she'd thought Buck would be at Kincaid's rodeo, and even more surprised to realize that the horse wasn't one of hers. It was a quarter horse, and not a very good one from what she could tell. Buck was standing beside the corral when she got out of her truck.

"Did you buy a horse?" she asked, walking over to the corral to take a look.

Buck's mind must have been a million miles away, because he hadn't heard her approach. He jumped now, a startled look in his wide eyes as if she were the last person he'd expected to see. "I thought you'd gone to Butte."

"I did," she said, climbing up the corral railing to get a better view of the horse. It was an older quarter horse and had a Kincaid Ranches brand on it.

Buck joined her on the fence. "I got it for Angel."

"She could have ridden any of the horses at the ranch," Delaney said, a little hurt he'd bought a horse from Jared Kincaid, especially when it wasn't necessary.

"Angel saw this horse over at Kincaid's while she was interviewing him about his ranch and just fell in love with it," Buck said nervously. "I tried to talk her into a Morgan, but she just had to have this one."

Delaney looked over at him. "I didn't know Angel rode."

"She doesn't. Yet," Buck said. "I'm going to teach her."

It struck Delaney again how different Buck had been acting lately. She blamed Angel and hoped that when this woman broke this poor man's heart, she didn't break his spirit, as well.

"It's not a bad-looking horse," Delaney lied. She hoped Buck hadn't paid much for it. And wondered why a man with such good horse sense would buy a horse like this from someone like Jared Kincaid. Because Angel had fallen in love with it, she reminded herself. Men! Love must make them stupid. She thought about Cooper and how she felt about him, and decided there was no doubt about it—love made a person too stupid for words.

"Delaney?"

Just the thought of Cooper brought back the mix of emotions she felt for the man. She'd gone from waking up in his arms to fearing he was dead. From relief that he was all right to wanting to kill him. If this was love—

It wasn't until he'd passed on that second ride that she'd admitted her true feelings. She would never have acknowledged them to anyone, let alone herself. But in that moment when she'd seen him decide not to ride because of her, knowing how much he'd wanted to, how much he needed to prove himself on that stupid horse, she knew she loved him.

Loved a rodeo cowboy. A rodeo cowboy with a police record. Conspiracy to defraud. Cooper McLeod was not only an ex-con, he was a con man. Boy, could she pick 'em. Admittedly he'd tried to tell her something last night and again this morning, but she hadn't let him. Not that she believed he was the one who was causing her troubles on the ranch. Admittedly he could have orchestrated the rock slide and the potshot with some help, but Delaney didn't believe it, not in her heart. She just hoped love wasn't as blind as Buck made it appear.

"Delaney? Is there anything I can do for you?" Buck asked, obviously antsy. "I was just on my way into town to see Angel, but if you need something—"

She shook her head. "I just stopped to see your new horse. How long have you had him?"

"A few days." Buck scratched at his jaw. He couldn't seem to meet her gaze. She figured he felt guilty buying a horse from Kincaid and not her. Heck, Delaney would have given him his pick of horses for Angel if she'd known he was looking for a horse. She could feel her ranch manager pulling away from the Rockin' L like a teenager getting ready to move out of the family home. She wondered how long it would be before he gave notice and moved into town with Angel.

"You sure I can't do something for you?" Buck asked again. He seemed reluctant to leave her there alone. He glanced at his watch.

"Go on and see Angel," she said. She blinked, did a double take as she looked over at him. "I thought Angel was with you at the rodeo earlier," she said, thinking she had seen Angel in the crowd when she first got to Jared's.

Buck nodded, fidgeting with a button on his shirt. "She had to leave."

"Well, go on. I might take another look through the stuff my father kept in the trailer," she said, knowing she wouldn't. Buck had helped her go through it, hunting for her father's will right after Hank died. It wasn't something she wanted to do again. Nor did she think even finding the original will would probably do any good anyway. But maybe she'd search for it. She knew she was just looking for an excuse not to go back to the ranch house because she was going to have to deal with Cooper.

"I guess I'd better get going—"

Buck stood for a moment as if part of him didn't want to leave but the other part was in a big hurry to get somewhere. She couldn't remember ever seeing him this nervous.

"If you need anything—"

As Buck walked off, she watched the quarter horse circle the small corral with Buck's horse, a Morgan she'd given him called Sugarfoot. It still bothered her that Buck had purchased a quarter horse, not a Morgan, for his girlfriend.

She heard Buck drive away and thought Jared must be laughing his behind off at Buck for buying this horse. Then she realized she couldn't care less about Jared, Angel's new horse or Buck's infatuation with the woman. What really worried her was what she going to do about Cooper.

Shooting him had been her first thought. Firing him and running him off with a shotgun was her second. But her heart kept arguing for clemency on his behalf.

She took one last look at Buck's new horse, promising herself she'd never let love make her *that* blind, and started back toward her truck. That's when she noticed the horse-shoe prints in the dirt near the corral. She stared down at the barred-shoe track, then turned to look back into the corral. It was full of barred-shoe tracks. And Delaney knew what she was going to find before she climbed into the corral with the quarter horse. Whoever had been riding this horse the last few days was the person who'd tried to kill her.

Chapter Sixteen

Cooper drove around for a while after he left Kincaid's, not sure where to go or what to do. He'd been cussing himself since Delaney had driven off, furious with him, not even giving him a chance to explain. Not that there was much explanation to give. He just wished he'd told her the truth himself. Now he figured he'd blown it with her. It didn't make him feel any better that he'd made a halfhearted effort to tell her the truth. And now if she was to find out he worked for Rattlesnake Range— He rubbed his thigh, the gunshot wound still fresh in his memory.

His head ached. From the rough ride on the bronc. From the look in Delaney's eyes. Damn. Cooper knew he was avoiding going back to the ranch because he didn't know what to say to her. There were so many things he needed to tell her, but he knew none of them would do any good right now. She would be just looking for any excuse to get him out of her life.

He should just pack up and move on. Delaney was bound to fire him the moment she laid eyes on him anyway. Why wait and have to see her face when she did? But as Cooper drove, he knew he couldn't just ride off into the sunset this time. He'd invested too much in this job. He laughed. He'd invested too much in this woman, more than he wanted to admit. And he couldn't leave her alone now to fend off

Rattlesnake Range and whoever else might be after her and her ranch.

He headed for the York Bar. The last thing he wanted was a beer. But he did want to talk to Dude. He kept thinking about Dude and the sheriff. He'd seen little more than a look pass between Dude and Jared Kincaid. There was something between them, something that Cooper recognized. Trouble. And Cooper was just curious enough to try to find out what it was.

When he pushed open the door, he found the place was empty except for Dude, who was behind the bar washing glasses. Everyone was probably out at Kincaid's rodeo, where the beer was free along with the barbecue and barn dance.

"Wanna beer?" Dude asked, and continued his glass washing.

Cooper shook his head. "Why aren't you out at the Kincaid rodeo?"

Dude stopped, a wet, dirty glass in his hands as he shot Cooper a look. "I had to work."

"Really?" Cooper said, glancing around the bar as he took a stool. "I hope you can keep up the pace."

Dude laughed and shook his head. "Hey, man, it lets me catch up on my cleaning."

Cooper nodded. "Not that you would go out to Kincaid's even if you weren't working."

The bartender put down the glass and dried his hands. "Is there a point to this?"

"Look, I don't blame you for not wanting to get involved, but all I'm asking for is a little help," Cooper said. "There are things going on out on the Rockin' L. I'm just trying to find out who's behind them."

Dude washed a few more glasses in silence. Cooper figured he was wasting his time. He was an outsider and Dude acted scared.

"I don't know what you're looking for, all right?" Dude said after a moment. "But the other night after you left, the sheriff was pretty happy with himself. Until the guy from the mining company came in."

"What guy from the mining company?" Cooper asked, his heart pounding a little faster.

Dude shrugged. "Some guy who's been around a few times. I overheard the sheriff arguing with him."

Cooper had a feeling Dude overheard a lot of conversations. "What were they arguing about?"

He appeared hesitant and Cooper wondered if he wanted money. Cooper started to reach for his wallet, when Dude stopped him.

"The sheriff pulled me over not long ago and read me the riot act. He thought I'd been drinking, but he was the one who was drunk. The guy's a loser."

"Yeah, Kincaid does have a way with people."

Dude flipped the bar rag onto his shoulder and leaned on the bar. "I heard what happened out at his ranch today." Bad news traveled fast. "I heard you almost got killed."

"I hate to think of it that way," Cooper said. He hated to think of it at all, especially when he remembered that Delaney had witnessed the whole thing. He'd never wanted to hurt her like that. "What were they arguing about?"

"The guy said that if Kincaid didn't take care of his end, the whole deal would be off. Then he left and Kincaid was real upset. That's when I decided to investigate the guy. I'd taken a check from him as a favor the day before but hadn't paid much attention. The guy was from Burton Mining Company."

Cooper had heard of it, a large company that was remining areas of the country. They dredged gulches that hadn't been mined for fifty years or more and chemically bleached the ore from the rocks. "Is there any mining going on around here now?"

Dude shook his head. "But there's been talk. That guy from the mining company—when he was in earlier in the week, he was asking me a lot of questions about the Rockin' L and Delaney Lawson. He seemed to think her ranch was for sale."

ALL THE WAY down the road, Delaney argued with herself over the barred-shoe horse. Somehow Jared had tricked Buck into buying the horse to shift the suspicion from himself to Buck. It was the only thing that made sense. But Buck's strange behavior the past few weeks made her have doubts she didn't like having. She'd known Buck all her life. He couldn't be responsible for her problems. He had no motive. If she sold the ranch or got killed, he'd be without a job. It wasn't as if he had the money to buy her ranch himself. And anyway, he'd been talking about marrying Angel and moving into town.

So why had he acted so strangely earlier? And why hadn't he wanted to leave her alone by the corral? She told herself Buck was in some kind of trouble. And if that was true— She knew what she had to do.

As Delaney drove to the ranch house, she passed Cooper's camp. His pickup was gone, but his horse trailer and Crazy Jack were still there. Her sudden relief brought tears to her eyes. In that instant, she realized he could have come back and cleared out before she got home. That would be the coward's way, and he'd already admitted he was a runner at heart. She told herself that if he'd taken off without even a word, she would have tracked him down. Tracked him down and what? she wondered. Tell him that she loved him? Fear made her heart ache. The last thing she wanted was to see Cooper get into his rig and drive off. But maybe in the long run it would be better for her heart, she tried to convince herself.

The sun had burned down to streaks of pinks and oranges against the mountains by the time she'd changed her clothes, putting on a dark shirt and jeans, tying her hair back in a ponytail. Instead of her usual western hat, she pulled on a dark old western hat of her father's. As she studied her image in the mirror, she couldn't help but think about what Marguerite had told her about her father. The anger she'd felt had lost a lot of its potency. If only he hadn't left the ranch to Ty, she thought. If he actually had, she reminded herself. Having the will proven a forgery was her only hope.

She glanced at her watch, then outside at the sky. It would be dusk before long. Delaney went out to saddle her horse, figuring it was going to be a long night, wondering where in the hell Cooper was.

THE FRONT DOOR of the York Bar slammed open with a bang and Buck stomped in, an obvious black mood hanging around him like a storm cloud. Cooper groaned.

Buck was the last person he wanted to see right now. He figured the ranch manager had heard he was an ex-con and had come looking for a fight. With Delaney mad enough at Buck for hiring a rodeo cowboy, she'd be real unhappy that Buck had hired an ex-con. And poor Buck wouldn't be able to tell her the truth, that he hadn't hired anyone. So the way Cooper figured it, Buck would want to take out his frustration on Cooper. And Cooper just wasn't in the mood.

Buck strode up to the bar. He didn't even act as if he noticed Cooper. "Have you seen Angel?" he demanded of Dude.

"Angel?" Dude frowned.

Cooper wondered why Dude was pulling Buck's chain. It didn't seem like a good idea right now.

"Blond. About this high." Buck held his hand out at his shoulder. "I've been in here with her a few times."

"Oh, Angel. The writer." Dude smiled. "She was in earlier. Had a couple of drinks, then got a phone call from some guy and left."

That was definitely not what Buck had wanted to hear. He glared at Dude for a moment. Cooper got the distinct impression he was deciding whether to pull Dude over the bar and pound him. Then Buck slammed a barstool out of his way and stomped back out, banging the door the same way he'd come in.

"Whew!" Cooper said, relieved Buck hadn't gotten into it with him.

He saw that Dude had picked up a baseball bat from behind the bar. He now put it back and smiled. "That cowboy is spoiling for a fight. He'll be back and meaner than ever when he finds out what's going on." He laughed at Cooper's puzzled expression. "Woman problem. It seems his Angel is keeping company with another man. You sure I can't get you a beer? It's on the house today."

Cooper declined the offer. "Any idea who the other guy is?"

Dude shook his head. "Voice was familiar, but I couldn't place it. Wasn't a great connection."

Cooper thanked Dude for his help.

"Just get Kincaid if he's the one," he said. "I don't trust that guy."

The feeling was mutual.

DELANEY SETTLED IN the draw above Buck's place, hiding among the ponderosas and rocks. She knew it was foolish. Buck might not be back until the wee hours of morning. And even then, he might do nothing more than go to bed for the night. Cooper galloped across her thoughts, making her groan. She couldn't help but wonder where he was and what he was doing. Maybe he was waiting for the cloak of darkness to sneak back so he could retrieve his gear. If that was his plan, she thought she would enjoy staking out his place more than Buck's. It would be worth it just to see the surprise on his face when she stepped out of the darkness and caught him.

For a moment, she wondered if he could leave that easily. She remembered their lovemaking under the pines, the stars overhead, the night breeze caressing their bodies. He'd held her so tenderly, she thought she'd seen love in his eyes as he'd bent to kiss her, his body warm and strong against hers—

She fanned herself with her hat and chased Cooper from her thoughts. Leaning back against a smooth rock, she stared up at the sky. The evening was warm. A gentle breeze stirred the pine boughs over her head. Night threatened to the east like a dark summer storm. It was summer evenings like this that made people do crazy things like fall in love, Delaney thought. Because for the life of her, she couldn't keep Cooper out of her thoughts, not the way he kissed her, not the way he held her, not the way he made love to her. Or the way he'd saved her life, the way he tried to protect her from herself, she thought with a smile, or the way he'd tried to tell her the truth about him.

Sitting up, she tried to concentrate on the corral below her. This was stupid. Surely she could have come up with a better plan if her mind wasn't so cluttered with unwanted thoughts of rodeo cowboys.

That's when she heard the pickup coming up the road. Of course her first thought was Cooper. He was finally headed home to face the music. Then she realized it wasn't Cooper at all but Buck. And he was alone, she noticed, as he pulled into his yard. He slammed the pickup door. The sound echoed up the draw. She expected him to head for the trailer. To her surprise, he headed for the corral, and instead of saddling his own horse, he saddled the barred-shoe horse.

With an aching heart, Delaney mounted her mare and followed at a discreet distance as Buck rode up into the foothills. It took her a moment to realize where he was headed. Johnson Gulch.

DAYLIGHT STILL HUNG over the treetops, but deep in the pines and rocks of the gulch, dusk settled in as Delaney followed Buck up the creek toward the lake. It didn't surprise her that he was taking a longer route that kept him hidden in the trees and rocky outcroppings. Her heart argued Buck's innocence, but her mind was busy compiling a list of suspicious facts that made him look guilty right now.

She wasn't far from the lake when she realized she'd lost Buck. Dismounting, she studied the ground, knowing it would soon be too dark in the pines to track him. That's when she heard the sound—not in front of her—but behind her. Quickly she pulled her horse in back of a large boulder and stood listening. A single rider. Coming cautiously up the mountainside. Tracking her. Could Buck have circled around? She pulled her rifle from its scabbard and crouched beside the rock nearest her trail to wait.

A few minutes later, she heard the horse approaching slowly. She waited until horse and rider came alongside her before she lunged out of her hiding place and jerked the surprised rider from the horse. The rider hit the ground with a *fffft*. She pointed her rifle at the slumped form and heard a familiar oath.

"McLeod?" she whispered angrily. "What are you doing here?"

He looked up, grimacing either out of pain or at the sight of her. She wasn't sure which. "Tracking you. What are *you* doing here?"

"I *was* following Buck until I heard you behind me."

"Buck?" He was surprised. "He's the one riding the barred-shoe horse?"

She nodded and lowered the rifle. "He says he bought the horse for Angel a few days ago—from Jared."

Cooper let out a low whistle but didn't say anything, and she was grateful. She didn't want to have to argue Buck's innocence. She really wasn't up to it.

"I've lost his trail," she admitted none too happily.

Cooper shoved back his hat and grinned at her. "He doubled back on you about a quarter mile ago."

She glared at him. "Did one of your criminal friends in jail teach you to track?" she demanded, trying to keep her voice down.

He winced as her remark hit right on target. "Actually, my father taught me." He got to his feet, meeting her direct gaze with one of his own. "You want to discuss my crime spree now, or do you want to find Buck and the barred-shoe horse?"

She glowered at him for a moment, then conceded. "Let's find Buck." She shoved her rifle back into its scabbard. "Then you and I are going to have a little talk, McLeod."

He tipped his hat to her. "You're the boss."

At least for the moment, she thought with a curse. She couldn't believe she was out there with a convicted felon. An ex-con.

As they rode, she studied Cooper's broad back, trying to convince herself he was dangerous. Dangerous to her heart—that was easy to believe. But to her ranch? To her livelihood? She refused to accept that, arguing he couldn't be trying to take her ranch because of the way he looked at her. The way he held her. The regret in his voice earlier at the rodeo, when he'd seen how much he'd upset her by his riding Hell's Fire. And the look on his face last night when he'd charged into her bedroom. She groaned, realizing she was just as besotted as Buck!

COOPER HURRIEDLY drew up Crazy Jack and swung around in the saddle at the sound of Delaney's pained groan. "Are you all right?" he whispered.

She nodded and seemed surprised that he appeared worried about her. Didn't she realize her safety was all that mattered to him right now?

"Are you sure you want to do this?" he asked. "It could be dangerous."

"Dangerous?" She laughed. "Believe me I just realized a few moments ago how *dangerous* it is."

He gave her a sideways look, thinking she was acting a little strangely. "So what do you want to do?"

"Do?" She stared at him. "What can I do now?" she asked, sounding as though she were on her way to the gallows but had to keep up a brave front.

"You sure you're all right?" He studied her for a moment, deciding she was acting more than a little strangely. Women. He'd never understand this one if he lived to be a thousand.

They circled back until Cooper found Buck's trail again. The ranch manager had dropped down into the gulch through a narrow opening in the rocks. They followed down below the band of rocks that ran the length of the gulch like a wall. Buck's trail stayed high above the creek bottom, winding through pines and rocks as if he hadn't wanted to be seen.

Suddenly a high-pitched whine filled the air. The horses danced nervously. A short distance farther, Cooper spotted the lights in Johnson Gulch Lake. He motioned to Delaney. Dismounting, he crept to the edge of the rocks to stare at the sight below him.

"I'll be damned," Cooper whispered as Delaney joined him. "There're Digger's space aliens, just as he said."

Chapter Seventeen

Delaney stared at the two creatures under the surface of the water. Illuminated by underwater lights, they seemed to be attached by hoses to a round craft that resembled a flying saucer. The saucer floated on the surface, its engine whining in the growing darkness. The whole thing looked much like the picture Digger had drawn.

"What is it?" she asked, knowing it wasn't from outer space, but equally sure it didn't belong there.

"A high-tech dredge for mining."

She looked over at him. "Mining?"

"It works like a giant vacuum cleaner," he said, the whine of the engine camouflaging their voices. Cooper pointed at the two divers. They swam beneath the water, rolling over boulders, then scouring the bedrock with a hose that was attached to the round floating dredge. "They're panning for gold, just using a little more advanced equipment than Digger."

The whine came from the motor on the floating dredge, where water and gravel spewed from the hose into what appeared to be a wire trap. "Later they'll sift through the gravel in the trap to get any color out."

"'Color'?" Delaney said, staring at the contraption. Cooper started to explain what color was. She made a face at him. "I know." The device was sucking up gold from the nooks and crannies in the rock that the old-timers like her grandfather had missed.

It wasn't that different from the dredging technique placer miners had used in the 1800s when their huge floating house dredges chomped through the nearby gulches to drag millions of ounces of gold from the creek bottoms. She knew all about that. She'd just never seen a small dredge like this one. And she was sure neither had Digger. The question was, what was it doing on her land?

That's when she spotted the barred-shoe horse some distance away in the trees. "There's Buck's new horse," she said, pointing at the poor old nag.

"Buck must be one of the divers," Cooper said. "The other one brings the gear. Buck meets him here on horseback."

Delaney nodded, finding it hard to conceive of Buck stealing from the Rockin' L under the cover of darkness. If she hadn't seen Buck ride that horse up here, she wouldn't believe it.

"Gold can make a man do stupid, dangerous, even illegal things," Cooper said, trailing her same thoughts.

"Gold. Or a woman," Delaney said, thinking of Angel.

"Yeah," Cooper agreed, looking over at her. "Or a woman."

She met his gaze and saw something that kicked her heart into gear. Love. She saw it as clearly as she'd seen the sun rise that morning. And she felt it at heart level. She warned herself that she wasn't seeing anything clearly, since she'd been bitten by that same bug herself.

"Boss, I think we should ride back to the ranch and report this to the sheriff," Cooper said. "Or someone."

Delaney stared down at the two divers. "I wonder who the other diver is." One diver moved the rocks while the other ran the vacuum system. Delaney thought of all the questions Angel had asked about mining and gold in the area, and wondered if Buck and Angel had been in cahoots from the beginning. It would explain a lot. "It has to be Angel."

Cooper frowned. "I don't know. When I saw Buck at the York Bar, he was looking for her. And making a big production of it. I suppose it could have been a cover."

"Are you thinking what I am?" Delaney asked. "That this little moonlighting venture is why someone has been taking potshots at us, dropping rocks on us? All for what little gold they could vacuum out of my creek bed?"

"I suppose," he said, unconvinced. "I think we'd better get back to the ranch and make that call."

"Go ahead," Delaney said, settling in behind the rock. "I'll stay here and make sure they don't get away."

"Sure you will," he said, looking over at her. "I'm not going anywhere without you."

"McLeod, I'm still the boss here."

He laughed. "I quit."

"You can't quit, not now," she snapped.

"Where do you think you're going?" he demanded as she got to her feet, pulled her rifle from her scabbard and started down toward the lake.

She stopped to look back at him. "I want to know who's been tormenting me."

Cooper let out an oath. "If they're the ones who've been trying to kill you, don't you think going down there and asking them could be a little dangerous?"

She smiled at him. "I'll just have to be more dangerous."

"*We'll* have to be more dangerous," he said with a growl.

"I thought you quit," she said sweetly.

"Damn you, woman."

He grabbed her before she could move and dragged her into his embrace, cutting off any further argument with a kiss. His kisses had been sweet and gentle, hard and passionate. But this one was pure possession. It laid claim to her in a way that she'd never realized she wanted to be possessed. She would have let him take her right there in the rocks. She didn't care for the moment about anything but Cooper and his mouth on hers. Then he raised his lips and looked down into her eyes.

"We do this my way or I'll turn you over my knee right now and—"

She leaned up on tiptoes and kissed him. "You're the boss," she said, brushing her breasts against him.

He groaned. "Right."

His gaze said everything she needed to know about how he felt, but still she wished he'd say the words.

"Are you trying to tell me something, McLeod?" she asked softly, heart pounding.

"Yeah." His lips brushed hers. His tongue trailed along her lips, teasing, tempting. "I'm telling you, Delaney," he said, his breath tickling her cheek. "That if you're thinking of firing me, do it now."

"I thought you already quit?" she asked with a low laugh. "But what if I don't plan to fire you?"

He pulled back a little to gaze at her. Darkness had filled in around the boulders, under the pines. She could barely see his expression. "I'm an ex-con, Delaney, just as Jared told you. I've lied and cheated and—"

"That isn't what you want to tell me right now, is it, McLeod?"

He groaned. "I'm trying to tell you, Delaney Lawson, that—"

The engine stopped. The whine dissolved into the still night. Delaney's eyes widened. They both scrambled to look over the rock to the lake below them.

The divers had come out of the water and pulled the dredge up on the bank at the edge of the trees. For the first time Delaney noticed a vehicle waiting in the trees. It was just too dark to tell whose it was. "They're going to get away."

"Dammit, Delaney, I love you," Cooper said quietly behind her.

She whirled around to smile at him. "I know, McLeod, but it's good to hear it anyway. Maybe we could continue this later?"

She started off the mountain, determined not to let the two claim jumpers get away. Behind her, she heard Cooper cussing, but nonetheless following her. She smiled to herself. "I love you, too, Cooper," she whispered, but knew he couldn't hear her.

As she hurried down through the trees and boulders, she stepped on a rock that rolled with her weight. Cooper caught her and kept her from falling, but the rock tumbled down the hillside, crashing into the lake. The two divers, still in their drysuits, masks and regulators, turned in surprise at the sound.

An instant later a rifle shot ricocheted off a rock to Delaney's left. The shot echoed through the gulch as Cooper pulled her down behind a large boulder. "Do you think they'll try to come up here after us?" she whispered, snuggling against him.

He wrapped his arms around her and pulled her between his thighs. "I don't know. I think it's getting too dark for them to find us."

She could feel his heart beating against her back. "Cooper?"

"Yes?"

His breath on her neck was as gentle as a caress. "I love you, too."

His laugh was sweet and warm. "Your timing is amazing, Ms. Lawson. If someone wasn't shooting at us, I'd—"

An engine roared to life. Delaney leapt to her feet in time to see the lights as a vehicle rumbled off into the night. The divers and their equipment were gone. So was Buck's new horse.

THEY LED THEIR HORSES through the rocky path to the lakeshore in the darkness, going slow and easy. When they reached the lake, Cooper stood beside Delaney as she stared down into the water. Darkness had settled in, making it impossible to see even tire tracks in the dirt.

All Cooper could think about was Delaney. She loved him. The thought made him want to smile and laugh, and take her in his arms and make love to her beside the lake.

Then he remembered that she didn't have any idea who he really was, what kind of man she'd fallen in love with. He worked for Rattlesnake Range, the agency trying to steal her ranch. And until she found out everything about him, her declaration of love meant nothing.

"I can't believe Buck would do this," she said, her voice full of hurt. "I have to find him and talk to him."

Cooper followed her, wanting to settle things between the two of them rather than track down Buck, but knowing he would have to be patient. Delaney had a lot on her mind right now. She didn't need any more disappointments at the moment. He admitted he was scared. How much more bad news could she take about him, Cooper wondered, and still love him?

They mounted their horses and headed down the old mining road. The moon had come up behind Hogback Mountain. It now lit the sky over the tops of the trees, making riding easier.

"Buck has changed since he's met Angel," Delaney said, riding beside him. "Buck told me he didn't make enough money for her. I guess he could have decided to do a little moonlighting in Johnson Gulch Lake."

Cooper couldn't think of anything to say to heal the hurt he heard in her voice. Nor did he have any doubt that Angel had changed the ranch manager. Loyalty meant everything to Delaney, he thought with growing fear. What would she do when she found out Cooper worked for Rattlesnake

Range? When she found out why he'd come to the Rockin' L in the first place?

"I just find it hard to believe mining the lake would be worth it," Delaney said. "There can't be that much gold in this creek to jeopardize his job."

That was the question, wasn't it, Cooper thought, remembering Dude's story about the guy from Burton Mining Company. "Maybe there's more gold here than any of us knows," he said, and told her what he'd heard at the York Bar from Dude about Burton Mining Company and the sheriff.

"I knew it. Jared told me things were going on under my nose and I was too dumb to see them. He acted as if he was angry with Buck. Now I know why. Jared's in this up to his eyeballs."

"For once, we agree," Cooper said. "When I was in his barn looking for the barred-shoe horse, I saw two guys hitting Ty up for money. They seemed to mean business. Then Ty headed straight for Jared and demanded money."

"And Jared gave it to him," she said, shaking her head. "That explains how the two of them knew so much about what was happening on the Rockin' L. They were sharing information."

"Yeah, that's what I was thinking. But if Ty's the one shooting at you, then I'd bet the sheriff doesn't know about it. He seemed genuinely concerned about your welfare, Delaney."

"Maybe," she said quietly. "Until recently."

Cooper shoved back his hat and looked up at the stars, trying to put the pieces together. "This all has to do with gold, Delaney. It's the only thing that makes any sense."

"Don't tell me you're buying into Digger's mother lode?"

Cooper wasn't sure what he believed anymore. "Well, Digger *was* right about the space aliens. Kinda. And now we find out there's a mining company asking about your ranch— What if Digger's right about Gus, too?"

"You know, McLeod, sometimes I worry about you." Suddenly Delaney reined in her horse. "Did you hear that?"

Cooper stopped to listen. A horse whinnied and a moment later, the barred-shoe quarter horse came trotting out of the trees, riderless.

"Why would Buck leave the horse behind?" Delaney asked as she watched the horse spook and take off down the road in the darkness.

"Maybe he decided he couldn't get away fast enough by horseback," Cooper said in answer. "Wait here." He and Crazy Jack went after the quarter horse the way Delaney imagined Cooper cut cattle out of a herd. Within minutes, he returned with the horse in tow.

"I just don't believe Buck would do anything to hurt me," she said. "I've known him all my life. But whoever's been riding that horse—"

"Buck has been spending a lot of time with Angel instead of on the ranch," Cooper said. "I guess someone else could have borrowed this horse."

Delaney was relieved Cooper was trying to help her defend Buck. But she couldn't help thinking about what Jared had said, and his obvious anger at Buck. Something was going on right under her nose, and Buck had been so odd lately. Delaney had just assumed it was Angel who made Buck act that way. And, she reminded herself, she'd seen with her own eyes Buck on the barred-shoe horse, Buck riding up to the lake tonight, skirting the lake as if he hadn't wanted to be seen. How much more evidence did she need?

"Who else would have had access to this horse?" Cooper asked.

"Angel, obviously. But Buck said she didn't know how to ride, that he planned to teach her. I figured that's why he bought her a hag like that one," she said, turning in the saddle to look back at the quarter horse.

They rode down to Buck's place in the moonlight. His pickup was still parked next to the trailer where he'd left it earlier. Delaney dismounted and handed her reins to Cooper as she went to the door and knocked.

"Buck?"

No answer. She knocked again.

Cooper had dismounted and was holding the horses. Delaney tried the door. It was open. She reached in and flipped on a light, then cautiously stepped inside.

"Delaney?" she heard Cooper call to her.

It didn't take but a moment to see that the trailer was empty. What stopped her from returning to the yard was a large cardboard box in the center of the living room area. One worn leather glove lay on the floor beside the box. The glove drew her, just the way it had as a child.

"Delaney?" Cooper asked behind her, making her jump.

She'd picked up the glove, and held it in her hand, the leather rough and ragged from use. Tears brimmed in her eyes as she looked up at Cooper.

"Your father's?" Cooper asked, glancing from the glove to the box. Cooper stepped past her into the room. "Is this his rodeo gear?"

"Please, I don't want to see any of it," she pleaded. "Not now." She handed him glove and swung around to leave.

"What was Buck doing with this box?" Cooper demanded as he began to rummage through it.

She stopped and turned slowly. "I don't know. I'm not sure where it came from."

"Delaney, are you telling me you've never seen it before?" he asked. "I thought you said you went through all of your father's things."

She frowned as she stepped closer. "I thought I did."

Cooper turned the flap up. "This was recently mailed to the Rockin' L. From Texas."

"That's where my father died. You don't think—"

But Cooper was already digging through the contents. "Does Buck pick up ranch mail?" he asked.

"Yes, we both do. Why wouldn't he have told me about this box?" The moment she asked the question, she knew. Buck had helped her go through her father's things right after his death. He knew how upset she'd been.

"Delaney, from the looks of it, these were the clothes your father was wearing when—" Suddenly Cooper stopped digging and turned. He held an envelope in his hand. Her name had been printed on it in her father's scrawl. She stared at it, unable to reach for it.

"You want me to open it?" Cooper asked.

She nodded as she dropped onto the couch, and Cooper sat down beside her. The sweet scent of summer drifted in through the open door on the night breeze. Delaney pulled her knees up and studied the carpet pattern as Cooper carefully opened the envelope and pulled out the papers inside.

"It looks like a note to you," he said.

"Please read it to me," Delaney said, resting her chin on her knees.

Dearest daughter,
Writing this is one of the hardest things I've ever done. I can't tell you what goes through a man's mind to find out at this age how little he really knows about himself. But the past few days I've learned a lot. And I've had to face things about myself. I wasn't much of a father to you, Delaney, and I'm sorry. You and your mama, you were the strong ones. 'Course you know that by now. Take care of yourself.

I love you, Dad

Delaney felt tears fill her eyes and flood over onto her jeans. He'd written her the letter trying to explain why he'd left the ranch to Ty, his son.

"There's more, Delaney. It's his will. It's short and to the point, but it's dated and witnessed." Out of the corner of her eye, she watched him scan the document. "He left you the ranch."

Her head jerked up. Her heart raced. "When was it dated?"

"The day before he died." Cooper smiled at her. "He left you everything, Delaney, all his earthly possessions, except for his rodeo gear. He left that to his son, Ty Drummond."

Delaney took the will Cooper handed her and read the words for herself, still unbelieving. "He loved me," she said, unable to stop the flow of tears. "I guess I never really knew that until this moment."

Cooper smoothed her hair back from her face. "There's another note in the envelope," he said, handing it to her.

It was to Ty.

Dear son,
I thought long and hard about everything you said to me the other day. The last thing I want is to leave a legacy of pain. You never had a father. Neither did Delaney. The ranch is more Delaney's than it ever was mine. She's loved it and worked it, two things I didn't. So, Ty, I'm leaving you all that I ever owned. I hope you see fit to live a different life than I did.

Your father

She looked over at Cooper. He smiled at her and pulled her into his arms. "It's going to be all right now," she said against his shirt. "The accidents will stop. It's over, Cooper. It's finally over." She leaned back to look into his face and her smile faded. "What's wrong?"

He glanced away. "I'm just not so sure about that, Delaney."

She looked out the door into the night. "You mean Buck? As soon as he comes back, I'm sure he'll have an explanation for what's been going on."

"Maybe you're right," he said. "I sure hope so." He released her and stood. "I'd better get that horse unsaddled and into the corral."

Delaney followed him, pressing the will and letters close to her heart. She thought of her father. All the hurts and resentments over the years. In time they would fade into soft memories like old photographs. She saw her father so differently through the eyes of Marguerite, through his own eyes at the end. She knew that for the first time in her life she would be able to forgive him. And that she had never stopped loving him.

"Delaney?"

She looked up to find Cooper standing by the barred-shoe horse, one hand on the saddle, the other resting on the horse's back.

"Delaney, would you turn on that other outside light for me?"

She stepped back to the trailer to accommodate him. The yard light came on, spilling over the corral. Delaney looked up and saw the expression on Cooper's face. "What is it?" she asked, her heart taking off at a gallop.

"I think you'd better call the sheriff," he said.

She stepped over to the horse. And saw the blood on the saddle. Too much blood.

Chapter Eighteen

"Buck could be out there, hurt somewhere," Delaney cried. "You have to go look for him."

Cooper stood in the shadows, trying hard to stay out of it. He watched Jared Kincaid glance out into the darkness. "I have men out searching, Del, but I can tell you right now, it won't do any good until we've got some daylight." He touched the blood on the saddle and studied it in the yard light. "It's warm out tonight. If he's just hurt, he'll survive till morning. If he's already dead, it won't make a difference."

"Damn you, Jared," she swore. "You knew about Buck dredging Johnson Gulch Lake, didn't you?"

The sheriff pulled off his Stetson, ran his fingers through his hair and let out a long, irritated sigh. "Del, I'm trying to be patient with you, but I'm getting real tired of your accusations." He turned his gaze on her, as steely and cold as the barrel of a gun. "You got proof, you want to file a complaint, then do it. Otherwise—"

If he thought to intimidate Delaney Lawson, he thought wrong. Cooper smiled to himself as he watched Delaney. What a little spitfire she was. He remembered the first time he'd seen her. The fire in her eyes. The determination in her stance. He'd put his money on this woman any day.

"Jared, I know you've been paying my brother to spy on me," she snapped.

The sheriff pushed back his hat. "I loaned your brother some money, if that's what you're talking about, Del." He frowned at her. "I felt sorry for him. I know what it's like to be the black sheep of the family."

"I'll just bet you do," she said, her eyes darker than the night. "You might want to tell Ty that I found my father's will. Dated just before he was killed. The Rockin' L is mine and it will stay mine."

Jared studied the ground but didn't say anything.

"You want to tell me what kind of deal you made with Burton Mining? I have a feeling the will changes your plans as well as Ty's," she said, anger making her voice break.

Jared let out a long sigh and looked again into the darkness. "Not that it's any of your business, Del, but I've been considering selling my ranch."

"And what about my ranch? Did you make a deal for it, as well?"

"Del, it's been a long day," the sheriff said. "We're all tired, so I'm going to overlook your behavior."

Delaney's eyes flashed like lightning in a bad thunderstorm. Cooper stepped over to touch her arm, afraid of what she was going to do next. She jerked her arm free, her gaze still locked on the sheriff, the threat clear in those dark eyes of hers.

"If I find out you're behind any of this—" She turned and mounted her horse. Without another word, she galloped down the road toward the ranch house.

Cooper mounted up and rode after her.

DELANEY HEARD Cooper come into the barn behind her. "I need to talk to you, Delaney," he said softly.

His tone made her heart feel as if someone were squeezing the life out of it. She feared what he had to tell her, feared it would break her heart and leave neither of them a choice.

"You hungry?" she asked as she led her horse to a stall.

"Dammit, Delaney, food is the last thing I have on my mind right now."

"I make the best chicken enchiladas you've ever tasted," she said, unable to hide the pleading in her voice as she turned to face him. "And I never talk on an empty stomach."

They unsaddled their horses in the cool silence of the barn. Delaney watched Cooper out of the corner of her eye, loving him, wanting him. Did it matter what he'd done in the past? She didn't want to know, but he was hell-bent on telling her. Whatever he had to confess, it was bad, she knew that in her heart.

She swung her saddle up onto the stall railing and turned to find him standing, his thumbs hooked in the front pockets of his jeans, his hat tipped back slightly, his blue-eyed gaze on her. "Coop." It came out a whisper. A plea.

Cooper stepped to her and took her in his arms, crushing her to him. "Delaney. My precious, Delaney." She hugged him, her arms wrapped around him with a fierceness that frightened him.

He knew he'd never be free of the aching desire inside him to hold her. Never. Just as he knew, no matter what happened here tonight, that he'd never get over loving this woman.

"Let's go up to the house," he said, taking her hand in his.

DELANEY FELT her heart break. It snapped like a branch in a strong wind. As he told her, she listened, knowing somewhere in her heart that he'd been too good to be true right from the start.

"I was twenty-two and working on a ranch in Wyoming," Cooper said quietly.

He had insisted she sit on the couch. He'd gone to stand by the fireplace, his body tense, and she was again reminded of a mountain cat. About to spring.

"Accidents started happening on the ranch."

She looked up at him, her eyes widening with the sudden rapid beat of her heart.

"At first they seemed like accidents," he said, his gaze avoiding hers. "Then the barn burned down and I decided to get the hell out of there." He looked up at her. "You know me. Always running. Well, I got blamed for it, and since I couldn't prove I didn't cause the accidents, I went to jail."

"Did you do it?" she asked, her voice no more than a whisper.

He shook his head. "But after that I had trouble getting jobs. I rode the circuit for a while. And then I got an offer from a company called Rattlesnake Range."

She stared at him. "Not the same Rattlesnake Range—"

He nodded. "I didn't realize it at the time, but my little brush with the law was what attracted them to me. And looking back, I think they probably set me up for the fall to begin with."

"You work for Rattlesnake Range?" she asked, her voice breaking, along with her heart. It was all so clear now. So damned clear.

He turned to face her. "Yes."

She felt her heart plummet. Angry tears rushed her eyes. "That's why you came to my ranch."

He didn't deny it, as she'd hoped he would, prayed he would.

"I came to make you an offer."

"One I couldn't refuse, no doubt." She glared at him as she got to her feet. "So you were behind my so-called accidents."

"No, Delaney."

He reached for her, but she stepped back out of his grasp. His blue eyes darkened, just as they did when he made love to her.

"There was a mix-up. I wasn't even supposed to get this ranch assignment. I stayed on just to make sure everything went according to plan."

"And what was the plan, Cooper? Scare me out? If that didn't work, kill me?"

He shook his head. She saw the pain in his eyes but refused to let it soften her heart to him. "I'm not the first, am I, Cooper?"

"I won't lie to you," he said. "I've done things on other ranches I'm not proud of. I've persuaded people to sell. I never cared what happened to them or their ranches. But I never burned any barns or threatened anyone's life." He held her gaze. "This was going to be my last job for Rattlesnake Range. I would have had enough money after this assignment to buy my own ranch. But when I met you, everything changed. I started wondering about the ranches and the people I helped take them from. I started caring. About you. About what I was doing with my life."

She stared at him, unable to think about anything but the ranches he'd taken, the ranchers he'd conned. "So who's behind the accidents on my ranch if not you?"

"I don't know. That's one reason I stayed around at first. To find out. I didn't want to see you hurt."

"Hurt?" She laughed, unable to hide her bitterness. "Don't you know that finding out you work for Rattlesnake Range would hurt me? Knowing that's why you got close to me, just to take my ranch away from me, would hurt me?"

"Maybe that's why I did at first, but—" He slashed his hand through the air. Pain welled in his eyes. "Good God, Delaney, can't you see that I love you? That I'd die for you?" He met her gaze, not flinching as she glared at him. "Why do you think I had to tell you the truth? Don't you think it would be easier to go on lying if all I wanted was your ranch? I'm quitting Rattlesnake Range. I'm quitting because of you. Hell, I didn't even earn my commission for this job anyway." He stepped closer. She moved back out of his reach, knowing that if he touched her now, she'd shatter like thin, old glass. "I knew we couldn't go on from here, without you knowing who I really am."

"'Go on from here'?" she asked with a shaky laugh. "And where is it you think we're going, McLeod?"

He stared at her. "I don't know. I just don't want to lose you. You said you loved me."

"I didn't know who you were then," she said, pain making her heart ache.

"And now that you know?"

"How could I possibly be in love with a man who came here to steal my ranch from me?" Her voice broke. "How could I ever trust you?" Tears rushed her eyes; she bit her lip, desperately trying not to cry. She stared at him, wanting to hurl angry words at him, wanting to pound her fists against his chest, wanting him to take her into his arms and hold her and never let her go.

"I want you off my property by morning," she said. It came out a hoarse whisper. "I want you out of my life."

He picked up his hat with an obvious reluctance from the chair where he'd thrown it. Then he turned and walked out, closing the door behind him with a finality that broke her heart.

Chapter Nineteen

Cooper awoke the next morning, after a restless night, to find Delaney nowhere around. Her pickup was still parked in front of the house, but she didn't answer the door. When he checked the barn, he found her horse and saddle were gone.

All night he'd thought of nothing but her and ways to get her back. He'd hoped that with the morning light she'd change her mind about him leaving. But he couldn't help thinking about the defeated look he'd seen in her eyes last night. He knew he'd destroyed her trust in him. Yet there had to be a way he could get it back, that he could prove to her his love, his loyalty.

He'd lain awake most of the night, wondering how he could make things right with her. How he could make her trust him again. Just before dawn he realized he couldn't make Delaney do anything. But he'd hoped that if he could see her this morning before he left, maybe talk to her, hold her in his arms— He swore as he remembered how easily his charm had worked on other women. But Delaney wasn't like any woman he'd ever known. Or would ever know.

He packed up everything and was just about to load Crazy Jack into the horse trailer, when he heard the phone ring inside the house.

The front door was open, so he let himself in and hurried to answer it, hoping it might be Delaney calling from the York Bar or—

"Where's Del?" Jared asked irritably.

"I don't know," Cooper said, unwilling to tell the sheriff even if he had known.

"Well, tell her Digger's taken off. He left the hospital sometime during the night. No one's seen him since he was rantin' and ravin' about Gus Halbrook coming back for revenge. Tell Del she'd best do somethin' about that old man before the county has to." He hung up.

Cooper stared at the phone for a moment, cursing Jared under his breath. He started to put the receiver back, when he remembered there was something he had to do.

"I just thought I should let you know, it's over," Cooper told Thom Jamison when he came on the line. "Delaney found the will that leaves her everything, including the ranch and the mineral rights. And she isn't selling. So call off your agent. *Now.*"

"I see," Thom said. "Can I assume that if we don't, we'll be fighting you, as well?"

Cooper smiled to himself, wishing the lie he was about to tell were true. "Yeah, you can assume that, Thom. And you might want to tell the board that I've officially quit."

"What about that ranch you were planning to buy? You won't have enough money now."

Cooper glanced around the room, seeing Delaney everywhere he looked. "It doesn't matter anymore." He was sacrificing his dream, but it was worth it. He had something more valuable, but he knew Thom wouldn't understand even if he tried to explain it to him.

"You were good, Coop."

"Too good. Goodbye Thom."

"Good luck. I have a feeling you're going to need it."

Cooper hung up, worrying what the businessmen at Rattlesnake Range would do now. Probably send their agent to tie up all the loose ends. Cooper McLeod was at the top of that list.

DELANEY RACED with the wind, her hair whirling behind her, the horse's hooves pounding the baked clay. She rode as if the devil himself chased close behind her. In truth, he did.

The devil in blue jeans. Wearing Cooper McLeod's handsome face. Grinning Cooper's grin. And calling her name. She rode faster, determined to outrun any thought of the cowboy. Riding had always calmed her, cleared her mind so she could think. It's what she did to solve problems. To get over hurts. To find herself.

But this morning all the ride did was make her think of Cooper. Of the way he looked straddling a horse; or standing against the horizon; his eyes as blue as the big sky; his body as familiar now as the land that stretched to that horizon. She brought her horse up and sat looking at her land. Once the deep green pines against the rocky bluffs and miles of reddish brown clay had offered her contentment. This morning they served only as a reminder of what the ranch would be like without Cooper in her life. She saw an emptiness she'd never noticed in the big sky before. A hollowness that echoed across the hard, dry clay. And no matter how hard or fast she rode, she couldn't seem to outrun it.

Delaney didn't even realize where she was until she heard a vehicle coming up the county road. She looked up, surprised to find she'd ridden to Cooper's old camp at the far side of the ranch. She stared at the stand of pines on the other side of the fence, remembering the night she'd driven him back here. It seemed like a lifetime ago instead of just days.

The vehicle she'd heard slowed, then came to a stop at the edge of the road. Delaney saw that it was a dark-colored van. Angel rolled down the passenger side window.

"I was just on my way to your place," the writer said.

She sounded a little shaken, and she looked as if she'd just woken up. The dark sunglasses she wore made her face seem especially pale.

"Have they found Buck?" Delaney asked hopefully.

Angel shook her head and Delaney realized why Angel looked so different. This was the first time she'd seen the woman without a mountain of makeup. Her hair, which normally was sculpted to perfection around her face, was pulled back in a no-nonsense twist at her neck.

"And they're not going to find Buck," Angel said, close to tears. "Buck sent me to get you. He has to talk to you. He said it's urgent."

Delaney felt a surge of relief. "Is he all right? Where is he?"

"He called me this morning."

Angel sounded frightened and a little breathless, Delaney realized.

"He told me to come get you and take you to him." She lifted the glasses long enough to brush at her tears. "He's in some kind of trouble, isn't he?"

"I think so," Delaney said. "The sheriff and his posse have been looking for him all night."

"Why?" Angel asked, surprised.

"His horse turned up without him and—" Delaney hesitated to tell her about the blood she and Cooper had found on the saddle or about the dredging for gold in the lake. "When was the last time you saw Buck?"

Angel frowned. "Yesterday at Jared's rodeo. I had to leave early to do some research. I was at the Helena library until it closed. Why?"

"I just thought you might have seen Buck sometime last night," Delaney said. She'd just assumed Angel had been the other diver.

"I didn't even know Buck was missing until this morning when he told me he was hiding out and that you were the only person he could trust," Angel said, as if she wasn't so sure about that. "You're going to help him, aren't you?"

The desperation in Angel's voice made Delaney wonder if she'd misjudged the woman. Maybe she actually did care for Buck. "Of course I'm going to help him."

"He insisted we come alone," Angel warned. "He sounded scared."

Delaney nodded. "Meet me at his place up the road. I'll leave my horse there."

Without waiting for a response, Delaney spurred her horse into motion and took off across the pasture. As she rode, she hoped mining gold illegally was the only trouble Buck was in. She had a bad feeling it wasn't.

AFTER HE'D HUNG UP with Thom, Cooper wandered into the living room, not certain what to do about the news on Digger. He had no doubt that the old prospector was headed for the Golden Dream mine in the hope of sending Gus back to the grave. The problem was, Cooper didn't have any idea where to find the mine. Cooper smiled as a thought struck him. He couldn't leave the Rockin' L as long as Digger was missing. He knew it was just an excuse to maybe see Delaney again. But at this point, he'd take anything he could get.

Not that he wasn't genuinely worried about Digger. While he doubted Gus had returned from the grave, someone dangerous was definitely out there. And he had a feeling Digger knew who it was.

The photo albums Delaney had gotten out for Angel were still stacked on the coffee table. He picked up one and opened it. Just as he'd thought, the albums were full of old photographs of the ranch. He started looking through them, hoping to find a photograph of the Golden Dream. Instead he found photographs of Delaney as a baby. Wild dark hair around the face of an angel. Cooper smiled as he caught that familiar twinkle in her eyes. Pure mischief. He thumbed through the book, watching Delaney grow, fascinated to see her go from a child to a beautiful woman.

Seldom was she without a horse in any of the photos. Her love for this ranch and her life-style were what had first suckered him in, he realized. He cursed himself for blowing it with her and wondered where she was. Probably hiding out, waiting for him to leave.

Closing the album, Cooper picked up what looked like an older snapshot book.

Bingo. Photographs of old miners. His heart pounded with hope. Maybe there were photos of the Golden Dream, something that would give him at least an idea where to look for Digger.

He was flipping through the book, when one of the photographs stopped him. It was a yellowed snapshot of a cowboy sleeping at the base of a large gnarled old tree, his hat over his face, his clothing dirty and worn as if he'd been working. But it wasn't the tree that captured Cooper's eye or the gaping mine entrance behind him. It was the man's spurs. They were identical to the one that Delaney found in Johnson Gulch Lake. He turned the photograph over. A date was written in faded ink. Nineteen thirty-four. And a name. Gus Halbrook.

DELANEY TURNED her horse into Buck's corral with the other two horses and threw her saddle onto the fence railing. Angel waited in the van, looking worried.

When Delaney climbed into the passenger seat, she noticed Angel fidgeting with the hem of her jean jacket. The scent of her perfume reminded Delaney of Buck's pickup that night he'd given her a ride home.

"Whatever trouble Buck is in, we'll do the best we can to get him out of it," Delaney said, hoping she sounded more confident of that than she felt.

Angel gave her a trembly smile as she got the van going, and Delaney had an odd wave of apprehension. She shook it off, blaming it on Angel's obvious nervousness. On Cooper's leaving. Cooper. By now he'd be gone. Her heart cramped with the thought. It was for the best, she assured herself. It would never have worked out. Never. And yet, suddenly she wished she'd told someone, even Cooper, where she was going. Except she didn't even know herself.

"Where are we supposed to meet Buck?" she asked.

Angel pointed toward the mountains. "Near Johnson Gulch Lake."

Johnson Gulch Lake? That was where the sheriff's posse and Jared were searching for him. How had Buck gotten himself into so much trouble that he had to hide from the law? And how much did Angel know about Buck and his double life? Delaney wondered. "Did you know that Buck has been running a small portable gold dredge in the lake nights?" she asked.

"Buck has?"

Angel seemed genuinely surprised. Maybe she hadn't known. "Someone was helping him," Delaney said. "Do you have any idea who that might have been?"

Angel stared at the road ahead. "The only person I can think of is Jared Kincaid."

"Jared?" Delaney tried to imagine the sheriff in scuba gear.

Angel shrugged. "Jared was real interested in what I found out about gold on the Rockin' L," she said. "He told me stories about the mother lode. I guess there's some gold on his property, but not the mother lode." Her painted red nails went to her lips. "What if that's it? What if Buck and Jared had been doing the dredging in your creek and Jared double-crossed him and that's why Buck's hiding now." She frowned. "Why else would Buck hide from the sheriff?"

Buck and Jared? Delaney had just assumed that Buck had been hurt last night trying to get away from her and Cooper. That's why he'd left his horse. Now she wondered if he *had* been double-crossed. But by Jared? Could Jared be that greedy for money that he not only was making deals with mining companies, but he was dredging her creek at night?

Delaney glanced back to make sure no one was following them, and frowned. It struck her: what was a writer doing with a cargo van? That's when she noticed the floor in the back was wet with water and sand. Her heart hammered, pulse rising with more than apprehension.

Angel glanced in her rearview mirror, then smiled as she saw what Delaney was looking at. "You caught me. I've been doing a little gold panning. Jared showed me how. But all I've found so far is fool's gold." Her smile faded. "Oh, no, you don't think the buckets of gravel and sand that Jared gave me were from your creek, do you?"

"Where did Jared say he got the gravel?" Delaney asked, trying to still her growing fears. Angel had used the van to carry the dredging equipment. How much more was she lying about? Delaney watched the country whiz by, wanting out of the van, not knowing how to accomplish that.

"I didn't even think to ask," Angel admitted.

"Don't worry about it," Delaney told her, noticing that Angel had taken the old mining road. Surely Buck wouldn't hide up here so close to where the sheriff and his men were searching unless—

"You're sure Buck isn't hurt?" Delaney asked.

Angel flipped her a look and Delaney realized if Buck was hurt badly he couldn't have gotten to a phone.

"I'm just surprised he's hiding up here, so close to the lake, so close to where Jared and the posse are searching for him," Delaney said, assuring herself her fears couldn't be justified. Angel wouldn't take her to the lake where Jared and the posse would be searching if she intended to harm her. So why didn't Delaney feel reassured by that? Why was this woman frightening her so?

Through the trees, Delaney spotted Johnson Gulch Lake, glistening in the sunlight. "I'm sure Buck will explain everything," Angel said, making Delaney wonder if that was true. If they were going to see Buck. Or someone else. Jared? Angel said Jared was teaching her to pan gold. Surely Angel and Jared hadn't gotten together to— To what? Delaney thought. Steal her ranch? What would a historical writer want with the Rockin' L, a horse ranch, when she didn't even ride, didn't seem to have any interest in horses. To steal her gold? The thought hit her like a rock upside the head. That's what Angel and Jared had in common. Angel, Jared—and Buck. Gold.

As Angel brought the van to a stop, a pile of papers and books slid from under the seat. Delaney picked them up without thinking. She looked down at the papers and books she held in her lap, then toward the lake. Her fear level increased drastically. There were no other vehicles up here. Where was the posse Jared had assured her was out looking for Buck? And where was Jared?

"What is it?" Angel asked.

Delaney shook her head. "Nothing." She tried to smile but had trouble meeting Angel's gaze. Warning signals were going off in her head. Only, Delaney didn't understand why. What could she have to fear from Angel? Even if Jared and Buck had been stealing gold out of her creek and Angel knew about it, Angel had nothing to gain by hurting her.

"Here, I'll take those," Angel said, reaching for her research materials.

As Delaney handed them over, one of the books slipped out and fell to the floor. Several pages fluttered out of the worn binding.

"I'll get it," Angel cried.

But Delaney already had it in her hand. Had already seen the writing and recognized it as the old prospector's diary she'd looked at in Angel's cabin. Only this time she saw the name. She gazed up at Angel in confusion. "This is Gus Halbrook's diary."

COOPER SEARCHED the photographs, trying to find another picture of Gus Halbrook. The only other one he'd seen was that dilapidated thing Digger had tried to show him at the hospital.

As he hurried through the album, Cooper kept telling himself that finding a spur in the lake that belonged to Gus Halbrook meant nothing. Gus hadn't come back from the dead. Then suddenly Cooper stopped flipping pages. He stared down at the one semiclear photograph he could find. His heart thundered in his ears. His fingers shook as he looked from Digger's smiling face to that of his best friend's, Gus Halbrook. Gus looked up at Cooper from over the decades, his face unsmiling. "My God," Cooper breathed. Why hadn't he seen the resemblance before?

Chapter Twenty

Cooper pulled the photograph out of the album and held it up to the light. Digger and Gus stood in front of a large, old, weathered boulder. In the background, Cooper could make out a gnarled ponderosa and, to the left of it, what looked like an opening in the rocks. The Golden Dream?

He stared at the photograph, his gaze returning to Gus. A tremor of fear surged through him as he dropped the photo of Digger and Gus. It fluttered to the floor. He had to find Delaney and warn her. He only hoped it wasn't too late.

"McLeod?"

Cooper spun around to find Jared in the open doorway.

"I knocked, but you didn't answer," he said, stepping into the living room. He glanced from the scattered photo albums to Cooper.

Cooper noticed the sheriff's hand was resting on his holster.

"What's going on in here? Where's Del?"

Cooper gave him his most innocent shrug. "I've been looking for her myself."

Jared shot a brow up. "And just where exactly were you looking for her? Her pickup's parked outside and her horse is down at Buck's—saddle is on the fence. And you're in here looking at pictures." He eyed Cooper for a moment.

"And I see you're all packed up like you're planning on going somewhere."

"What's her horse doing at Buck's?" Cooper demanded, trying to imagine why Delaney would ride to Buck's, unsaddle her horse and leave it there. Unless Buck had returned. Or someone else came by—

"That's what I'd like you to tell me," Jared said.

Cooper noticed he flipped the tab off on his holster and settled his hand on the pistol handle.

"First Buck was missing. Then Digger. Now Del—"

"*Was* missing?" Cooper asked. "You found Buck?"

"That's what I came to tell Del. We've called off the search. Buck's fine. He fell off his horse last night. He's with Angel. Now, what I want to know from you is what you've done with Del."

"Wait a minute, how did Buck explain what he was doing at Johnson Gulch Lake last night?" Cooper asked.

Jared let out a sigh. "Never mind Buck. I just got a call from Del's attorney. It seems you work for a company by the name of Rattlesnake Range. I think you'd better tell me what's going on here, McLeod."

Cooper watched Jared's hand, wondering just how little it would take to provoke the sheriff into shooting him. Very little, he decided. "I used to work for Rattlesnake Range. I quit. But Delaney knows all about that."

"Sure she does. Why don't we just ask her about that when we see her." Jared pulled his pistol and pointed the barrel at Cooper's heart. With his other hand, he reached for his handcuffs. "I think you'd better come with me. Peacefully, of course."

Cooper raised his hands slowly. "We don't have time for this right now, Sheriff. We've got to find Delaney. And warn her."

"Warn her about what, McLeod?" he asked.

His trigger finger looked a little too itchy. Cooper wondered how deep Jared was in this mess. And how much it would be safe to tell him.

"Gus Halbrook," Cooper said. "Digger was right. Gus is back from the dead and after revenge. And unless I miss my guess, Delaney is his target—and always has been."

ANGEL SMILED as she took the diary from Delaney's trembling fingers. "You didn't know Gus kept a diary?" she asked, turning in her seat to face Delaney. "He wrote in it right up until the day of the cave-in. It makes for very interesting reading." She pushed her sunglasses up onto her hair and settled her gaze on Delaney. "He wrote about the people who were trying to steal his gold. He was tormented with their plots to take what he'd worked so hard for. Toward the end, he feared for his very life. And rightly so, as it turns out. He would have been seventy-seven this fall, if he'd still been alive, of course."

Delaney stared at Angel as if she'd never seen the woman before. In a way she hadn't—not this woman at least. Angel looked so different with her hair pulled back and no makeup. It was the eyes, Delaney realized. They were no longer deep green but a pale, pale green. "The damnedest eyes you've ever seen." Digger's words jarred Delaney's memory. She blinked and sat up a little straighter. Her heart rate soared as realization set in. Fear rippled through her. Cooper, her heart cried out. If she was right about this woman, Delaney knew she might never see him again. She had to do something. And quickly.

"What's Cooper doing here?" Delaney bluffed, gazing past Angel to the window behind her.

Startled, Angel spun around to look. Delaney threw open her door and ran.

"GUS?" JARED FROWNED and stepped back. "You're not going to try to tell me Gus's ghost is who's been causing all the trouble around here, are you, McLeod?'' He shook his head. "Everyone knows how Rattlesnake Range operates. All those *accidents*. I think you'd better move away from that coffee table. Put your hands behind your head and spread 'em on the floor.''

Cooper stared at Jared. Why hadn't he realized it before? No one outside of Rattlesnake Range knew how the agency operated. Jared wouldn't know unless he had either hired them—or worked for them! It was like a light going off in his head. No wonder Rattlesnake Range had hired a local. The sheriff was the perfect person.

But right now Cooper's only concern was Delaney. If her horse was at Buck's— "Listen to me, Kincaid, I think I know what's been going on around here—''

"Yeah? Well, I think I know what's been going on about here,'' he said, as he moved closer. "You've been using those scare tactics, something you Rattlesnake Range people are known for, huh? But maybe this time you went too far and I got me a murderer on my hands.'' Jared kicked the coffee table out of the way. "Get on the floor, McLeod.''

Cooper stared at the sheriff, having watched him work himself up to the point where he could—what? Kill someone? Jared didn't really believe Cooper had killed Delaney. In fact, Cooper thought just the opposite. Jared was looking for a way to get what he wanted. And what he wanted was Delaney's ranch. Unless Cooper missed his guess, Jared had made a deal with the mining company that involved Delaney's spread. Without Delaney's ranch, the deal would fall through.

But it still didn't add up. How would killing Cooper get Jared Delaney's ranch? Cooper felt a cold sliver of fear pierce his heart. Unless Delaney was dead, too. And it appeared that Delaney's ranch hand had killed her. Then Ty would get the ranch and gladly sell it to Burton Mining.

"On the floor, McLeod,'' Jared shouted, bracing the pistol with both hands. "Or you're a dead man.''

Cooper dropped to his knees.

"All the way down," the sheriff yelled.

Cooper looked at Kincaid, saw the way his gun hand shook, saw the scared expression in his eyes and knew Jared planned to kill him. The only chance Cooper had was a slim one and the very last one he'd take under normal circumstances. But Delaney was out there somewhere, her life in grave danger from either a lunatic or a murderer. Or both. He had no choice. Cooper let out a piercing whistle as he flattened himself to the floor.

Jared jerked back in surprise. "What the hell? You dumb rodeo cowboy, son of a—"

Crazy Jack burst through the screen door in a shower of splintered wood and ripped screen. Jared swung around, pistol first, his trigger finger way beyond nervous. Cooper grabbed the edge of the coffee table and swung it around on the hardwood floor. The table hit Jared about midcalf and dropped him like a sack of grain. But not before Cooper's fears were realized. Jared got off one shot.

DELANEY'S ONLY ESCAPE was straight up. She scrambled up the rocky bluff next to the van, hoping that once she reached the top and dropped over the rim, Angel wouldn't be able to find her. She doubted the woman could climb the rocks fast enough to catch her. Running toward the lake or down the road would only allow Angel to chase her in the van.

Delaney was almost to the top of the rock bluff, when the first pistol shot ricocheted off a rock to her right.

"Don't make me kill you," Angel called from below.

Delaney climbed higher, frantically trying to reach the last few rocks that rimmed the bluff. The second shot hit closer and on the left. Rock chips stung Delaney's bare arms. Several cut her face. She felt blood trickle down her cheek as she clung to the rough boulders, her arms weak with fear and exertion. She fought to catch her breath, her heart pounding in her ears.

"Keep going and the next shot will be in your back," Angel said, anger and bitterness making her voice hard as the rocks around them. "Have you forgotten? Buck is waiting for us. You don't want to let Buck down, now do you?"

Delaney looked up at the rock bluff, estimating her chances of getting out of Angel's line of fire before the woman could get off another shot. They weren't good. And Angel knew it. "I'm coming down."

"Wise decision," Angel said. "Back down slowly," she instructed. "And please, no rock slides. They're very unpredictable and not all that reliable."

When Delaney reached the ground, she turned to face Angel, and the barrel end of the pistol the woman held pointed at her chest. Where was Jared and the posse who were supposed to be searching for Buck? Was Jared part of this, just as she'd suspected? She fought the feeling that she was alone on this mountain with a madwoman. And Buck— the traitor who'd helped Angel set her deadly trap.

By now Cooper would be packed up and off the ranch. Just as she'd ordered him. She closed her eyes, fighting tears of defeat. "Who are you? You aren't Angel Danvers—the writer."

"Actually, I am. That's how I stumbled across Gus's diary—researching a historical piece on the Halbrook family. I'm just not the blond bimbo you thought I was."

Angel frowned as Delaney opened her eyes. "What gave me away?" Her hand went to her hair. She felt the sunglasses she'd pushed back onto the top of her head and smiled. "The eyes. A family legacy. All that *my* grandfather had to leave me." She laughed at Delaney's expression. "That's right. I'm Gus's granddaughter. Angel Halbrook Danvers. Gus had a young woman hidden away in Helena. She's the one who had his diary. Unfortunately, she died in childbirth."

"It's been years since I've seen a photograph of Gus," Delaney said. But now that she'd seen Angel's eyes, she remembered that haunting look of Gus Halbrook's. "The resemblance between the two of you is remarkable."

Angel smiled. "Digger saw it right away. The old fool thought I was my grandfather. I really wish I'd known Digger was crazy, before I tried to kill him the second time. It would have saved me a lot of trouble."

"How could you do that to a harmless old man?" Delaney demanded, her heart breaking at the thought of this woman hurting the prospector. "Your grandfather was his best friend. Digger has never gotten over Gus's death."

Angel let out a snort. "And why do you think that was? Because Digger and your grandfather, Del Henry, killed Gus. Murdered him in the Golden Dream."

"That's not true," Delaney cried, feeling a little of her old fight come back. "Gus got himself killed in a cave-in. He thought he'd found the mother lode. He went crazy in that mine. Just as Digger did watching it happen to his best friend."

"We'd better not keep Buck waiting any longer," Angel said, her eyes as cold as the river ice in winter.

Delaney looked toward the mountainside. "I can't believe Buck would fall for your lies."

"Why not? You did," Angel said, jabbing Delaney in the ribs with the pistol.

Delaney took a breath, heart pounding. "You're the one who's been trying to kill me?"

"If I had wanted to kill you, I could have. No," Angel assured her, "I just wanted to torture you for a while. The way your grandfather tortured mine before he killed him. I wanted you to see what it was like to know someone was after you."

"And Buck? What part did he play in all this?" Delaney said.

"Why don't you ask him when you see him?" Angel suggested. "Come on. Let's get moving. We don't want to keep Buck waiting."

COOPER GRABBED the sheriff's pistol and turned it on him. "Blink, Jared, and I'll shoot you."

"They're going to put you back in jail for this little stunt, McLeod," Jared warned, but had the good sense to look concerned about Cooper and the gun he was holding.

"Maybe," Cooper agreed, as he checked his horse. Crazy Jack was still standing, but Jared's wild shot had left a notch in the horse's left ear. "At least I won't be in jail for murder the way you planned." He narrowed his gaze at Jared. "That is, unless you don't do exactly what I say. Slide those handcuffs over here, then let's go out on the porch real slowlike."

"You won't get away with this," the sheriff grumbled but did as he was told.

"Tell me something, Jared," Cooper said as he had Jared sit in Delaney's oak rocker and put his hands behind his back. "Did you go to Rattlesnake Range or did they come to you?"

"What are you talking about?" Jared asked.

"Rattlesnake Range. There is no way you could have found out how they work, about the small accidents they use to get ranch owners to sell. Not unless you hired them or worked for them. Which is it?"

Jared looked down at the floor. His jaw tensed. And Cooper had to laugh. How could he have been such a fool not to realize it before? The sheriff. No wonder Rattlesnake Range hired Jared. He was perfect for the job.

"What was the deal? Your ranch *and* Delaney's? And Rattlesnake Range hired you to bring in the Rockin' L. Sweet deal, except you underestimated Delaney. And now you're going to get blamed for not only the accidents, but the murder attempts on Delaney's life."

"But I didn't do it!" Jared cried. "Yes, I made a deal with Burton Mining. I needed Delaney's property or Burton Mining wouldn't buy mine. It was Rattlesnake Range who asked me to help things along. But I didn't hurt anyone."

Cooper smiled. "Right. Been there. Done it. Jail time. Only I was innocent." He looped the cuffs through the porch railing beside the chair, then snapped one cuff on each of Jared's wrists.

"I never would hurt Del," he said angrily as Cooper took his keys. "Selling the ranch was the best thing for her. But I knew how stubborn she was—"

"So you cut her fences, drugged her horses, took a potshot at her, ransacked her office, burned down her barn—and almost got caught—and put a snake in Delaney's bed—"

"I didn't put any snake in her bed or drug her horses," Jared contended. "I looked through her office, trying to find something to help me figure out who was after her. But I didn't have anything to do with cutting the brake line on her stock truck or that rock slide. At first, when I found that barred-shoe print up at the rock slide and near the lake, I thought it had to be Buck. Then when I found out you worked for Rattlesnake Range, I figured you were doing those things. I swear to God I don't know who's behind it."

Cooper looked toward the mountains. "Unfortunately, I think I do. And if I'm right, Delaney could be in a world of hurt right now. I need to find the Golden Dream, the mine Gus Halbrook died in. If you have any idea where it is—"

Jared shook his head. "Only Digger would know. And he's run off with that blamed mule of his, probably searching for the mother lode or Gus Halbrook's ghost—"

"What?" Cooper glanced toward the barn, then back at Jared. "How do you know Digger's got his mule with him?"

"I saw the mule tracks."

"Where?" Cooper demanded.
"Down by Buck's place."

DELANEY CLIMBED UP the hillside above Johnson Gulch
Lake, weaving her way through the tall ponderosas and the
rocks, knowing all along that Angel had a pistol trained at
her back.

"There never was a mother lode," Delaney said, desperately trying to find some way to reach Angel. She'd looked
into those pale-green eyes and glimpsed the insanity there.
Gus had left Angel more than a legacy of pale green eyes.
"Gus died in a worthless mine, digging for something that
doesn't exist."

"Lies," Angel said behind her. "That's just what Del
Henry told people."

Delaney knew her only chance was to reason with the
woman. "Then what happened to the gold?" she demanded, turning to look behind her.

Angel's smile was more frightening than the pistol she
clutched in her hand. "The gold's still there. Del Henry only
dynamited the entrance to keep anyone from getting it." She
motioned with the gun for Delaney to keep moving.

"That doesn't make any sense."

"He thought he could keep the gold a secret, but it's
coming out in Johnson Gulch Lake," Angel argued. "And
now it's my inheritance instead of yours."

Delaney looked over at the creek, running down through
the rocks and trees as it dropped to the lake. Could it be
true? Delaney wondered. Gold often washed down from
rich veins upstream. That's how the original miners had first
discovered the larger deposits.

"Just because there's a little gold dust in the creek
bed—"

"Don't lie anymore," Angel said, suddenly right behind
her. "I know you were planning to sell the ranch to a mining company and cash in on the gold. But what you don't

know is that Del Henry promised my grandfather one-third of anything he and Digger found in the Golden Dream. And I'm here to collect.''

''Who told you I was going to sell the Rockin' L?'' Delaney asked. ''I'd never sell the ranch.''

''It doesn't matter now.''

They'd reached a flat spot beside the creek. The boulders were large. Pines towered over them. ''I'm tired,'' Delaney said, stalling for time as she looked around for a possible weapon. A tree limb. Small rock. ''How much farther is it? I have to rest for a while.''

''Nice try,'' Angel said, prodding Delaney with the cold steel of the pistol. ''You wanted to see Buck, didn't you? Well, he's waiting. Right through there.''

Delaney gazed past a massive boulder to see a gnarled old ponderosa. Beyond it lay the shadow of a small opening in the rocks. Her heart quickened. The Golden Dream mine.

ON CRAZY JACK, Cooper followed the mule tracks in to the mountains, trailing Digger and Tess as they headed for the Golden Dream. Cooper had known the moment Jared told him about the old prospector taking his mule that Digger had left the hospital to find Gus. He'd be headed for the mine. But where was Delaney? She'd tied up her horse and saddle at Buck's. All Cooper could figure is that someone had picked her up. He just hoped it hadn't been Angel.

As Cooper and Crazy Jack climbed, the sun climbed Montana's big sky with him. All Cooper's fears escalated when he saw Angel's rented van parked near Johnson Gulch Lake.

Cooper looked up the mountainside, hoping to catch a glimpse of Delaney, wondering how much of a head start Angel had, hoping it wouldn't matter. He tried to rein in his apprehension. He knew running scared wouldn't help Delaney. But just the thought of Delaney with Angel—

He urged Crazy Jack up the mountainside, praying he would find Delaney and the mine in time.

"WELL, BUCK, we made it," Angel said deep in the cool, damp darkness of the mine. "Your precious Delaney was a real pain in the neck, though."

Delaney stood where Angel had left her, in the middle of the pitch black mine tunnel, wiping cobwebs from her face. The mine smelled moldy, as if it had been closed up for years. Angel had forced her through the small opening, then down a series of tunnels, with only the faint beam of Angel's flashlight to guide them.

Delaney rubbed the elbow she'd scraped on the rocks in the darkness and tried to get her bearings. She considered making a run for it, but even if she could see, she didn't know which way to run and realized she wouldn't get far in the dark, not with Angel and Buck after her.

She heard Angel strike a match. It glowed brightly for a moment before she touched it to an old lantern. Slowly the light radiated out from the lantern to fill a small section of the mine.

"Buck doesn't seem all that happy to see you," Angel noted, motioning for Delaney to come a little farther into the mine.

Delaney did, aware that she could reason with Buck. At least the Buck she used to know before Angel came into his life.

Delaney hadn't gone far, when she saw Buck sitting in the shadowy darkness. She felt her heart break as she looked at him. Buck sat against the rock wall, his head back, his feet and hands bound. He lifted his gaze to Delaney's.

"I'm sorry." The words came out in a choked whisper.

Delaney went to him, kneeling next to him. The side of his head was soaked in something dark that plastered his hair to his head. "Are you all right?"

He nodded, then grimaced as if the simple movement caused him a great deal of pain.

"He needs to get to a doctor," Delaney said over her shoulder to Angel.

"He'll live. Maybe."

Angel didn't sound as if it made a difference to her one way or another, Delaney realized.

Buck's eyes filled with tears. "I've been such a fool."

Delaney hushed him. "We all have, Buck." She thought of Buck's plans to marry Angel and wanted to scratch the woman's eyes out. She brushed angrily at her own tears and stood to face Angel. "And to think I was worried about you breaking his heart."

Angel shook her head in disgust. "At first he was so easy to control. Totally malleable, like so many men."

Delaney thought of Cooper. The opposite of malleable. Hardheaded. Impossibly determined. Totally inflexible. Her heart stopped with a jolt, then kicked back into high speed. Cooper. Had he done what she'd told him? Had he packed up this morning and left? Or had he done just the opposite and stayed? A faint glimmer of hope shone through the darkness of the mine, through the madness of the situation she found herself in. Cooper. He'd never done anything she'd told him. She just prayed he hadn't this time.

"You didn't have to hurt Buck," she said to Angel.

"He didn't give me a choice. He started snooping around in business that didn't concern him."

"I found the horseshoe tracks at the rock slide and at the spot where the sheriff said someone had taken a potshot at you, Delaney," Buck said, his voice barely above a whisper. "I knew it couldn't be Angel, though." He leaned his head back, as if the effort of talking had been exhausting.

Denver stared at the woman, confused. "Buck said you didn't know how to ride a horse—"

Angel made a face. "Or shoot a gun? Or tie my own shoes? What do you think, boss lady?"

Delaney looked down at Buck. "Then you didn't know what she was up to when you bought her the horse?"

Buck shook his head.

"He bought me the quarter horse because I insisted it was the one I wanted. The old fool thought if I learned to ride, I might marry him and stay down on the ranch."

"What a fool, huh, Angel?" Buck said, glaring up at her.

Delaney stared at the woman. "Why would you insist on such a horse? Unless— You knew we'd be able to track the barred shoe. Who were you setting up? Jared or Buck?"

Angel laughed. "Just clouding the water a little. I didn't want you to figure out who was after you too quickly."

"She's sick," Buck said, sounding as if he almost felt sorry for her.

Delaney had to agree. "I can't believe you'd go to all this trouble for—"

"Revenge?" Angel asked, her eyes bright in the lantern light. "I think of it as justice. Your grandfather killed mine. Now I will take your ranch, your life and your gold. *That* is justice."

"Killing me won't get you my ranch or this mine," Delaney said, but noticed Angel wasn't paying any attention. Instead the woman had glanced at her watch, then back down the mine tunnel. "Who are you waiting for?" Delaney asked, suddenly more frightened than ever.

Angel raised one perfect brow. "Think about it, boss lady. The perfect revenge. Who's missing?"

Delaney felt her legs turn to water beneath her and fought to keep her feet. "Digger."

"You got it on the first guess." She shot Delaney a thumbs-up sign. "I stopped by to see him last night at the hospital and told him I had his precious Winnie, as he calls you, at the mine." She glanced down the tunnel again, then back at Delaney. "Don't worry. He'll come, and then it will all be over."

Delaney tried to think of something to do as she looked over at Buck, and bit her lip to hold back the tears. And her growing terror. She was with a madwoman in a mine tunnel, a mine Digger believed cursed. And Buck was hurting and needing immediate medical attention. Her heart went out to him now. He'd fallen in love, proving just how blind it could be.

A thought whizzed past. Delaney blinked, remembering the lathered horse she and Cooper had found in the corral that day after the rock slide. If Buck hadn't been the one, and Angel was on the barred-shoe horse, then who had ridden it?

And— Delaney stared at Buck's body propped against the wall of the mine, then at the dirt on the mine floor. No drag tracks. Who had helped Angel get Buck's body up here to the mine? There was no way Buck could have gotten here by himself. Someone else was involved.

Suddenly Delaney remembered what Angel had said about having no choice but to stop Buck because of his snooping into her business. "Buck caught you and your accomplice dredging Johnson Gulch Lake last night," Delaney said, the pieces starting to fit.

"Very good, boss lady." Angel smiled. "Too bad you didn't figure it all out sooner."

So why didn't these pieces feel as though they fit together? "It *was* you and Jared in the lake last night, right?" Delaney asked. "I mean, how many other poor fools could you have suckered into your deranged plot?"

Angel turned to look back up the dark mine tunnel at the sound of footfalls on the mine tunnel floor. She smiled. "I believe that's another poor fool now."

Chapter Twenty-One

The mule tracks led up the mountainside overlooking Johnson Gulch. Then disappeared. Cooper stood in a clearing of rocks and pines, staring at the ground. Then he looked closer and saw that someone had brushed away the tracks with a limb. Cooper circled the area, knowing he must be close to the mine entrance, but wondering at the same time just what Digger O'Donnel was up to. Maybe he still believed there were space aliens who had brought Gus back from the dead and he was hiding from them.

Cooper found the boot tracks in the dust about the time he lost Digger's tracks. Small feet. Two women. Then he noticed it. The weathered old tree. The large boulder. He climbed off Crazy Jack and walked to where he thought the entrance to the mine was from the photograph. Only all he could see were thick brush and rocks. No entrance. Could Del Henry have dynamited *both* entrances to the mine?

Cooper shoved aside some of the brush where he estimated the opening should be. What he found made his heart rumble to a halt. Sweat beaded on his forehead instantly. His heart threatened to pound its way out of his chest. He swore as he gaped at the tiny, confining entrance to the Golden Dream. It was little more than a hole, just large enough for a small person to squeeze through. Behind the hole was nothing but darkness. Cooper felt his claustrophobia constrict his heart, squeezing each breath he took the way the opening would squeeze his body. He swore again. Then started moving the brush. Delaney was in there. With Angel. He had no choice.

DELANEY STARED down the dark tunnel, waiting for a figure to emerge. Ty Drummond appeared in the lantern light, dragging someone with him.

"Hello, Sis," Ty said as he gave Digger a shove. The old prospector stumbled and fell at Delaney's feet. "Look who I found on my way in."

Delaney knelt to help Digger to his feet. His eyes were wild; his voice was shrill. "Cursed. Nothin' but evil in this mine, Winnie. Pure evil." His eyes darted around the mine tunnel, then settled on Angel. "I told you Gus was back, didn't I?"

"That's not Gus, Digger. It's his granddaughter, Angel." Not that it seemed to make a lot of difference, she realized. Angel was much more dangerous than any ghost.

"I heard you found the will," Ty said.

"I figured Jared would tell you," Delaney said.

Ty nodded. "Yeah, well, it changes my plans."

"'Our' plans, don't you mean, Ty?" Angel asked.

Delaney looked from Angel to Ty and back. "So the two of you are in this together?"

"While I was doing my research, I found out about Ty being Hank Lawson's son," Angel said sweetly. "I thought it was just something else I could hurt you with, Delaney." Bitterness and hatred oozed from her words.

Delaney caught movement out of the corner of her eye. Someone was sneaking up the tunnel to her left. While she hadn't gotten more than an impression, she knew in her heart it was Cooper. She'd been right about his hardheadedness. Thank God she'd fallen for a man who didn't do anything she told him to. Angel still held a pistol trained on her and now Ty was here and probably armed, too. And there was no doubt that they planned to kill her and Digger, and likely leave Buck for dead, as well, and steal the

Rockin' L. If she could just keep them talking and distracted—

"And let me guess," Delaney said. "The snake was your idea, right, Ty?"

He smiled. "Someone mentioned your fear of snakes."

"Jared," Delaney said with an oath. "And how does he fit into all this?"

Ty smiled. "Well the sheriff has come in handy."

"Why don't I believe he's been giving you money out of the goodness of his heart?" Delaney said, seeing things clearer. "Blackmail? What did you have on him?"

"He's been working with Rattlesnake Range to take your property away from you, Sis. All those little accidents around the ranch? Jared."

"Why?" Delaney asked.

"Seems he needs to sell his ranch and the only way Burton Mining will buy it is if they can get the Rockin' L," Ty explained. "I just happened to catch him in the act of cutting some of your barbed wire."

Delaney shook her head. "Angel wants revenge. But you, Ty—"

"I just want what's mine. My father's ranch," he said.

Delaney gritted her teeth. "The only way you can get the Rockin' L is to kill me, and you know it."

Ty shrugged. "You're right. You've left me no other option."

"But you'll never get away with it." Delaney moved so Cooper could get behind Ty and Angel. "You'll be the number-one suspect."

"Who's been salting the Johnson Gulch Lake?" Digger asked out of the blue. "There ain't no gold in that lake."

Angel frowned. "Salting?"

"Me and Tess seen it. Gold flakes where there shouldn't have been none," Digger said. "Gus, you're too smart to fall for that."

Ty groaned. "Come on, Angel, let's get this over with."

"Wait a minute," Angel said to Ty. "What's he talking about?"

Delaney could see Cooper edging along the wall of the tunnel, an old shovel in his hand. She needed to create a diversion, but it wouldn't be easy, because Angel wasn't about to fall for another "Geez, isn't that the calvary behind you" trick.

Delaney looked over at Digger and saw that he, too, had seen Cooper and was doing his level best to help. She glanced down at Buck. His eyes were closed, his head back. She hoped he'd only passed out and not died.

"Somebody put gold flakes in the lake to make it seem like there was gold upstream," Digger said. "Only a fool would fall for an old ruse like that."

Angel looked over at Ty, her eyes wide. "He's saying someone tried to trick us?"

"The guy's loonier than a pet raccoon," Ty said to Angel. "You know there's gold in this mine. It's in the diary." Angel appeared doubtful. "Here, give me the pistol," Ty said. "And I'll finish this."

"I wouldn't do that if I were you, Angel," Delaney cautioned. "Don't you see what he has planned? I couldn't figure out how Ty thought he could get away with my murder. But he has the perfect scapegoat. You. Crazy, revengeful Angel Halbrook."

"Don't listen to her, Angel," Ty said, stepping over to her, his hand out. Angel retreated, waving the gun to keep him back.

"Ty wouldn't double-cross me," she said.

"Sure he would," Delaney argued. "You think he ever planned to split the money with you? He's too greedy. He kills me and gets the ranch, but you get the blame and he gets all the money to himself."

"Angel," Ty said, moving closer to her. She backed up against the rock wall of the mine and pointed the pistol at Ty's chest. "Don't you see what she's trying to do? She's trying to play us against each other."

"You said Buck would be blamed," Angel accused. "You said we'd share the money. But *you* had to be the one to salt the lake. There wasn't any color at all in the gravel Jared gave me from his place."

As Ty went for the pistol, Cooper broke from his hiding place. Cooper swung the old shovel, hitting Ty in the back just as Ty made a grab for Angel's pistol. The gun went flying. Ty fell to his knees. He cursed at Angel and swung around to slam his elbow into Cooper's knee. Cooper dropped, taking Ty to the ground with him. As the two wrestled in the dirt, Delaney made a leap for the pistol. But Angel reached it first.

"Get back," Angel said, her pale eyes eerie in the lantern light. Her gaze darted past Delaney. "Where the hell did he go?"

Delaney turned to see that Digger was gone.

COOPER SAW HIS opening. He buried his fist in Ty's stomach, then came back with a shot to his jaw. Ty's eyes crossed. He fell back with a groan. As Cooper stumbled to his feet, all he could think about was holding Delaney in his arms. He grabbed her and pulled her to him, breathing in the familiar scent of her, holding her tightly as if he'd lose her forever if he let her go. He'd forgotten about his claustrophobia the moment he saw Angel with the pistol trained on Delaney. He'd forgotten everything—the rotten timbers, the danger of being in an old mine deep in the ground. Forgotten everything but saving Delaney. He knew at that moment that he'd give his own life if that's what it took.

He looked up to see Angel, the pistol clutched in her hand, madness in her eyes. He turned Delaney, sheltering her in case Angel got off a shot before he could reach the woman.

"He tricked me," Angel cried, swinging the pistol back and forth from Ty to Cooper and Delaney. "You tricked me!" she yelled at Ty.

"Give me the gun, Angel," Cooper told her softly. "It's all over. I called the county marshal before I came up here. He and his men will be here any moment."

Angel met his gaze and smiled. "Nice try, cowboy, but you're not all that good at lying."

Cooper wondered if that was true. Since Delaney, he'd lost a lot of his old skills. They just didn't come as naturally as they used to.

"Get up," Angel said, turning her anger and the pistol on Ty. "You lying bastard, get up. That's why you suggested killing them in the mine. You were setting me up from the start."

Ty got to his feet, licking his lips as he eyed Angel. "You were already set on getting revenge when I met you. I just offered to help, that's all."

Cooper started to advance on Angel, but Delaney grabbed his arm.

"Why did you salt the lake?" Angel demanded, all her attention on Ty. "Tell me the truth, damn you!" She cocked the pistol and pointed it at his heart.

"All right," he said, raising his hands in surrender. "I put some gold in the lake. But just to get the price of the ranch up. It didn't have anything to do with you."

"You planned to double-cross me—" The pistol shot roared through the mine like a cannon blast. Dirt and gravel began to fall from the timbered shoring over head.

Ty clutched at his chest he dove for Angel and the pistol. "You're going to ruin everything!"

Cooper grabbed Delaney as the timbers groaned overhead. Dirt began to pour down in a dark shower of dust and gravel.

"We've got to get out of here," Cooper cried, pulling Delaney down the tunnel toward the entrance.

"We can't leave Buck," Delaney cried, breaking free to turn back.

Cooper reached for her, and saw that Ty had stumbled to his feet and was holding the gun. Angel was sprawled on the floor near him. As Ty advanced toward them, the pistol cocked and pointed at Delaney, Cooper saw Buck open his eyes. He nodded at Cooper, then reached out to grab Ty's leg.

"Run!" Cooper cried to Delaney as Ty's shot went wild, ricocheting through the tunnel.

DELANEY HEARD the first timbers give way behind them. Heard the roar and felt the wind as the earth caved in after them. She'd seen the look Buck had given her. "Run," he'd said. And she knew it was his way of paying her back for the pain he'd helped Angel cause her. She knew in that moment, she couldn't save Buck, could never have saved him from Angel. Or the cave-in. She ran, Cooper right behind her, for the tiny hole of light at the end of the tunnel, afraid they would never reach it in time. Just as they neared the opening, she saw Digger and Tess waiting outside. An instant later, the entrance opened like a golden door as Tess pulled a large rock from the opening, and Delaney and Cooper rushed out into the sunshine.

Behind them, the Golden Dream seemed to explode, sending dirt shooting out over them. Cooper pulled Delaney into his arms as they looked back at what was left of the Golden Dream. Nothing but a wall of rock.

"Buck. Ty and Angel—" Delaney buried her face in Cooper's shoulder and cried. "Buck saved our lives."

Cooper held her. "I've got you, Delaney. It's all right now. I've got you."

Epilogue

They rode out across the wide-open land, the sun climbing high over Montana's big sky. Cooper rode behind Delaney on Crazy Jack. The morning air smelled fresh. Tall wild grass brushed her boots as she rode. Delaney knew where Cooper was taking her long before she saw the large pine tree and the flat smooth shadowed rock beneath it. She smiled over at him. This was the spot they'd first met. It seemed like a lifetime ago.

Cooper dismounted and, taking Delaney by the waist, lifted her down from her horse. He held her for only a moment before he released her and turned to look out across the land.

The Rockin' L stretched across the horizon below them. In a far pasture, the two-year-old Morgans raced on the wind, their hides dark against the sea of tall grass and wildflowers that grew beneath their hooves.

"I heard from the county attorney this morning," Cooper said. "They're willing to drop the charges if I turn state's evidence against Rattlesnake Range. I've decided I have to do it. Not to save my own hide as much as to put them out of business for good."

Delaney nodded but didn't say anything. She'd already talked to the county attorney and knew he'd made Cooper an offer. She just hadn't been sure Cooper would take it. He'd stayed around after the mine cave-in, helping her get through the days that followed, all the funerals. He'd been there whenever she'd needed him and yet neither of them had talked about him staying.

"With Rattlesnake Range gone and Jared out of the picture . . . well, you shouldn't have anything to worry about," Cooper said.

Jared was now facing misdemeanor charges for the accidents he'd caused on the Rockin' L and abuse of power. She'd been surprised to learn about his financial troubles. That was why he'd made the deal with the mining company, in an attempt to keep from losing his ranch after a series of bad investments. But without Delaney's land, the mining company had said it wouldn't be financially feasible to mine Kincaid's property.

Delaney heard Cooper had made an offer on Kincaid Ranches. Jared had needed a fast sale to keep from losing everything and Cooper had picked up the ranches for a song. But Delaney wasn't sure what he planned to do with the land. For all she knew he might turn around and sell them at a profit.

"I know how you feel about this place," Cooper said, taking off his hat to turn it in his fingers.

Delaney looked across the wide expanse of pines and rocks; rolling hills and mountains; long, wide pastures and grassland as far as the eye could see. Home. The place she'd put all her dreams. All her hopes.

She shifted her gaze to the cowboy standing beside her. It wasn't until recently that she'd realized the land meant everything to her. And nothing without Cooper. But she wasn't going to make the same mistake her mother had, trying to tie a rodeo cowboy to that land. A rodeo cowboy who wasn't ready to settle down. It had to be what he wanted.

"Something on your mind, McLeod," she asked.

He grinned. "The deal I made with the county attorney is dependent on one small thing." He settled his baby blues on her, letting all that charm just pour out of him like a warm summer rain shower. "I need a job."

"A job?" she asked. "Didn't I hear that you've just bought a ranch of your own?"

He nodded. "But I was kinda hoping there still might be something for me at the Rockin' L."

"You were?" She pushed back her western hat to give him the once-over. "You look like a rodeo cowboy to me, and I make it a rule never to hire 'em."

"What about reformed bronc riders?" Cooper asked, as he closed the distance between them.

"Sorry," Delaney said, taking a spin with the devil dancing in those eyes of his. "I have only one opening on the ranch and it's not for a hired hand."

"No?" Cooper asked.

He was so close she could feel his breath against her cheek. "No."

"I thought about the ranch-manager job," he said, the devil jitterbugging away in his gaze. "But maybe I'm more upper-level management than that. And you've got Digger and Tess back at their summer camp keeping an eye on things, so you don't need me for that."

Delaney raised a brow. "So what position were you considering?" she asked with a grin. "I should tell you, when I take on a man here at the Rockin' L, I expect something from him."

Cooper grinned, but it faded quickly. A seriousness came into his eyes, into his stance. He cupped her face in his hands. "Delaney?"

His voice was soft and deep with emotion. She realized he was nervous and had to fight a smile. Cooper McLeod. Nervous.

"Yes, Coop?" she said.

"Have you ever considered marrying a former rodeo cowboy?" he asked.

"No, Coop, I never have."

He eyed her for a moment. "You're not going to make this easy for me, are you?"

She smiled. "No."

He took a breath. "Just tell me if there is anything about me that you like, so I know what my odds are."

She pretended to think for a moment. "I like your horse."

"You do?" Cooper asked in pleased surprise.

She wrapped her arms around his neck. "And I think you can tell a lot about a man by his horse."

"Yeah?" He grinned again.

"Say it, McLeod. You've never had any trouble telling me what you thought before." She leaned back to look up at him. "So just say the words. If you're sure it's what you want."

"Oh, it's what I want. It's all I want."

He met her gaze. He looked as if he thought she might run him off with a shotgun. Or worse yet, say no.

"Delaney Lawson, would you marry me?" he asked, his voice breaking with emotion.

"Yes, Cooper McLeod," she said, pulling him down for a kiss. "I certainly will."

Behind them, Crazy Jack let out a long whinny. They both laughed as Cooper lowered Delaney to the smooth, flat rock beneath the pine tree.

CELEBRATION 1000

SILHOUETTE
Desire®

Publishes it's 1000th title!

Join the festivities as Silhouette® celebrates Desire's 1000th title next month.

Look out for our special competition in the end pages of Silhouette Desire titles in October—and you could win a year's worth of seductive and breathtaking Silhouette Desire novels—absolutely FREE!

Celebration 1000

Come celebrate the publication of the 1000th Silhouette Desire, with scintillating love stories by some of your favourite writers!

COMING NEXT MONTH

BEAUTY VS. THE BEAST M.J. Rodgers

Justice Inc.

When psychologist Damian Steele killed off the nasty half of
his dual-personality patient, he never expected that the
'widow' would file a wrongful-death suit. Nor did he expect
that a breathtaking beauty, attorney Kay Kellogg, would be his
saving grace…

LUCKY DEVIL Patricia Rosemoor

Dangerous Men

JoJo Weston tried not to be impressed by the obviously
dangerous man standing before her, oozing sensuality. Lucian
was a Donatelli—not to be trusted, not to be messed with.
Could he possibly even be the one who'd been waiting,
watching, moving in on her?

TRIPLECROSS Linda Stevens

Lizzy Green's charity case of the month was playing detective
for a sweet little old lady who'd misplaced an heirloom. But
suddenly Lizzy became the target of someone whose idea of
fun was stalking and terrorizing her. Michael Cook insisted she
leave the case to him—the little old lady in question was his
grandmother—but Lizzy was determined to play it to the
end…

TANGLED VOWS Rebecca York

43 Light Street

Private investigator Jo O'Malley had two men in her life, and
she didn't know which one to trust: her husband, Cam, or a
ghost from her past who wouldn't rest in peace. Jo's life was a
nightmare, shaped by events from beyond the grave. Between
her love for Cam and her loyalty to the past, Jo was
trapped…trapped in a ghostly triangle.

GET 4 BOOKS
AND A SILVER PLATED
PHOTO FRAME

Return this coupon and we'll send you 4 Silhouette Intrigue™ novels and a silver plated photo frame absolutely FREE! We'll even pay the postage and packing for you.

We're making you this offer to introduce you to the benefits of Reader Service: FREE home delivery of brand-new Silhouette® romances, at least a month before they are available in the shops, FREE gifts and a monthly Newsletter packed with information.

Accepting these FREE books and gift places you under no obligation to buy, you may cancel at any time, even after receiving just your free shipment. Simply complete the coupon below and send it to:

SILHOUETTE READER SERVICE, FREEPOST, CROYDON, SURREY, CR9 3WZ.

No stamp needed

Yes, please send me 4 free Silhouette Intrigue novels and a silver plated photo frame. I understand that unless you hear from me, I will receive 4 superb new titles every month for just £2.30* each postage and packing free. I am under no obligation to purchase any books and I may cancel or suspend my subscription at any time, but the free books and gifts will be mine to keep in any case. (I am over 18 years of age)

161E

Ms/Mrs/Miss/Mr _____

Address _____

_____

_____ Postcode _____

COMING NEXT MONTH FROM

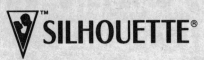

Sensation

A thrilling mix of passion, adventure and drama

GUARDING RAINE Kylie Brant
KEEPER Patricia Gardner Evans
HOMECOMING Sally Tyler Hayes
PERFECT DOUBLE Merline Lovelace

Special Edition

Satisfying romances packed with emotion

MOLLY DARLING Laurie Paige
EXPECTANT FATHER Leanne Banks
SUMMERS PAST Laurey Bright
NEW BRIDE IN TOWN Amy Frazier
RAINSINGER Ruth Wind
MARRY ME, NOW! Allison Hayes

Desire

Provocative, sensual love stories for the woman of today

BABY DREAMS Raye Morgan
THE UNWILLING BRIDE Jennifer Greene
APACHE DREAM BRIDE Joan Elliott Pickart
CONNAL Diana Palmer
INSTANT HUSBAND Judith McWilliams
BABY BONUS Amanda Kramer